GW01403350

The Letter

The Letter Series, Volume 1

Shelly Meyer

Published by Shelly Meyer, 2024.

THE LETTER

First edition. November 4, 2024.

Copyright © 2024 Shelly Meyer.

ISBN: 979-8227622440

Written by Shelly Meyer.

The Letter: Part One
By Shelly Meyer

Chapter One – Sarah

"I shouldn't have sent it," I said, shaking my head. "I wonder if I can stop the mail before it gets picked up." I hurried toward the door, but Kelly came after me and grabbed me by my arm.

"It's done, Sarah," she told me. I sat down on the chair in the lobby and put my face in my hands. "Besides," she said, sitting down at her desk, "I think it's sweet." I eyed her, and she smiled at me.

Kelly Frost, our company's receptionist, radiated positivity and warmth. She made friends with everyone she met. Her youthful beauty was undeniable, with her bouncy curls of golden blonde hair and sparkling hazel eyes. Her laughter was infectious, which caused her hair to bounce and her eyes to dance with joy. She had recently graduated college and was full of optimism, ready to start her career as a real estate agent. She had a supportive nature and always had a smile on her face.

"What was I thinking sending a letter to a twenty-five-year-old movie star? I'm thirty-five, for Pete's sake."

"So? It's not like you asked him to sleep with you. You only asked for an autographed picture. I thought the letter was funny. If nothing else, he'll laugh about it. The worst that could happen is that you'll find photos in your mailbox sooner." She grinned at me again.

"You're right." I sighed and stood up. "He doesn't even have time to read the letters himself." I walked toward the door to the back office. "I need to go back to work."

Back at my desk, I pulled a copy of the letter I sent out of my desk drawer and read it to myself.

Dear Andrew:

First, I want to introduce myself. My name is Sarah Miller. I'm certain I'm one of a million women who send these letters to you every day. First, I'm not a fanatic teenage girl, and if I were ten years younger, I wouldn't feel so much like a creepy old lady hitting on a young guy.

Without sounding like that creepy old lady, I'm thirty-five. I wanted to say I think you're a beautiful person, inside and out. You're down-to-earth and real. You also have great taste in burger joints. I believe you're a fantastic actor, and they couldn't have found a better Will (the character he played in his latest movie) if they tried.

Okay, so I've seen 'Two Hearts' and 'One Life' and I'm wondering when the third movie is coming out?

Can I ask you a huge favor? Can you please send an autographed picture? Everyone asks for that. At least I didn't ask you to come to Denver to sign my chest. Ha ha. (I groaned at that).

It would mean the world to me.

Okay, now for the creepy old lady stuff...my contact info. I'm not expecting to hear from *you*, but a lady can dream, right?

I included every bit of my contact information.

I groaned again and shoved the letter in my purse, hoping it would never again raise its evil little head. But Kelly felt the need to remind me of it every single day for a month.

"Have you heard anything yet?" she would ask every day.

"No," I would answer. "And I hope I don't. I feel so weird about it."

"Feel weird about what," my friend and co-worker, Chris Keller, asked one day in late January. He had been oblivious to what I had done for an entire month. I wrote the letter on December first.

"Boy, you're with it, aren't you?" As I stood in front of him, my laughter bubbled out. I looked up at him, taking in his striking features. His hair was the color of sun-kissed wheat, and his eyes were a vivid blue, drawing me in with their intensity. The firm lines of his square jaw and long nose made him rugged and handsome. He had an almost Nordic air about him, and he exuded a sense of strength and confidence.

Standing next to him, I felt small. He towered over me, and I had to tilt my head back to meet his gaze. Yet, despite his imposing stature, he had a gentle calmness about him. I found it hard to believe he could be anything but kind and understanding. But then, I remembered how his ex-wife had described him. He had a bit of a temper and was prone to bouts of jealousy.

"What's going on, Sarah?"

I sighed, searching for the best way to explain my stupidity without sounding stupid. Kelly's bubbly voice piped in before I opened my mouth. "She sent a letter to a movie star. She thinks it was creepy, but I think it's sweet."

"You would," I smirked at her.

Chris laughed. "How old are you? Fifteen?" I punched his arm. "Ouch," he groaned, rubbing his arm, still laughing.

I walked away, but I wasn't mad or hurt.

To be honest, I only acted my age when it I had to. Acting thirty-five made me feel old, and I didn't like that feeling. I had always appeared younger than my actual age, although I had been fighting the fine lines with anti-aging creams and make-up.

My hair fell in loose waves, reaching just below my shoulders, its auburn hue shining in the fluorescent lights. I had countless freckles scattered across my face, each one a unique mark on my skin. My eyes, a vibrant shade of green, sparkled with curiosity. The slight tilt of my nose gave me a mischievous air, while my thin mouth held a constant hint of a smile. I wouldn't say I was stunning, but I was content with my ordinary appearance.

Chris knew I wasn't upset, so he didn't bother coming after me. I went back to work. It was almost five o'clock anyway.

***

I drove home that evening, hoping there would be something from Andrew Collier in the mail. I had a feeling there wouldn't be anything there, but I had hoped something wonderful would happen for me. I had been single for five years, and I deserved some happiness again. Then I thought about Chris. I'd had a crush on him for more than a year. He knew it, but neither of us ever acted on it. We had always been friends. He never failed to help me when I needed it, and he was always there for me.

I drove up to my mailbox at the end of my street and opened it. Nothing, which is what I had expected. Movie stars as famous as Andrew Collier didn't have time to read the thousands of letters they received every day. It had been almost two months since I sent mine. I gave up hope on this one.

When I pulled into my driveway, I saw Chris's truck parked in front of my house. He never mentioned he was stopping by. It was too cold outside to move anything into my storage shed out back. He had planned to come by this weekend to help with that, so I wasn't sure why he was at my house.

"Hey, goofball. What are you doing here?" I greeted him with our usual friendly ribbing.

"I wasn't planning on coming over, but I wanted to apologize for hurting your feelings earlier." He walked into the house behind me. As usual, my house was freezing. The furnace wouldn't start, and I couldn't keep my space heater on all day.

"You didn't hurt my feelings. You were joking, and so was I." I turned on the space heaters and the oven to get the house warm faster. "Would you like some coffee or soda or something?" I turned on the kitchen faucet. "Dammit!"

"What's wrong?"

"The pipes froze again. Was it really that cold today?"

Everything in my house was falling apart. If I could have afforded to move, I would have in a second.

"I'm going to buy that fuse for your furnace."

"It's not your problem, Chris, but thank you," I smiled and sat down on the couch next to him and handed him a bottle of water I pulled from the fridge.

"Are you sure everything's okay?" He put his arm around my shoulder, and I leaned in close to him, more to get warm than to hint at anything romantic.

"Yeah," I answered inaudibly, and looked up into his blue eyes. He was so adorable. He hadn't shaved in a couple of days, so he was a little scruffy. His smile was sweet, and he smiled often. I liked that about him. He was always optimistic, and I wanted to be more like that.

He still had his arm around my shoulder, and I was still looking up at him with a smile on my lips. "You didn't come over to apologize, did you?"

He shook his head. "No."

"Why *did* you come?" I sat up and faced him.

He sucked in a deep breath. "Do you remember when you told me you had a crush on me?"

"Oh, jeez." I laughed, embarrassed, and glanced away. "Yeah, but let's not go there, please."

"*That's* why I'm here, Sarah." He took my chin in his hand and pulled my face toward his. I had no choice but to look at him.

"Chris..."

"I should have said something a long time ago, but I'm a coward."

"What are you talking about?"

"I like you, too."

"You don't have to..." He stopped me with his lips on mine. I let out a quick, nervous laugh.

"You okay?"

"Um, yeah." I smiled at him. "Are you?"

"Yes." He smiled back and leaned in again.

The second kiss was a little more passionate. His hands cradled my face. I put my hands on his.

"Wow," I sighed when he pulled away.

"*This* is why I came over here." He took my hands in his. "I should have told you months ago."

"Isn't it going to be weird at work now?"

He rolled his eyes and pulled away. "Why do you have to look at it that way?"

"What way?"

"All negative? I tell you I like you and I kiss you, and you're worried about things being weird at work." He shook his head and chuckled.

"I'm sorry."

"This isn't a bad thing, Sarah. Be happy, would you?"

"I can do that," I said with a smile and a nod.

"Listen, I can't stay long, but I had to come over here and tell you how I feel."

"I'm glad you did. Thank you."

"Anytime." He pulled me off the couch and put his arms around me. "Yeah, I need to fix that furnace for you. It's freezing in here."

"It is."

"And I'm going to insulate those pipes, too. Are you going to be alright here tonight?"

"Yeah. It was colder the night I went to watch Two Hearts."

Chris rolled his eyes again. "Can we *not* talk about Andrew Collier again, please?"

"Yeah. I've given up on that whole thing."

"Good." He chuckled and kissed me. "I'll come by this weekend and fix that furnace."

"Thank you." He kissed me one more time and stepped outside.

"Jeez, woman. It's warmer out here than it is in your house."

"I could always sleep in my car tonight." I winked at him. "Text me when you're home."

"I will." He smiled and headed for his truck.

I closed the door and leaned against it, a huge smile on my lips. I felt warm at that moment.

I slept well that night and woke up feeling refreshed. In the morning, I had my mocha, checked my emails, and took a long, hot shower. I was thankful the pipes had thawed overnight. It was casual Friday, so I put on a pair of jeans and my black cashmere cardigan. I applied my makeup with care and made sure everything was perfect. I even took the time to curl my hair and pulled it back off my face. I was feeling better about myself than I had in months.

For the first time in weeks, I didn't complain about the other drivers on the road, and I made it to work in record time. It would be a beautiful day. I could feel it.

Chris was already at the office. "Morning, beautiful." He was standing behind me in the kitchen as I fixed my coffee. He wrapped his arms around my waist.

I turned to face him and smiled up at him. I had never thought much about how tall he was. He was over six feet. "Morning."

He bent to kiss me. I had seen no one else in the office, so I wasn't worried about getting caught.

"Did you stay warm last night?" he asked, stepping away from me so I could finish making my coffee.

"Yes." I sighed, remembering the passionate kiss of the night before.

"I should have stayed with you."

"Something might have happened if you did."

"Your point?" He chuckled.

"It wouldn't have been a bad thing." I said with a smile.

He stepped toward me again and put his hands on my face. I loved that feeling. He stooped and kissed me again.

"Don't mind me," we suddenly heard someone say from the kitchen doorway. We stopped. Our boss, Valerie Wilson, was standing in the doorway.

Her presence filled the room as she stood, leaning against the door frame. Her hair flowed down her shoulders in a river of chocolate brown, framing her face. As she met my gaze, a glint of mischief danced in her warm brown eyes, revealing her acceptance of Chris and me. Valerie was more than just a figure of authority. She was a natural leader, guiding us with a friendly hand while maintaining her position of power. Her approachable demeanor made her easy to talk to about anything.

"Uh, yeah," Chris stammered. "We, um..."

She waved it off. "I saw nothing." She winked at me, made her coffee, and walked back to the door. "Please, continue."

"We should go back to work before we're busted again," I told Chris.

***

The day was flying by. It was almost noon, and I was about ready for lunch. Valerie was rushing to my desk as I was getting up. She had a huge, mischievous smile on her face. I figured she was stealing a minute to talk to me about the incident with Chris. "What's up?"

"There's a young man at the front desk with an enormous bouquet. He says he has to give them to *only* you."

Puzzled, I stood up and walked to the front office, with Valerie at my heels. "Who would send me flowers? Chris?"

"They're not from Chris," she told me.

I stopped short and turned around. "Who are they from?" I was suspicious.

She was still smiling. "You'll see."

I glanced at her and opened the door to the outer office. Atop Kelly's desk sat an enormous arrangement of the most beautiful and fragrant flowers I had ever seen. They made the entire room smell incredible.

At that moment, he stepped out from behind the vase and showed himself. "Sarah?" His smile was breathtaking. I recognized him at once.

I felt light-headed. I couldn't catch my breath. "Will you excuse me for a minute, please?" I ran back to the kitchen and sat on a nearby chair. I bent over, trying to breathe. Valerie, Kelly, and Chris were right behind me.

"Are you okay?" Kelly asked. "You look like you're going to pass out."

"I'm alright. I need to sit for a minute."

"What happened?" Chris asked, sitting down next to me.

"What do you want me to tell your...um...friend," Valerie asked, concern in her voice. She glanced at Chris.

"Sarah, that's...," Kelly said, setting a glass of water on the table in front of me.

I looked up at her but spoke to Valerie. "Could you ask Mr. Collier to come in here?"

Chris groaned, and I looked up at him. He appeared hurt. "Andrew Collier?"

I nodded. "Chris, I did not know. I'm sorry. I didn't expect him..."

He stood up, pushing his chair to the floor, and stormed out of the room. A few seconds later, I heard his office door slam.

Andrew was standing in the doorway. "Are you alright, Sarah?" The sound of his voice made my head spin. I nodded and took in a deep breath. He stepped inside the room and picked up the chair and sat down next to me. "Are you sure?"

"Yeah." His presence alone was enough to make my heart race. The way his dark hair fell in disarray and the slight stubble on his jawline added to his charm. His full lips curved into a smile, and it lit up the entire room, outshining the fluorescent lights above us. His piercing blue-gray eyes held me captive, making it hard to look away.

He stood tall and confident, his lean frame exuding strength and grace. As he looked at me, I felt weak. His intense gaze had the power to render me speechless. It appeared his arms ached for me, as if he wanted to pull me into an embrace. "What are you..? I mean, how did you... um, why?" I stammered. I couldn't understand why he was here, and my mind struggled to make sense of it all.

"I needed to bring you the flowers. I'll tell you; this office is difficult to find. GPS is a lifesaver. And to answer your why...because your letter intrigued me, and your picture, well, you're more beautiful in person."

I chuckled. "So are you." I peered toward the door. We were being watched by everyone in the office. When they saw I had noticed them, they scattered, mumbling to each other. "I, um, need some air. Do you mind?"

"Not at all." He stood up and helped me to my feet. I was still a little dizzy. I had to crane my neck to look at him. Six feet, one inch. Damn, he was tall and beautiful.

We stepped into the elevator and walked outside when we reached the first floor. Andrew held the door for me. It was warm today, not at all like yesterday. Not usual for late January, either, but this was Colorado. The weather here was often bi-polar. I didn't mind one bit. At that moment, I could have been standing in the middle of a blizzard in shorts and a tank top, and I don't think I would have noticed or cared.

Andrew and I sat down on a patch of grass at the far end of the parking lot, facing each other. "So, are you surprised?" he asked.

"That's the understatement of the year." I shook my head and smiled. I was having a hard time looking at him. His eyes were hypnotizing. I could have gotten lost in them. I was playing with the grass, thinking of something witty to say to him. "I'm wondering..." I had to make myself look at him. He had his head cocked, and he was grinning. Oh, God, stop! "Why are you here?"

"I told you. Your letter intrigued me. I had to meet the woman who wrote it." He took my hands in a friendly gesture.

"Disappointed," I asked.

"Not at all. You're more than I expected." He was still smiling. "What about me?"

"Are you kidding?" I tried not to chuckle. I failed. "Remember I said, 'You're beautiful, inside, and out'?"

"Yes, but pictures don't always do a person justice. Yours didn't."

"Neither do yours." I shook my head and grinned. "I feel like an idiot."

"Why?"

"I'm thirty-five years old. You're twenty-five. What was I thinking? Jeez, what were *you* thinking coming here?"

"Are you sorry?"

"Not at all. But I didn't even expect the pictures I asked for. I hoped, but I never thought I would be sitting here with you, having an actual conversation. This is what girls dream about, but it never happens in real life."

"Well, I'm thrilled to be here. I'm glad I came, Sarah." He stood up and pulled me to my feet. I glanced at him with apprehension.

"I'm glad, too."

"I had better let you go back to work." I frowned, and he chuckled.

"Where are you staying?" I asked.

"The Brown Palace, downtown. Do you know it?"

"Everyone knows the Brown Palace."

"How far is it from your house?"

"Twenty minutes, maybe, when there's no traffic."

"That won't do." His forehead creased as he thought about that.

"Well, my house is a piece of crap, but..." I stopped, thinking about how run down my place was.

"But what?"

"I was going to ask you if you wanted to stay at my place while you're here, but I'm too embarrassed by it. You're used to mansions and luxury hotel suites."

"Sarah," he laughed again. "I lived in an RV while we were filming 'Two Hearts' and 'One Life.'"

"That may be, but my place is falling apart. It's...gross." I wrinkled my nose, and he touched it. It sent a shiver up my spine.

"I don't believe that."

"Fine...would you like to stay with me while you're here?" I asked him.

"Yes, I would." He smiled and put his arm around my shoulder, and we walked to the front door of the building.

We went upstairs, and he walked me to the door. "So, I'll see you later?" I think my knees were shaking.

"Of course. I'm going to have some lunch, then check out of the hotel, then I'll meet you here later and follow you to your house."

"Okay." I looked down at my feet, too nervous, again, to look at him.

"Hey," he whispered.

"Yeah?" I gazed at him, and he stooped and kissed my lips. My entire body tingled. Some kind of electric shock ran through my body. I thought I was going to faint. I was light-headed again, and my legs felt like jelly.

"You okay?"

"More than okay." I gave him a huge smile, and he walked backward toward the elevator. I watched him until the doors closed. I walked to the landing and watched him walk to the front door.

"Bye," I called to him.

He smiled and waved at me, then he walked outside. I went inside and had to sit down. I was panting, and every muscle in my body was weak.

Kelly was at my side. "Oh my God, Sarah. He kissed you."

I could only nod and try to breathe. There was a huge, stupid grin on my face. I wondered if Andrew was feeling the same as I was.

"What did you two talk about?"

"I asked him what he was doing here. Then I started babbling about how weird it all was. Oh yeah, then I invited him to stay with me while he's here."

Kelly gasped. "Oh, my!"

"Stupid, huh?" I shook my head.

"Andrew Collier is staying at your house. You're going to spend an entire weekend alone with him." Now she had an enormous grin on her face.

"Beautiful," I heard Chris growled in an angry tone from the inner office door.

Both Kelly and I eyed him. He scowled at me, then walked away.

"What was that about?"

I shook my head. "I'll deal with that later." I frowned. "I can't do this. What am I thinking?"

"He's gorgeous, and it appears he's into you. If you don't make a move, you're crazy."

I shook my head and stood up. "I have to deal with this Chris issue."

"Yeah, what is that about?"

"I'll fill you in later." What was I going to do? I had to talk to Chris, but he was angry. Should I give him some time to cool off?

No, we needed to work this out. "Can I talk to you?" I asked him as I stood in the doorway of his office.

"Why don't you go talk to your new *boyfriend*?" He didn't even look up at me. This was hurting him. It hurt me knowing he was hurting.

"That's not fair. I wasn't expecting Andrew would show up."

"You didn't have to kiss him."

I sucked in my breath. "*He* kissed me." I couldn't believe he was spying on me.

"Of course he did." He glared up at me and stood up. "You left with him, and you were acting like a teenage girl when he showed up."

"I was in shock." I walked toward him. "If you remember, I told you yesterday that I had given up on even a picture of him."

"I guess I'd act the same way if it were Sandra Bullock."

"Sandra Bullock, huh?" I cocked my head and grinned.

"Can we forget it?" His expression was somber. He stood and walked toward me.

"Yes."

"I think I found the fuse for your furnace. I'm going to pick it up tomorrow morning and bring it by in the afternoon."

Worry was clear on my face. I bit my bottom lip. "About that."

Chris rolled his eyes and turned away. "He's staying with you," through gritted teeth. "Awesome." He spun around to face me again.

"It slipped out."

"Sure, it did." He leaned in close. I could feel the heat of his breath on my face. "What do you want, Sarah? Me or him?"

"Are you joking? This isn't a competition. I just met him. I thought you and I were trying to make something happen?"

"We were...until Mister Perfect showed up." He paced. "How old is he? Sixteen?"

I chuckled. "You're jealous."

"You think?" He closed the door before the entire office heard what was going on.

"You have no reason to be jealous. And, for your information, Andrew is twenty-five."

"Oh, that makes it okay?"

"Chris, please. You have no reason to be jealous."

"You asked him to stay with you."

"I told you; I blurted it out. I guess I thought it was better than some lonely, impersonal hotel room."

"Which hotel?"

"What difference does it make?"

"A lot. Which hotel?"

"The Brown Palace."

"And that's worse than your house?"

"That was low." I walked away and started toward the door.

"I'm sorry." He walked toward me and put his arms around me. "I didn't mean it. I *am* jealous. I'm sorry."

I turned around and wrapped my arms tight around him. "You don't have to be. I've been waiting a long time for you."

"Me, too." He bent to kiss me. I stood on my toes as he did. He pulled away. "We had better stop before we start something we can't finish."

"Alright." I sighed and opened the door.

"I'm still coming by tomorrow to put that fuse in."

"I hope so," I smiled at him.

"Hey, one last thing," he stopped me.

"Yeah?"

"Who's a better kisser?" He was grinning.

"You have to ask?" I didn't have an answer to that question. "I'll see you later," I smiled at him and left. I could hear him laughing as I walked to the front office to talk to Kelly.

"Okay, so what's going on with Chris?" Kelly asked me when I got to her desk.

"Please don't tell anyone, alright," I told her. "I'm not one hundred percent sure what's going on or what's going to happen now, with Andrew showing up here like that."

Kelly was like a giddy little kid about the entire Andrew Collier situation. "Sarah, what are the chances of this happening? Things like this don't happen."

"Yeah. I'm still kind of shaking."

"I was right."

"About what?"

"I told you the worst thing that could happen was that you would receive an autographed picture. I think you got the better deal." She grinned at me, and I had to laugh.

"Did I?" I let out a deep sigh and began my explanation about Chris. "I'm not joking, Kelly. You can't tell a soul."

"I swear."

"The only other person who knows is Valerie, and that's only because she caught us this morning."

"What were you doing?"

"Kissing."

She gasped and grinned. "You're kidding!"

I shook my head. "No. He came over last night after work. I wasn't expecting him to show up. I already told you he shows up at my house out of nowhere to help me with stuff around my house."

"Yeah." She was leaning forward in her chair.

"Okay, so he shows up out of nowhere last night. He was waiting for me when I got home."

"No way."

"Yeah. I thought it was funny, too. It was too cold to move anything out to my storage, so why was Chris there?"

"He liked you already." I cocked my head and smirked. "He told me yesterday he was going to talk to you."

"And you said nothing to me?"

"He swore me to secrecy. I can keep a secret." She gave me another toothy grin.

"Well done," I smiled back. The phone rang, so I waited for the call to end.

"Go on," she told me when she hung up.

"Yeah. Last year, I told Chris I had a crush on him, so he already knew I liked him. It went no further than that. I was okay with that until he showed up last night. He told me he had been too afraid to say anything to me back then. We were both going through so much."

"I remember. That's about when I started here."

"Right. So, now everything has changed. We talked for a little while, then he kissed me. I couldn't believe it. It was so sweet."

"Did you guys...?"

I knew she was hinting at sex. "Oh, no," I assured her. She appeared to be deflated. "No way, Kelly. Come on."

"What?" she asked with mock innocence. "I didn't want details or anything. I figured..."

"I suppose it might have this weekend if I hadn't had asked Andrew to stay at my house."

"How did Chris take that news?"

"How do you think? I think he's tolerating it, though. I guess that would be the right word. I mean, it's not as if he asked me to be his girlfriend or anything. He told me he liked me and said he would come by tomorrow to put that fuse in my furnace."

"He's checking up on you, isn't he?"

"I guess he is now, but he *was* planning to put the fuse in the furnace this weekend."

"That's going to be kind of weird with the two of them in your house, isn't it?"

I shrugged and inhaled the sweet fragrance of my bouquet. "I suppose, but Chris and Andrew will have to deal with it, or I'll kick them both out." I laughed and peered down at my feet.

"You like them both, don't you?"

"Well, yeah. I mean, as much as I can, I guess. Chris is my friend. He's funny and sweet and generous."

"And handsome," Kelly added.

"Yes. And Andrew, he's also sweet and funny, and he flew thousands of miles to see me."

"He's also gorgeous."

"Thank you for pointing that out. I was not aware." I smirked at her.

"What are you going to do?"

I shook my head. I had Chris, who had always been there for me, helping me out without me even asking and then telling me he had feelings for me. Then I had Andrew Collier, the mega movie star, who I never expected to meet in a million years.

"What am I going to do? The minute Andrew steps one foot in my house, he's going to run screaming."

"Chris wouldn't do that. He hasn't done that, and he's been there hundreds of times."

"Yeah and cleaned some nasty crap for me."

"I can't tell you what to do, Sarah, but I would make the safe choice."

"The safe choice." I pondered that for a moment.

"Yeah." She smiled.

"I need to go back to work. Valerie is going to kill me if I keep slacking."

Before I got to my desk, Valerie called me into her office. I knew she wanted to know about Chris and me.

I closed the door behind me and sat down across from her.

"What's going on with Chris?"

"He's jealous. He thinks I'm going to run off and be with Andrew. I'm not."

"What are you going to do if something happens with Andrew?"

"I don't see anything happening. I'm too nervous to even look him in the eyes. Besides, the second he steps foot in my house, he's going to regret ever coming to Colorado."

"I doubt that, but I want you and Chris to be careful and take it slow. You've both been through so much."

"I have no intention of hurting Chris. He doesn't want to hurt me, either."

"Please be careful." She gave me a thoughtful expression.

Valerie had become a loyal friend in the last year, despite her position as my boss. She had always been easy to talk to. Valerie was the best boss I had ever had. She was concerned about everyone in the office. She knew when something was wrong, and she listened. Valerie cared. I loved that about her.

"I'd better go to work." I stood up and went to the door. "Thank you."

"Anytime." She gave me a sweet smile, and I walked to my desk.

I tried to work, but it wasn't possible. Anita Ortiz and Marie Vallejo, two of my co-workers who had been waiting all day to grill me about Andrew, stopped by my desk to chat with me.

Anita was the first to grill me. She and I usually talked in the morning before we started our day. We talked about family and random work stuff.

Anita radiated compassion. She exuded vibrancy and youth, despite being near forty. Her tall, lithe figure moved with grace, her dark curls bouncing with every step. Her eyes, a deep shade of brown, twinkled with kindness and understanding. I cherished our morning talks, where her words and genuine interest never failed to uplift me.

"Tell me everything," she demanded with a smile, leaning on my desk. Because Anita was only a few years older than I was, we related to each other.

I sighed and smiled up at her. "Everything?"

"Everything, girl. Come on. I've been waiting to talk to you all day about this young man."

"His name is Andrew Collier. He's..."

"Why does that name sound so familiar? He looks so familiar to me, too."

I pointed to the picture of him I had taken out of a magazine and pinned up on my cubicle wall.

"No," she said in disbelief.

"Yes. Andrew played Will in "Two Hearts"."

"That's the guy who was here. How?"

"Yeah, I wrote him a letter in December. He felt he needed to come to Denver to meet me."

"Wow. What's he like?"

"He's nice. I only know what I've seen in interviews and magazines, but we talked for a while when he was here."

"Are you going to see him again?"

"He's going to be staying with me this weekend."

Anita gasped and almost fell off my desk. "You're kidding!"

I shook my head. "Nope. I asked him, and he agreed."

"Well, what is he doing here besides bringing you beautiful flowers and causing you to almost pass out?"

"I don't know." I realized I hadn't asked him if he had another purpose for coming to Denver. "He kept insisting he was here to meet me because my letter 'intrigued' him."

"That's amazing, Sarah. Are you nervous?"

"That's an understatement. He seems so sweet, and he's gorgeous, but..." I bit my bottom lip. I wasn't sure I was ready to tell her about Chris yet.

"But what?" She was waiting for the entire story.

I waved it off. "I have a lot going on right now."

"Sarah, what's going on?"

I groaned. "It's Chris."

"What about him?"

"You didn't hear us arguing in his office earlier?" Their offices were next to each other.

"No. I had an appointment this morning. I wasn't here. What about Chris? I thought you liked him. Why were you arguing?"

"He showed up at my house last night and told me he liked me, too."

"Oh, wow." She averted her eyes. She was staring into space. "Perfect timing, huh? I knew he was going to tell you, but..."

"Excuse me?"

"Yeah. It's nothing." She waved it off.

"No, it's not nothing. Spill."

"Chris asked me yesterday if you still had your little crush on him. When I told him you did, he said he liked you, too, and wanted to make sure you still felt the same way before he made a move."

"You've got to be kidding me. Does everyone know about this?"

"I think it's only me, Kelly, and Marie."

"And Valerie."

"Valerie?"

"She caught us kissing this morning."

"Oh, my," Anita giggled.

"Shh. It's not funny," but I was laughing a little, too.

"I'm sorry." She was attempting to control her giggling. "What are you going to do now?"

"I've never been in this situation before. I don't know what to do."

"You'll figure it out." She patted my shoulder and stood up. "Keep me posted."

"Sure." I put my head on my desk and groaned in frustration. Anita left, then, and headed back to her office.

"Sarah." Marie's voice shocked me back into reality. I jumped.

"What?" I groaned.

Marie was one of my closest friends at work. I could tell her anything, and I knew she wouldn't tell another soul. She told me her secrets and was certain I wouldn't tell anyone else. We would never betray each other's trust.

Marie Vallejo stood in my cubicle; her height matched mine. Her dark, straight hair cascaded down her shoulders and framed her stunning face. The rich brown of her eyes sparkled with vitality, and her smile was radiant and infectious. Even without a trace of makeup, she was a vision of beauty. I couldn't help but envy her youth and natural allure.

"Come on, buddy, spill." Marie knew who Andrew Collier was. She, too, was a "Two Hearts" fan. "Andrew Collier?"

I had told her about my letter ages ago. Neither of us would have ever dreamed Andrew would show up here.

"I can't believe it, either," I said after I had told her the same story I had told Anita.

"You are, like, the luckiest woman on Earth."

"I wouldn't say *that*."

"You've got this hot British actor flying from England to see you for no reason, and then you have Chris admitting he likes you."

"You call that luck?" I laughed.

"Uh...yeah."

"Confused is more like it." I put my head back on my desk. "What am I going to do, Marie?"

"Well, I'm still shocked Chris isn't freaking out about Andrew staying with you this weekend. He knows, doesn't he?"

"Yeah," I sighed and ran my fingers through my hair. "He *did* freak out. What am I going to do?"

"See how things go this weekend."

"What about Chris?"

"Yeah, what about Chris?"

"I don't want to hurt him. I have been waiting for a year for him to tell me how he feels, and now..."

"Andrew shows up."

"Why did I write that damn letter?"

"You didn't know this was going to happen."

"Yeah, but now I'm stuck. I wish Chris would have told me last year how he felt. I would never have written that letter."

"I think he was trying to tell you, Sarah. He was at your house all the time, helping you. I think that was his way of telling you."

"I know. Neither one of us pushed it."

"He told me so many times he wanted to grab you and kiss you."

"No, he didn't."

She nodded and smiled. "Yeah, he did. I think he loves you."

"No, no. I'm not ready for *that*."

"Neither is he. Listen, Andrew is sexy, sure, but you have no emotional attachment to him, although that might change after this weekend." Her forehead creased. "Don't sleep with him, okay?"

"I'm not planning on it. My head is too messed up to put myself in that situation."

"Don't." She glanced at her watch. "It's four. I don't suppose you've gotten any work done, have you?"

"No, and I most likely won't, either."

"It will be okay. You'll figure it out and by Monday, you and I can gossip at lunch." With that, she grinned and walked away.

Between the friendly interruptions and my brain in a fog, I couldn't concentrate on my job. There was no way any of this was happening to me. I had to have fallen asleep at my desk and was dreaming the whole thing. I pinched myself. Nope, I was awake.

***

The hour dragged on, but when five o'clock arrived, I rushed out the door. Chris had left two hours earlier to pick his kids up from school, but I hoped Andrew would wait, either in the front office or downstairs in the lobby. Kelly had told me earlier he called and said he might be late.

He had kept his word, though. Andrew was chatting with Kelly at the front desk. She was in complete awe of him. Who wouldn't be? He was gorgeous. He peered over his long lashes and gave me a knee-weakening smile. "Are you ready?"

"Yes." I breathed deep and picked up my flowers.

"Let me take those for you." I opened the door for him. "Have a nice weekend, Kelly," he said as he walked out.

"You, too." She smiled at me.

"Are you sure you want to see my crappy house?" I asked him as I guided him onto the elevator.

"It can't be that bad."

"You'll see. It's not too late to run away."

"I'm not running away." He laughed and followed me to my car.

"Do you need a ride, or do you have a car?" What a stupid question. Of course, he had a car. I didn't think he'd take an Uber.

"I rented a car." He didn't even acknowledge my stupid question. What a gentleman. "I'll follow you."

"That works out perfectly. This way you can drive away." I put the flowers on the floorboard of the passenger seat.

"Please stop." He grinned and shook his head, then he walked to his rented compact car.

"I drove home a little slower than my normal, careful pace. Andrew wasn't familiar with the city, and I didn't want him getting lost. I lived only a few miles from the office, but it was still dark at five.

He parked in the driveway next to my Nissan. I got out of my car and grabbed my flowers and waited for him. "Are you ready to see my meager living arrangements?"

"I doubt it's meager." He grinned and took the flowers out of my arms and followed me up my paint-chipped front porch steps. I opened the door and let him go in first. He set the flowers on the coffee table.

"Well, this is it." I held the door open. "You're free to run now."

He walked toward me, smiling, and closed the door. "Shh." He leaned down and kissed me, the same way he had this afternoon. It made my entire body tingle. "Now, are you going to give me a tour, or do I have to get nosy on my own?"

"Uh, yeah. Sure." He held my hand. "Well, this is my living room, obviously. Couch, chair, television. The basics. I have cable, of course."

"Of course." He smiled. "The fireplace is beautiful."

"Thank you." I took in a deep breath. I could smell his intoxicating cologne. "To the left is my computer room. This is where I spend most of my time on the weekend." I opened the door, and he peeked into the room.

"Not this weekend, I hope?"

"Of course not."

"What's with the seventy's linoleum floor? This has to go."

I rolled my eyes and pulled him toward the master bedroom. "This is my bedroom, which I never use. Oddly enough, I'm more comfortable on the couch. The master bath doesn't work, so I use it for storage."

"Sarah, you can't live like this."

I showed him the other two bedrooms and the bathroom, and he critiqued everything that was falling apart. He wasn't mean about anything. He seemed more concerned about my safety and well-being.

I told him about the dilapidated roof and the broken furnace, but Chris was going to fix the furnace this weekend. He listened to my every word. I figured he was making mental notes about what needed to be fixed.

We were sitting on the couch when he asked, "Are you and this Chris fellow dating?"

I shrugged. "I have no clue what we're doing. We've been friends for a long time, then yesterday, suddenly, he..."

He nodded. "I ask because you've mentioned him several times."

"I didn't realize. I'm sorry."

"Don't be. I don't want to intrude if you two have something going on."

"I'm not sure what we have. We haven't even been alone for anything more than a kiss to happen."

"Do you *want* something to happen?"

"Yes...and no. I mean, Chris kind of freaked out when you showed up today. The jealousy thing bothers me. When I told him you were staying here this weekend, he freaked. He thought you and I were planning to..." I chuckled.

"If he's not comfortable with this..."

"He'll be fine." I put my hand on his knee, then pulled away, realizing what I had done. "I explained it to him. It's fine." I smiled.

"I hope so." He smiled back at me and caressed my face. My stomach flipped. Why did he have to do that? This was difficult for me. In my whole life, I had never been confronted with this kind of situation. I had never had two men vying for my affection before.

We spent the next few hours talking about how and where we grew up, our likes and dislikes, and where we wanted our lives to go.

I already knew about Andrew from reading about him. He grew up with two loving and supportive parents who encouraged him in whatever he did. He had two older sisters. He grew up in Barnes, an upper-middle-class suburb of London. The rumors about him and Karen, his co-star in 'Two Hearts' and 'One Life,' were untrue. They were only friends. He traveled back and forth between London and Los Angeles, but he wanted to settle in L.A. soon and bring his parents out to live there with him. He was a sucker for redheads with green eyes, but I think he was humoring me with that one.

I was afraid of what he was thinking of me as I told him about my sad life. There was no way he would want anything more to do with me after tonight. If he left in the middle of the night, I wouldn't have blamed him. I wouldn't think about that now. I let him talk, and the more I learned about him, the more I wanted to learn. It was getting harder and harder to fight my attraction to this sweet, caring, sexy man.

Before I knew it, it was nine o'clock, and neither of us had eaten dinner.

"What are you hungry for?" I asked him. He raised his eyebrows and had a seductive grin on his face. "Quit." I giggled and pushed his shoulder. Even touching him in jest sent a current of electricity through my body. What was wrong with me?

"I'm teasing. How does pizza sound?"

"I love pizza." I ordered a large pepperoni and some soda, then grabbed some cash from my purse."

"My treat," he told me. "Come, sit down." He patted the couch seat next to him. I sat down and watched him. His expression was somber. He wasn't going to stay. I had scared him off.

"Is something wrong?" Wait for it.

"No. Not at all." He took my hands and put his lips on my palms. Every time he touched me, my insides had spasms. "I'm enjoying myself with you. I'm honoured that you've allowed me to stay with you."

But? "I'm glad you agreed," I smiled at him and waited for the let-down. It never came.

"I want to be your friend, a close friend, maybe even a best friend. You're such a wonderful person, Sarah. I feel terrible that you've had such a long run of bad luck. I want to change that for you. I want to make it better for you." He sighed. "I look at this place, and I want to fix it. All of it."

"Andrew, you..."

"Shh." He put his finger to my lips. "Let me finish, please." I nodded. "You can't live here like this anymore. So much around here needs to be fixed, and I want to be the one to do that for you."

"No." He appeared hurt by my unintentional acidic tone. "I can't let you do that." My tone softened, and he relaxed. "I could never afford to pay you back."

"I'm not asking you to. I don't want you to."

"Please don't spend any money on me. Why would you..."

"I want to spend this weekend learning everything about you. I want to learn more about you long after this weekend has passed."

"I do, too, but I still can't let you spend thousands of dollars on me or my house. I can't give you anything in return."

"You already have. Don't you see that? Your friendship is all the payback I want."

It was apparent I wasn't going to win this debate right now. It would have to wait for another time because the pizza arrived. We sat on the couch and ate and talked about other things.

"I have a radio interview on Monday morning to promote the third movie. We're going to film 'Silence' next month.

"This whole thing must be so overwhelming for you. I can't imagine how you're dealing with this sudden fame."

"It's crazy. I hide out a lot." He laughed. "I never expected it to be this massive."

"I'll tell you, I've read the books, and I saw 'Two Hearts' and 'One Life' at the midnight openings. I became obsessed.

"I was going to ask you how you're able to get around town without being mobbed."

He leaned in close and whispered. "No one knows I'm here. Shh."

"All of Denver will before the weekend is over. Kelly will announce it to everyone on her Facebook." I frowned. "She means well, but still."

"It's alright." He patted my knee.

He finished his slice of pizza and went to the kitchen for another slice. I watched him and still couldn't believe Andrew Collier was in my kitchen, stuffing his face. Again, I felt as if any second, I was going to wake up like this was some kind of surreal dream. If it was a dream, I didn't want to wake up.

Andrew caught me looking at him and smiled, a mouthful of pepperoni pizza puffing his cheeks out like a squirrel. "Sorry." I blushed and looked away.

"No." His mouth was still full. He came back and sat down next to me again and took a drink of his soda. "It's fine. I like it."

"You have teenage girls staring at you and chasing you and screaming your name all the time. I'm sure you're sick of it."

"They aren't you." He grinned again and leaned over and kissed me. I blushed. "Does that bother you?"

"Not at all. I keep wondering..." I was afraid to ask.

"What?"

"Well," I took a breath and continued. "Why? What's the real reason? You've seen me, you're sitting with me in my run-down house, and we have talked for hours, but you aren't running away."

"Why would I want to? You are unbelievable. You're funny and smart and beautiful. I'm enjoying all of it."

"Are you?"

"I am." That beautiful smile again.

"And you aren't disgusted?"

"Not in the least." He took my hands. "Stop this now, alright? I'm having fun with you. I want to continue to have fun with you."

"Okay."

He kissed me and kept his lips on mine for what seemed like an eternity. When he moved away, I was out of breath, and my heart was racing again.

"So, what do you have planned for tomorrow?" I asked once I had found myself. "I mean, it's not like you can go to many public places without being spotted and mobbed.

"I've gotten used to that. I'm open to whatever you have planned."

"Hmm. I need to go to the grocery store, but I'm sure you don't want to go." I chuckled. The image of being surrounded by crazy teenage girls made me a little uneasy.

"I want to go with you."

"No, you don't. It's crowded and obnoxious for ordinary people. I don't even want to imagine what's going to happen if a celebrity of your caliber is spotted."

"I want to go with you," he insisted. "It's not like I've never been to a grocery store."

I couldn't help but laugh. "It's your funeral, buddy."

"I'll risk it," he told me, "As long as you stay by my side."

"Do you think I'd leave you alone?" We both laughed.

***

Before I knew it, it was after one in the morning. I got up and went to change into some sweats and a t-shirt.

"We should get some sleep. I don't do well with no sleep."

"Do you mind if I stay up and watch the telly for a while?"

I shook my head and grinned. Someday I would get used to his sexy accent, but I was certain it wouldn't be soon. "I don't mind at all," I told him as I lay next to him on the couch and closed my eyes.

I got comfortable under the covers on the sofa. Andrew took my feet and put them on his lap and began rubbing them. My eyes shot open. He was looking at me with a sweet smile on his lips. "Too much," he asked.

"No way. It feels wonderful." I grinned and closed my eyes and got comfortable again. If Andrew Collier wanted to rub my feet, I would let him. It didn't take me long to fall asleep.

Chapter Two – Andrew

I sat on Sarah's couch, rubbing her feet and watching her sleep. She was too beautiful for words. Not in the classic supermodel way, but her heart and her soul were so open, despite her hard life.

I saw myself with her for a long time if she'd let me. It didn't matter that she was ten years my senior, or that she was interested in another man. She was an amazing woman; so smart and funny. I would accept being her friend if that was all we were meant to be.

I felt the need to take care of her, to give her better than what she had. I glanced around the room. She deserved better than this, and I was going to make sure she got it.

I started thinking about the day in early January when my agent, Susan Rael, handed me Sarah's letter. I had been so busy with movie premiers and press conferences. Susan usually sent out autographed pictures to my fans because I didn't have time to do it anymore. That bothered me. Apparently, she thought this letter was unique.

"You have to read this letter, Andrew. This woman is too much." She handed me the two envelopes, one of which contained her picture. She was beautiful.

Susan's face was set in a stern expression. She had a certain air about her, one which suggested she was not to be messed with. She was past her prime, in her forties, and had never been married. The lines on her face told a story of disappointment and resignation. It was clear she had given up on finding love, whether it be with a man or a woman. Her sexual identity was a mystery, but it didn't matter to me.

It was clear she didn't care about frivolous things like appearances. As she sat at her desk, I noticed how her hair, once a bright blonde, was now faded and streaked with strands of gray. Her once bright hazel eyes had lost their sparkle and seemed to fade with age. She was the same height as me, and despite her height, her figure was hidden beneath layers of shapeless clothing that looked as if they had come from the reject bin in a thrift store. It was as if she had given up on taking care of herself, both physically and emotionally.

I wondered about her life outside of being a talent agent. Did she have any hobbies or passions? Did she have any friends or family?

The walls of her small office were bare, the furniture was old and worn, and the air was heavy with the smell of neglect. The room mirrored Susan's own life, one that lacked color and joy.

As I read the letter and admired at Sarah's picture, I knew I had to contact her. There was something about her. I wasn't sure what it was, not only her beauty, but I knew I had to talk to her. Anyone who put this much effort into a simple request for an autographed picture had to be extraordinary.

"I have to meet her," I told Susan.

"You're kidding? She might be some psycho. I didn't show you her letter so you would run off and get yourself hacked up by some loon."

"I doubt she's a psycho. Besides, if she is, that will be *my* problem. If you don't help me, I'll go on my own." I sat down across from her at her desk. "Are you going to help me or not?"

"No. I will not assist you with this. You're insane."

"Please do this for me, Susan. Please."

She sighed, frustrated. I think she knew I would go to Denver on my own. "Fine. I'll try to arrange some kind of interview to promote "Silence"."

"Thank you, Susan," I smiled at her and left her office.

The next couple of weeks were dragging for me. I was doing a few more press conferences with Karen Steele and Trevor Landers, my co-stars in 'Two Hearts' and 'One Life.' I was also acting in a couple of small venue productions and playing music on the weekends. I needed to pass the time. I was eager to go to the states.

***

One cold Saturday I went home to my parent's house. I hadn't seen my mum in over a week. That was unlike me, and I was feeling guilty about it.

"Andrew, it's so good to see you," my mum chirped when she saw me at the door.

"I'm sorry it's been so long."

She hugged me. "Come in. It's freezing." I followed her to the kitchen where my family spent lots of time when I was growing up. A lot of broken hearts had been mended, and quite a few punishments had been doled out at this kitchen table.

"Would you like some tea?" she asked.

"That would be perfect," I said as I entered the kitchen, the comforting scent of Earl Grey greeted me. My tall, slender mother stood at the stove, her delicate hands preparing the tea. Her blonde hair fell in a straight curtain, framing her piercing blue eyes. She seemed ageless, as if time had no hold on her. Growing up, I had always seen her as twenty-five years old.

Her strength was clear in every move, her unwavering presence filling the room. She never needed to raise her voice. Her firm but fair demeanor commanded respect. As I watched her, a warm smile spread across my face. "Is dad at work?" I asked, breaking the silence.

"Yes. Your father has been working so hard for the past several weeks." My father was a bank manager. With the global economic troubles, Roger Collier. was working extra hours to ensure that his branch stayed afloat.

"You remember I suggested he retire? I can take care of the family now."

"Yes, dear, but your father is a proud man. Besides, he would go mad if he didn't work." She brought the tea to the table and sat down next to me. "So, tell me, son, what has been going on with you?"

"I've been working, too. I've had some gigs. They have been going well. "Silence" begins filming next month. I'm planning a quick trip to the states in a couple of weeks." I smiled at her.

"What is that all about?" She sipped her tea and glanced at me over her cup.

"Susan is getting me an interview to promote the new movie."

"That's fantastic."

"And I met someone. Well, sort of."

"Sort of?"

"I haven't exactly *met* her yet. That's part of the reason I'm going to Colorado."

"Colorado?"

"Yes."

"Who is this girl?"

I pulled Sarah's picture from my coat pocket. I carried it with me all the time. Then I handed her the letter.

"She's beautiful," she said, giving the picture of Sarah back to me. She scanned the letter, chuckling. Then she frowned. "Thirty-five? Andrew, I don't know..."

"Mum, it's not an issue."

"Of course it is. I would like to have a grandchild someday."

I sighed. "I didn't say I was going to marry Sarah. I only want to meet her."

"My goodness, Andrew, she might be a crazy woman. I'd much rather see you with Karen."

I laughed. "You sound like Susan."

"Susan is a smart woman." My mother patted my hand.

"Mother, I love you, but I'll be fine."

"Alright. Enough of this." She grinned at me. "You need a shave."

"No, I don't."

"You're scruffy. I don't care for it." She sipped her tea. "And your hair..."

I ran my fingers through my messy locks. "My hair is fine."

"You need a cut, too."

I rolled my eyes and glanced at the clock on the wall. "I need to go. I'm playing at the Bellvue tonight."

My mother walked me to the door. "Please be careful while you're in the states."

"I will, mum. I promise." I kissed her cheek and gave her a hug. "I'll come by before I leave."

"Make sure you do." She smiled at me, and I got in my car and drove back to my flat in Chelsea.

***

It had been a long night. I had played my heart out, one acoustic love song after another. I couldn't stop thinking about Sarah Miller. I wanted to meet her. I *needed* to meet her. It was taking too long for Susan to arrange this interview.

The next morning, at six, Susan called with the news. A Denver radio station would interview me on a popular morning show the last Monday in January.

"You're scheduled to promote "Silence" next Monday. You'll be leaving Heathrow on Thursday evening. You'll have an entire weekend with your psycho lady, as long as she doesn't kill you first."

"Would you stop? I'll come by the office later to pick up my tickets. You're a lifesaver."

"I had to pull a lot of strings for this interview. Don't make me regret it, Andrew."

"You know that will not happen."

"You need to be back here on Tuesday. You have a photo shoot Wednesday morning."

"I know. I'm coming back. You and my mother should have tea together."

She laughed and hung up.

I tried to go back to sleep, but my head was racing. I was going to meet Sarah Miller; that charming woman who was making me impatient.

I wasn't able to fall asleep, so I showered and shaved; the shaving was a rarity for me. Around nine-thirty, I drove to Susan's office. I couldn't wait to for those plane tickets.

"I owe you, Susan," I told her as she gave me the itinerary. I would arrive in Denver early Friday morning. A limo would pick me up at the airport. That wouldn't work for me. Someone would spot me if I rode around in a limo. I frowned at her.

"What's the matter now?"

"Please cancel the limo. I would rather rent a car. I don't want anyone to know I'm in town until I'm on the radio."

"The DJs are already promoting your interview. How do you plan on avoiding it?"

"No one has to know I'm there until I'm in the building."

"Don't you suppose Ms. Miller will tell everyone she knows she has met the monstrously famous Andrew Collier?"

"I don't think she's like that. I don't believe she would do that."

Susan let out an exasperated moan. "You know nothing about her."

"I have a feeling about her."

"A feeling?"

"Yeah."

"Oh, okay. That makes me feel so much better." She rolled her eyes and shook her head and sighed. "Fine, Andrew, I'll cancel the limo. You can attempt to sneak around an enormous city like Denver until you arrive at the radio station." She shook her head again. "I still don't feel right about this."

"You don't have to."

"What do they call male divas?"

"Charming," I said with a smirk as I walked to the door. "Love you," I called out as I left.

"Go home, Andrew." I heard her chuckling as I left the outer office.

***

Back at my flat, I went over my itinerary again. I would stay The Brown Palace Hotel. Very high class, and too conspicuous. Was Susan trying to get me noticed?

Winter in Colorado was like England, so I would need sweaters and wool trousers. I had less than a week to prepare for this trip, and only two and a half days with Sarah to make the same impression on her she had made on me. I only hoped I lived up to her expectations. I wasn't worried about her living up to mine. I was certain she would exceed them.

The week was dragging, but on Wednesday evening, I paid a visit to my family before I left for the states.

My dad and older sisters, Veronica and Laura, were there, and we sat in the kitchen, as we often did, and had a long chat.

My sisters had a lot to say about my trip to Colorado.

"I cannot believe you're flying all the way to the states to see some woman you've never met," Veronica complained.

"Andrew," Laura began, "what do you know about her?"

"I wish all of you would stop. I'm a grown man. I can take care of myself."

"You're Andrew Collier, not just *some guy*. There's a difference," Laura piped.

My father almost never said a word, but when he did, he made sense. But it was too late for me to change my mind. "Son, we realize you can take care of yourself, but you are also famous. Please be careful. Don't get emotionally attached to this woman."

My dad stood tall at an impressive six feet three inches, towering over my mother and me. His full head of grey hair was always combed back, revealing his sparkling blue eyes and bushy eyebrows. He seemed to radiate happiness, always wearing a permanent smile. He was a man who exuded joy and contentment. His happiness and love for life were infectious.

"I think I already am."

"Good grief, Andrew." Veronica's eyes widened in disbelief as she gazed at me. She let out a heavy sigh, her patience already wearing thin. "How is this even possible?" Her voice was tinged with frustration. Veronica was the eldest of us Collier siblings, and her resemblance to our mother was uncanny. Her long, straight blonde hair and piercing blue eyes were a mirror image of our mother's. Standing tall and slender, with curves in all the right places, she radiated beauty. However, unlike the rest of our family, Veronica carried herself with a demure grace.

"There is something about her. I can't explain it. You've all seen her picture and read her letter. Can't any of you see that there is something exceptional about her?"

Laura studied the picture for a moment before shaking her head. "I don't see it," she said, her eyes never leaving the portrait. "She's thirty-five," Laura continued, her tone conveying a sense of disbelief. "Practically a spinster." My sister Laura bore a striking resemblance to our mother, as well. She possessed the same tall and graceful figure, with long, flowing blonde hair and captivating hazel eyes. But unlike our sister Veronica, Laura exuded an air of lightheartedness and humor. She was the life of the party, always ready with a witty remark or a playful joke.

"I want you to promise me you'll be careful, son," my dad told me again. "Claudia, will you please bring me my address book? It's on my desk in the study," he asked my mum.

"You're crazy, Andrew. I would never fly thousands of miles to meet up with some guy," Veronica told me.

"I would hope not. I don't think your husband would care for that very much," Laura joked. We all laughed, and the mood lightened a little.

My mother came back with my dad's address book. He opened it and wrote a name and address on a piece of paper, then pushed it across the table toward me.

"This is my friend, Lawrence, in Boulder, Colorado. Please ring him if you need to," my dad told me. "I'll give him a ring and let him know you may be in contact."

"Thank you, dad, but I'm staying in a hotel. Susan has planned my entire trip."

"That's good to hear," my mum said, relieved.

"I'll be alright. I promise." With that, I stood up and walked around the table to hug my mother. "I need to head home. I have to pack, and I need some sleep."

Everyone followed me to the door, and I hugged each of them.

"Call Lawrence if you find yourself in any trouble," my dad told me again.

"I will," I said, then walked out to my car.

***

I couldn't sleep again. It was after one in the morning, and I was awake. I had to go for a walk or something to burn off some energy. It wasn't doing me any good sitting in my dark flat with my mind racing the way it was.

It was raining, and I was sure it was freezing, so I bundled up and headed out. I hadn't planned a route; I wanted to walk and made it several blocks before realizing I was cold.

I was on King's Road and found myself in front of Gypsy Souls, a twenty-four-hour café. I went inside and ordered a coffee and sat down near the front window. I wanted to watch the misty rain and think.

I was thankful it was the middle of the night. No one was on the street or in the café. I was alone and didn't have to worry about being hounded by the press or fans.

I peered up and saw my ex-girlfriend, Natalie Brennan, walk in. She didn't see me until she was on her way out.

"Andrew," she squealed, surprised to see me, and sat down at my table.

"Hello, Natalie. How have you been?" I hadn't seen or wanted to see her in almost a year.

"I've been spectacular. Thank you for asking." She smiled and flipped her blonde hair off her shoulder. "What are you doing out in public?"

I sighed. I didn't want to talk to Natalie. "It's the middle of the night. I couldn't sleep. I think I'm safe."

"I finished a photo shoot. I'm doing very well for myself." She batted her long eyelashes over her deep blue eyes and showed me her perfect white smile.

"That's great." I didn't care.

"I hear you're doing well for yourself."

"Yeah."

"You sure aren't very chatty."

"I have a lot on my mind." I wished she would go away.

It had been a nasty breakup. Natalie had always been so full of herself. That hadn't changed.

Natalie had cheated on me, and when I caught her with her lover, I lost it. We yelled, we cried, we screamed. She tried to blame me for her infidelity. She said it was because I was never around, but neither was she. Natalie was always traveling around the world on photo shoots. Her modeling career came before anything, including me and our relationship. Those were easy to live with, but not the cheating, so I threw her out and hadn't seen her since, until that night in the café. It annoyed me I had to on this occasion.

"I need to go," I said and stood up. "Goodbye, Natalie."

"Andrew?"

I turned and glared at her. "What?"

"You're still angry?"

"Not angry. Annoyed."

"Well, I thought since we ran into each other we might talk and maybe..."

I sat back down and, through gritted teeth, growled, "not if you were the last woman on earth."

She appeared shocked and hurt. "But, why?"

"Aside from the fact that you cheated, I'm seeing someone."

"Who?"

"None of your business." I stood up and walked to the door. "Goodbye." I pulled my coat collar up and walked out into the freezing rain. I didn't look back.

***

I had only gotten a few hours of sleep, and I was finding it difficult to fill my day before I had to leave. I packed my carry-on bag, took a shower, then called Susan around five thirty to let her know I would leave for the airport soon and to thank her again for doing this for me.

"Call me when you land in Denver," she told me before we hung up.

"I will, and I promise, everything is going to be fine."

"I hope so, Andrew. Do you want me to send you a car?"

"No, I'm going to take a taxi."

"Alright. Have a safe trip."

"Bye, Susan. Thanks again." I hung up and watched the telly for another hour before I heard the cab driver honking out on the street, then I hurried downstairs with my bag.

***

No one gave me a second glance at Heathrow. No paparazzo was waiting for me because no one knew I was leaving. I was safe from the cameras and flashbulbs and the hordes of fans, who always seemed to know where I was every minute of the day.

After an hour of waiting at the gate, first-class passengers were called, and I got on the plane and found my seat. I wanted to sleep, but I still had a lot to think about. I wasn't paying attention to the flight attendant's announcement of the emergency procedures. I had heard them a hundred times.

Once the plane was in the air, I reclined my seat and closed my eyes. My first order of business was to buy an enormous, very aromatic bouquet. I would find a florist near Sarah's office after I checked in at the hotel. I drifted off and didn't wake until we were descending upon Denver International Airport almost ten hours later.

Despite the busy terminal, I remained inconspicuous as I went to the rental counter to rent my car. The rental agent assigned me a nice, ordinary compact car. I picked up my bag and took a van to the rental lot and found my car. I was afraid someone was going to recognize me in the swarm of travelers.

With the GPS in the car, I found The Brown Palace Hotel with no problem. I parked in the underground car park and checked in. The cute blonde behind the concierge desk gave me only a hint of recognition, but she never said a word. I assumed she had met several celebrities, and she was professional enough not to make a scene.

"Here's your card key, Mr. Collier. You'll be in room seven-oh-six. Have a pleasant stay with us," the girl told me with a perky voice and lovely smile.

"Thank you," I replied and took the elevator up to my room on the seventh floor.

I made my promised call to Susan but cut it short because it was almost ten a.m. I didn't have time to waste. I needed to find a florist and go to Sarah's office.

I found a small family-owned florist called Cherry Blossoms, a few blocks from Sarah's office.

The kind, older woman running the shop most definitely did not recognize me.

"How may I help you?" she asked with a bright smile.

"Good morning," I smiled at her. "I need a big, beautiful bouquet."

"What are you looking for?"

"The most fragrant flowers. I want my girlfriend to be intoxicated by the aroma." This woman would never know that Sarah wasn't my girlfriend.

"There are several in bloom this time of year," she told me as she pulled a book from under the counter with pictures of flowers from which to choose.

By the time I left the shop, I had a beautiful crystal vase filled with Calla Lilies, Chrysanthemums, Freesia, Gardenias, Orchids, and White Roses. There were other flowers, but I couldn't recall their names, as well as Baby's Breath and other garnishments for filler. The arrangement was exquisite and the scents blending together took my breath away, the same way Sarah had the first time I saw her picture. I hoped the bouquet did the same for her.

Damn, but that vase was heavier than I thought.

I checked the clock on the dashboard. It was eleven forty-five. I still had a few minutes to take in a few deep breaths and calm my nerves before I went inside.

Two women stood behind the reception desk in the office where Sarah worked. One was older than the other, and she was leaning on the counter next to the younger girl. They both glanced up when I came in with the heavy vase. Both women smiled, and they stared at me as if they knew me from somewhere.

"No way," the younger girl said, her mouth agape.

The older woman tapped her on the shoulder and cleared her throat. She never looked away. "May I help you?"

"Yes, I have a delivery for Sarah Miller, and I must give these to her myself."

"Of course," the older woman said, still smiling, still staring. "I'll bring Sarah out," the woman backed up and disappeared behind the door.

The young girl behind the desk remembered herself and said, "can I offer you something to drink?" Still, she kept her eyes on me.

It occurred to me. Had I made a mistake by coming to Sarah's place of business? Was it possible that my cover was blown? It was clear these two women knew who I was.

At that moment, I heard the door open, so I stepped behind the bouquet I had placed on the receptionist's desk. I saw Sarah walk out. She was more beautiful in person. She saw the flowers and gasped. That was my cue to step out from my hiding spot. "Sarah?" She saw me and her eyes widened. She appeared to be ill.

"Will you excuse me for a minute, please," Sarah forced out, then ran out of the room through the door to her right. The two other women followed behind her.

They left me in the reception area alone. I wasn't sure what to do. Was this a mistake? I shouldn't have come. But as I was about to go, the older woman came back.

"Mr. Collier, would you follow me, please? Sarah would like to see you."

"Certainly." I gave her a quick smile and followed her. A very upset man crossed my path and scowled at me. He glared at me as if he wanted to kill me.

"Are you alright, Sarah?" I asked when I reached the door of what appeared to be the employee kitchen. She only nodded.

I picked up a dropped chair. I assumed the guy who appeared as if he wanted to kill me had abandoned it. I sat down next to her.

"Are you sure?"

"Yeah." She gave me a quick smile, so I smiled back. At that moment, I felt the need to put my arms around her. I didn't, but she appeared so small and fragile to me at that moment. "What are you... I mean, how did you... um... Why?" She had her head tilted, shock and confusion in her eyes.

"I needed to bring you the flowers," I smiled, and I heard her breath catch in her throat. "I'll tell you; this office is difficult to find. GPS is a lifesaver." She gazed up at me. The colour was returning to her face. "And to answer your why... because your letter intrigued me, and your picture, well, you're more beautiful in person."

"So are you," she said with a quick laugh. She watched the door. My eyes followed hers. We were being watched by her co-workers. They were standing at the door, and when they noticed us watching them, they all departed. "I, um, need some air. Do you mind?"

"Not at all." I stood and helped her to her feet. She seemed a little unsteady.

We took the lift downstairs, and I held the door for her.

We walked to a patch of grass on the other side of the lot and sat down, facing each other. "So, are you surprised?" I asked.

"That's the understatement of the year." She shook her head and smiled. She played with the grass. "I'm wondering..." I cocked my head, interested in what she had to say. She glanced at me. "Why are you here?"

"I told you. Your letter intrigued me. I had to meet the woman who wrote it." I took her hands in mine. It felt as if she was shaking.

"Disappointed," she asked.

"Not at all. You're more than I expected. What about me?"

"Are you kidding?" she chuckled. "Remember, I said, 'You're beautiful, inside and out'?"

"Yes, but pictures don't always do a person justice. Yours didn't."

"Neither do yours." She grinned at me and shook her head. "I feel like an idiot."

"Why?"

"I'm thirty-five years old. You're twenty-five. What was I thinking? Jeez, what were you thinking coming here?"

"Are you sorry?" I asked. I had no concern about the age difference.

"Not at all. But I didn't expect the pictures I asked for. I hoped, but I never thought I would sit here with you, having an actual conversation. This is the kind of thing girls dream about, but it never happens in real life."

"Well, I'm thrilled to be here. I'm glad I came, Sarah." I stood up and pulled her to her feet. I gazed into her eyes. She appeared nervous.

"I'm glad, too."

"I had better get you back to work." She gave me a little frown, and I chuckled.

"Where are you staying?"

"The Brown Palace, downtown. Do you know it?"

"Everyone knows the Brown Palace."

"How far is it from your house?"

"Twenty minutes when there's no traffic."

"That won't do." Too far. I had to think about this. Perhaps the hotel across the street from her office building would be closer.

"Well, my house is a piece of crap, but..." She stopped with concern on her beautiful face.

"But what?"

"I was going to ask you if you wanted to stay at my place while you're here, but I'm too embarrassed by it. You're used to mansions and luxury hotel suites."

"Sarah," I began with a chuckle, "I lived in an RV while we were filming 'Two Hearts' and 'One Life.'"

"That may be, but my place is falling apart. It's... gross." She wrinkled her nose, and I tapped it. I felt a bit of a spark when I did.

"I don't believe that."

"Fine... would you like to stay with me while you're here?" She was reluctant to agree, but gave in.

"Yes, I would," I smiled and put my arm around her shoulder. That spark again. What was that? It didn't matter. I liked it, so I squeezed her shoulder as we walked back toward the building.

"So, I'll see you later," she asked once we were back upstairs in front of her office.

"Of course. I'm going to have some lunch, then check out of the hotel, then I'll meet you here later and follow you to your house." I had already confirmed that she left work at five o'clock.

"Okay." She peered down at her feet. Why wouldn't she look at me?

I was inches from her. "Hey," I whispered.

"Yeah?" She gazed at me, and I stooped and kissed her. That incredible shock had turned into a current of electricity.

"You okay?" I asked when our lips parted. I wasn't sure I was.

"More than okay." She grinned at me, and I walked backward toward the lift. We watched each other until the doors closed in front of me. I took a deep breath, and when the doors opened and I was near the front of the building, I heard her say goodbye from the landing above. I smiled at her and waved, then walked out.

Was she feeling what I was feeling? I thought as I started the car and pulled out of the lot. Did she feel the sparks, too? I reflected on those questions as I drove along the highway toward the hotel.

I didn't want to screw this up. I didn't want to push Sarah or scare her away. Sarah Miller was an amazing woman. I intended to spend the next two days showing her how incredible I thought she was.

I had never unpacked my bag, so when I got to the hotel, I took a shower, grabbed something quick to eat in the hotel restaurant, then checked out of my room.

"Were our accommodations unsatisfactory, Mr. Collier?" the girl behind the desk asked when I told her I was checking out early.

"Oh, no. A friend of mine offered to let me stay with her."

The girl appeared deflated when I said 'her,' but she remained professional and said, "Thank you for staying with us."

"Thank you," I grinned at her and headed for my rented car. I pulled out my phone and rang Susan as I walked. She would not be happy with this, but I needed to let her know there would be a credit on her agency account. I didn't care if my staying with Sarah pissed her off. I was doing what my heart was telling me to do.

"You're doing what?" Susan shouted into the phone. I knew that would be her reaction.

"You heard me. Listen, I didn't call to fight with you about it. I wanted to let you know about the credit."

"Andrew, I swear to Almighty God. You've gone insane."

"Crazy would be the correct term." I was sitting in the car with the engine running.

"Beyond crazy. You're risking your career, Andrew. You can't imagine what will happen if the press gets wind of this." She was still shouting.

"Susan, I'm crazy about her." Saying that out loud made my heart race. I was crazy about her already, but I couldn't explain why."

"No! No! NO!"

"I'll be all right, Susan. I have to go."

"Andrew, I'm not kidding. I..." That was the last word I heard because I had hung up on her and drove out of the car park.

It was rush hour, and the motorway was congested when I got on it. The cars were at a stand-still and I was afraid I wouldn't make it back to Sarah's office before she left. She might think I had decided not to come and go home. I could find her house. After all, I had GPS and her address, but I would have rather followed her home. I called the office and let the receptionist know I was in heavy traffic and to let Sarah know.

"Please ask her not to leave if I'm not there. I *will* be there."

"I'll let her know, Mr. Collier."

Now the traffic had stopped completely, and the woman in the car to my left was staring at me. I was sure she recognized me. I saw her shake her head in disbelief, then look back at me. I smiled in her direction.

The cars were moving so slow, but I reached my exit and made my way round the corner to Sarah's office building. I had several minutes to spare, and I made my way upstairs to her office.

It was almost five o'clock when I arrived at the building. I went inside to wait for Sarah. The receptionist, who I learned was Kelly, again asked me if I wanted something to drink. I politely declined.

"She's sweet," Kelly told me.

"She is," I agreed.

"She has been through a lot." Kelly sighed. She closed down her workstation as she spoke. "She's coming out of some personal issues, and then there's that business with Chris."

"I'm sorry?" I was confused, but she couldn't finish. Sarah opened the door and stepped out. I couldn't help but smile at her. "Are you ready?" I asked her.

"Yes." She walked to the vase to carry it out.

"Let me take those for you," I told her, and she held the door for me. "Have a nice weekend, Kelly," I called as Sarah guided me out the door.

"You, too," she smiled at Sarah.

"Are you sure you want to see my crappy house?" Sarah asked as she guided me to the lift.

"It can't be that bad."

"You'll see. It's not too late to run away."

"I'm not running away," I chuckled and followed her to the car.

"Do you need a ride, or do you have a car?" She appeared sorry for asking that question, so I gave her a quick answer.

"I rented a car. I'll follow you."

"That works out perfectly. This way you can drive away." I watched her put the flowers on the floor of her car.

"Please stop." I grinned and shook my head. It couldn't be as bad as she was making it out to be.

I walked to my car and followed her to her house.

It didn't take long to arrive at Sarah's house, even with the excess of rush hour traffic. On the short drive, I had time to ponder that last statement Kelly made about Chris. I guessed Chris was the man who gave me the evil eye this morning. I had to ask Sarah what was going on with him.

I parked my car next to Sarah's Nissan in her driveway and went around to help her with the vase. "Are you ready to see my meager living arrangements?" she asked, only half joking, I was sure.

"I doubt it's meager," I smiled and took the vase from her and followed her up the porch steps. She opened the door and let me go in first, and I set the vase down on the coffee table.

"Well, this is it." She held the door open. "You're free to run now."

I walked toward her, smiling, then pushed the door closed. "Shh." I leaned down and kissed her the way I had earlier. The electricity raced through me again, and I wondered if she felt it, too. "Now, are you going to give me a tour, or do I have to get nosy on my own?"

"Uh, yeah. Sure." I held her hand as she led me from one room to another. "Well, this is my living room, obviously. Couch, chair, television. The basics. I have cable, of course."

I smiled at her. "Of course," I said. Her silly sarcasm was going to grow on me.

I glanced up and noticed a lovely fireplace on the back wall. I loved it. "The fireplace is beautiful."

"Thank you. To the left is my computer room. This is where I spend most of my time on the weekend." She opened the door, and I took a peek inside.

"Not this weekend, I hope?"

"Of course not."

"What's with the seventy's linoleum floor? This has to go."

She rolled her eyes at me and guided me toward the bedroom. "This is my bedroom, which I never use. Oddly enough, I'm more comfortable on the couch. The master bath doesn't work, so I use it for storage."

I was sad for her. "Sarah, you can't live like this."

She showed me the other two bedrooms and the bathroom. I couldn't help but critique everything. I didn't want to hurt her feelings, but I knew she couldn't live in this house with it in such disrepair. I had to help her, especially when she told me about her broken furnace and leaky roof. She said Chris was bringing a part this weekend to fix the furnace. It was then that I realized people cared for her, and she deserved it and needed it. It also made me wonder if she and Chris were an item. Maybe that's what Kelly had been talking about.

We sat together on the couch, and I had to ask. "Are you and this Chris fellow dating?"

"I have no clue what we're doing. We've been friends for a long time, then yesterday, suddenly he..." She didn't finish, but I understood.

I nodded. "I ask because you've mentioned Chris several times."

"I didn't realize... I'm sorry."

"Don't be. I don't want to intrude if you two have something going on." I wouldn't intrude, but the idea of not being able to be with her made me a little sad.

"I'm not sure what we have. We haven't even been alone for anything more than a kiss to happen."

"Do you want something to happen?"

"Yes... and no. I mean, Chris kind of freaked out when you showed up today. The jealousy thing bothers me. When I told him you were staying here this weekend, he freaked. He thought you and I were planning to..." she chuckled.

"If he's not comfortable with this..." She stopped me.

"He'll be fine." She put her hand on my knee, then removed it. I felt the spark of her touch at that moment and wished she hadn't pulled away. "I explained it to him. It's fine." She eyed me and smiled.

I smiled back at her. "I hope so." I caressed her face with my fingertips. I couldn't help myself. I knew I wanted to be with this woman. I was falling for her already. What an odd feeling this was.

For the next few hours, Sarah and I talked and got to know one another. I told her about my life growing up, about my family and my music. I explained to her the reasons I became an actor. As much as being in the spotlight made me nervous, I wanted to explore different avenues of the entertainment industry and how, when 'Two Hearts' became such an enormous hit, I hid out as much as possible when I wasn't working. It was getting harder and harder to do because my face had become so recognizable. I ebbed her concerns about the rumours of Karen and me. We were only friends. Sarah seemed happy to hear that. I explained how I had a thing for redheads with green eyes. I don't think she believed me.

Sarah told me about her childhood as well. It sounded so lonely. Her parents didn't seem to encourage her to pursue her dream of being a writer. The only people who appeared to encourage her were her English teachers. She told me when she turned fifteen; she found an after-school job, so she had some kind of life. As she got older, her priorities had to change. She moved in with her aunt. She wanted to go to college to become a journalist, but she soon met and married a man whom she thought she was in love with. He cheated on her, so she left him. She and her aunt moved from California, where she grew up, to Colorado, where she had been living for fifteen years.

She had one failed relationship after another, never finding true happiness. She felt as if her aunt was discouraging her from bettering herself when she went to college, so at her first opportunity, out of spite, she married the first guy who showed her any interest. That man abused her, so she left him, too.

She had several more failed relationships, but here she was now, living on her own, paying her own way, and getting better. She had friends at work, but not much of a life outside that. I was going to make sure that changed.

After hearing her story, I wanted to hold her and let her cry if she needed to. I didn't care how long it took; I was going to do my best to heal this woman. She needed me, and I believed I needed her, too.

I was falling hard for her.

Before we realized it, it was nine o'clock, and neither of us had eaten dinner.

"What are you hungry for?" she asked me.

I gave her the proverbial eyebrow raise and smiled at her with mock seduction. I needed to lighten the mood. Our conversation had been so intense.

"Quit." She giggled and pushed me.

"I'm teasing," I told her. "How does pizza sound?"

"I love pizza." She ordered a pepperoni pizza and some soda, then got some money out of her purse. She thought she was going to have to pay.

"My treat." I smiled at her and patted the couch next to me. "Come, sit down." She seemed to be a little scared.

"Is something wrong?"

"No. Not at all," I assured her. I took her hands in mine and kissed her palms. I didn't know what possessed me to do that. I only knew I needed to be near her and touch her. "I'm enjoying myself with you. I'm honoured that you've allowed me to stay with you." She was breathing again, but I didn't think I had convinced her I wouldn't run.

"I'm glad you agreed." She gave me a tiny, unsure smile.

"I want to be your friend, a close friend, maybe a best friend." I didn't want to push a relationship with her. "You're such a wonderful person, Sarah. I feel terrible that you've had such a long run of bad luck. I want to change that for you. I want to make it better for you." I glanced around the room, then sighed. I felt almost helpless for her, but I knew I wanted to help her. "I look at this place, and I want to fix it. All of it."

"Andrew, you..."

She tried to protest, but with a finger to her soft lips, I stopped her. "Shh. Let me finish, please." She agreed and was quiet. She was watching me with sad, grateful eyes. She wanted to protest, but there would be no winning for her. "You can't live here like this anymore. So much around here needs to be fixed, and I want to be the one to do that for you."

"No," she told me in a harsh tone. "I can't let you do that." Her tone softened. "I wouldn't be able to pay you back."

"I'm not asking you to. I don't want you to."

"Please don't spend any money on me. Why would you..."

I cut her off. "I want to know you. I want to spend this weekend learning everything about you. I want to learn more about you long after this weekend has passed."

"I do, too, but I still can't let you spend thousands of dollars on me or my house. I can't give you anything in return."

"You already have. Don't you see that? Your friendship is all the payback I want."

The pizza arrived, and I let this conversation go for the time being. I was here to learn about my new friend, and I was happy with that.

"I have a radio interview on Monday morning to promote the new movie. We're going to film 'Silence' next month."

"This whole thing must be so overwhelming for you. I can't imagine how you're dealing with this sudden fame."

"It's crazy. I hide out a lot." I laughed. "I never expected it to be this massive."

"I'll tell you; I've read the books and saw 'Two Hearts' and 'One Life' at the midnight openings. I'm obsessed."

"I was going to ask you how you're able to get around town without being mobbed."

I leaned in close to her and said, "No one knows I'm here. Shh." I grinned at her, and she smiled, too. I was growing to love her smile.

"All of Denver will know before the weekend is over. Kelly will announce it to everyone on her Facebook." Sarah frowned at that thought. "She means well, but still."

"It's alright." I patted her knee, then stood and went to the kitchen to grab another slice of pizza.

I caught her looking at me. I didn't mind. I was watching her, too, twirling her hair around her finger.

"Sorry." Her eyes widened, and she was blushing.

My mouth was full of pizza. "No," I said, heading back to the couch for a drink of soda. "It's fine. I like it."

"You have teenage girls staring at you and chasing you and screaming your name all the time. I'm sure you're sick of it."

"They aren't you," I smiled at her and leaned close to her and kissed her. She was blushing again. "Does that bother you?"

"Not at all. I keep wondering."

"What?"

"Well, why? What's the real reason? You've seen me, you're sitting with me in my run-down house, and we have talked for hours, but you aren't running away."

"Why would I want to? You are unbelievable. You're funny and smart and beautiful. I'm enjoying all of it." I was.

"Are you?"

"I am," I assured her. I smiled at her again.

"And you aren't disgusted?"

"Not in the least." I took her hands in mine. "Stop this now, alright? I'm having fun with you. I want to continue to have fun with you."

"Okay."

I knew she would continue to worry about it. I kissed her and kept my lips on hers for some time. They were warm and soft, and the electricity was welling in me. When we pulled away from each other, I felt my heart beating in my chest. I had to take a couple of deep breaths to slow it down.

"So, what do you have planned for tomorrow?" she asked after a long silence. "I mean, it's not like you can go to many public places without being spotted and mobbed."

"I've gotten used to that. I'm open to whatever you have planned."

"Hmm. I need to go to the grocery store, but I'm sure you don't want to go." She chuckled.

"I want to go with you."

"No, you don't. It's crowded and obnoxious for ordinary people. I don't even want to imagine what's going to happen if a celebrity of your caliber is spotted."

"I want to go with you," I insisted. I felt like a child begging his mother for something before having a tantrum. "It's not like I've never been to a grocery store."

She laughed but gave in. "It's your funeral, buddy."

"I'll risk it. As long as you stay by my side."

"Do you think I'd leave you alone?" We both laughed.

***

It was after one in the morning when Sarah announced she was getting tired and went to change into her pajamas. She came back in sweatpants and a baggy t-shirt. She was so sexy.

"We should probably get some sleep. I don't do very well with no sleep."

"Do you mind if I stay up and watch the telly for a while?" She grinned and shook her head.

"I don't mind at all," she told me as she closed her eyes.

I watched her as she nestled under the blanket beside me. Her face was calm and at peace. She was more beautiful to me at that moment.

I pulled her legs up on my lap and started rubbing her feet. Her eyes shot open then. I didn't realize I had been smiling. "Too much?"

"No way. It feels wonderful." She smiled at me, then closed her eyes again.

Here I was, in Colorado, the United States, thousands of miles from home, not a care in the world. I watched Sarah sleep. The corners of her mouth turned up. It was wonderful to see. I was falling for her, but there was no logical explanation for it. I had only met her, but I felt as if I had known her for years.

As I watched her sleep, I knew what I wanted. I wanted Sarah Miller, and I intended to make her world a better place, no matter what I needed to do.

When I was certain she was in a deep sleep, I went into the bedroom to put on my pajama bottoms and a clean t-shirt. She had told me I could sleep in her bed, but I wanted to stay close to her. I slipped in behind her on the couch, and she stirred. I put my arms around her and held her hand. I kissed her head and closed my eyes and fell asleep.

Chapter Three – Saturday

Sarah woke up on Saturday morning and found herself pinned down by Andrew's arm. Without waking him, she pulled away, got up and started the coffee, turned on her computer, and went to the bathroom.

It annoyed her she had woken up before him. She wanted to stay safe and warm in Andrew's arms all day.

As she left the bathroom, she glanced in the mirror and groaned. Her eyes were puffy. She couldn't allow Andrew to see her like this, so she washed yesterday's make-up off her face and applied her creams and lotions. In her own eyes, no matter how much work she put into her appearance, she would never perceive herself as anything more than ordinary.

Once satisfied with her appearance, she went to the kitchen and fixed her morning mocha. Andrew was still sleeping. She let him sleep to until he woke up on his own. She checked her emails; nothing important, so she took her cup and went to the chair in the living room and turned the television on low to catch the weather.

Andrew was even more handsome when he was asleep, with his tousled hair. He was grinning at something in his dreams. She continued to watch him sleep.

The weather was supposed to be mild, in the fifties again. It was warm for January. She would still need a sweater. Sarah didn't like winter in Colorado. It seemed to always be too cold for her. She used to love walking in the snow, sledding in the park, snowball fights, and making snow angels.

Winter was a sad time for her now. It meant short, wintry days. She hated the cold now since her furnace broke. It never got warm in this house, except in the summer.

Most mornings were so cold, the hairs in her nose were freezing. And when her pipes froze, she couldn't even take a hot shower to get warm.

Sarah had decided a long time ago that if she were rich, she would run away to Australia and live on the beach until she died. Sarah knew that would never happen, so, as fast as the idea came into her head, she pushed it away. There was no point in dwelling on things that would never happen.

That's when she thought about Chris. She never thought he would tell her about his feelings for her, but he had. And he had kissed her to prove it; something he had never even attempted to do in the past. He did nothing more than hug her. It took her a while to realize that's all that was going to happen, but she finally accepted it for what it was: a potential lifelong friendship. Now it was something else, and she wasn't sure what to do about it since Andrew Collier had shown up in her life.

She gazed at Andrew again. He was still sleeping. What was she going to do about him? Here was this gorgeous twenty-five-year-old movie star insisting he fix her life for her. What were the odds of this happening? One in a bazillion? But here he was, asleep on her couch and, only hours earlier, telling her he was going to improve her life. He was sincere.

He was funny and honest and caring and amazing and sexy, and he wanted to be her best friend.

These kinds of things didn't happen, not to her anyway, the habitual pessimist and unwilling holder of bad luck. God must have had sympathy for her because this never happened to her before and she was sure it would never happen again, so she wasn't about to screw it up.

Sarah had a choice to make. She had been waiting for Chris for a long time, and now he was ready to be with her. She also had

Andrew, who had appeared out of nowhere and was already setting her heart on a whirlwind.

Someone would get hurt, she knew, but she would prefer it be herself. She was used to it. She couldn't hurt either of these sweet men who wanted to be with her. That was a new sensation for her, too.

"What had you so deep in thought?" Andrew asked.

She glanced at him and smiled. "Did the TV wake you?"

"Not at all. I have to use the loo." He got up and went to the bathroom. He was amazing looking in the morning. "So, what were you thinking about?" he asked when he came back.

"Nothing. Checking the weather. It's going to be in the mid-fifties today."

"Nice." He smiled and leaned over and kissed her. "Do you mind if I have some coffee?"

"Help yourself. You don't have to ask." He went to the kitchen.

"You drink your coffee with hot chocolate?" he asked. There was a smile in his voice.

"Is there any other way to drink it?"

"A girl after my heart." He meant that. He walked back to the couch and sat down next to Sarah. She was staring into space again. "Are you alright?"

"I'm terrific." She was, but she still had her concerns. "We should hit the store early, before it gets too crowded. It would have been nice to go in the middle of the night, but since COVID, the stores aren't open twenty-four hours anymore."

"It will be okay, as long as we stick together." He sipped his mocha.

Sarah sighed. "I guess you're right." Her smile was weak as she stood up and went to get dressed.

"What's wrong, Sarah?" Andrew asked when she came back into the room.

She sat down next to him on the couch. "I don't want to hurt you. I don't want to hurt Chris. I don't want to get hurt. I'm afraid someone will get hurt in all this mess."

"Why are you worrying about this?"

She shrugged. "I like you both, and you both like me, and I don't want anyone getting hurt."

"We're friends, Sarah, and if that's all it's meant to be, so be it. I'm happy with that. No pressure."

"Are you sure?"

"Yes. We don't need to worry about this. We're okay. You and Chris will be all right."

"Alright." He hugged her and gazed into her eyes. Something was stirring in him. The look in her eyes told him she was sensing it, too.

"I want to kiss you," he whispered, "but I'm afraid if I start, I won't be able to stop."

Sarah's breath hitched as she leaned in, her lips trembling with anticipation. His hand found her nape and guided her closer. Her hands reached up to cup his face as their lips met in a fiery kiss. Every touch and movement was like an electric shock, igniting a fire within her. Andrew's lips inched down her face, leaving a trail of tingling sensations in their wake. She could feel his desire matching her own as his lips found hers once again. This time, the kiss was more profound and passionate, and Sarah could feel her body responding to his every touch. The intensity of their connection was overwhelming, making her heart race and her body ache for more. Andrew could sense her desire, and he knew if he didn't stop now, he would lose control and give in. But as much as he wanted her, he also wanted to respect her boundaries. So, with great effort, he pulled away, leaving them both breathless and wanting more.

He pulled away. "We have to stop." They were both out of breath.

"I'm sorry," Sarah told him, looking away.

"Don't apologize. I want it, too." He laughed short. "Believe me."

"You're right. We can't do this now." It wasn't easy controlling her urge to kiss him again, but she kept her hands, and her mouth, away from him. "Why don't you get dressed? I need to call Chris and tell him we're leaving, so he doesn't show up while we're gone."

Andrew nodded and went to the bedroom. Sarah grabbed her cell phone and dialed Chris's number.

"Hey, it's me," she said when he answered.

"Hey you." He sounded happy to hear from her. "What's going on?"

"I wanted to tell you we're going to the store soon. I need food."

"We?" His tone changed to disappointment and suspicion.

"Yes. Andrew didn't want to stay here alone."

"Hmph. Sounds like Andrew wants to be with you twenty-four-seven."

"Please don't be all weird, Chris. Nothing's going on, okay," she lied.

"Yeah, sure." He sounded sad.

"I'll call you when we're back. You're still coming by, right?"

"Do you think I'm going to leave you alone with him any longer than I have to?"

"Please don't do this."

"Yeah, yeah. So why is Andrew risking being out in public and getting spotted?"

"He said he wanted to go with me."

"Fine, Sarah. Call me when you're home."

"I will. Bye." She hung up. Chris's mild jealousy was *almost* cute. Almost. He was acting as if he was being forced to let the new kid play with his toy.

The moment Andrew walked out of the bedroom; he took Sarah's breath away. There was nothing extraordinary about what he was wearing; dark turtleneck and gray slacks, or his appearance; his disheveled hair and smoky blue eyes, and that alluring half-smile. It was all of him. It was the way he walked; it was the way he ran his fingers through his hair. It was his lean, tall body.

"Is everything alright," he asked. Sarah's knees went weak, and she almost collapsed. Andrew ran and grabbed her before she fell to the floor. "Are you alright?"

"Fine. Fine. Way to ruin a moment, eh?" She felt stupid and clumsy.

"You should eat something before we leave."

"No, it's not that. It was your fault, actually." She smiled at him.

"My fault?"

"Mm-hmm. You came out of the bedroom and made me dizzy."

Andrew's broad smile assured her he was taking it in jest. "I wasn't aware I had that effect on women."

"Liar."

"Well, not beautiful women."

"Okay, whatever. Let's go."

***

"Are you sure you still want to do this?" Sarah asked as they sat in her car in the store's parking lot.

"I'm sure." He squeezed her hand.

"Nervous?"

"A little."

"We can leave."

He shook his head. "No, I can do this."

"Okay, but if it's too much for you, tell me and we'll leave."

"Alright." Andrew took a deep breath, and he and Sarah got out of the car and walked, hand in hand, toward the entrance.

The automatic doors opened, and they went inside. The only person near the door was a little old lady who checked bags.

Andrew's stomach was turning. "Are you going to be okay? We can still leave," Sarah told him.

"No. It's fine," he told her unconvincingly.

She wasn't sure about that, but grabbed a cart anyway, and they started into the store. "We'll do this quick." Sarah had forgotten how far the walk from the entrance to the grocery section was. Andrew was sure to be spotted. The store was crowded already.

"There are so many people here," he whispered.

"I told you there would be."

Most of the people were older folks who wouldn't recognize him. Until they turned down the dairy aisle.

Three teenage girls were standing right in front of Sarah and Andrew, almost running into the cart.

The three of them looked up at once, and Sarah tried to hide Andrew from the girls before they recognized him. Too late.

"Crap," Sarah cursed under her breath.

"You're... Oh my God!" one girl shrieked. He gave them a weak, scared smile.

"Oh, my God. You're Andrew Collier," one of the other girls squealed.

"Shh," he pleaded.

"Can I have your autograph?" The girls were crying. "Is this your mom?" she asked.

Sarah was angry. The minute he had signed his autograph for them, and they had scampered away in a hysterical frenzy, Sarah snapped, "let's go. Now!"

She stormed off ahead of him. He had to run to catch up with her. When they reached the car, she got in and slammed the door.

"What is wrong with you?" he demanded.

"They thought I was your mother." She cried.

"Oh, Sarah. Come here." He pulled her toward him and held her as she cried.

"I can't do this, Andrew. I'm sorry." She pulled away and wiped her eyes. "That's going to happen all the time."

"They're teenage girls. Everyone over the age of thirty looks old enough to be someone's mum or dad."

"It's not only that. This is the thing you're going to deal with every time you go out in public here."

Andrew laughed it off. "It happens all the time in L.A. I don't like it, but I'm used to it. At least there aren't any photographers following us around."

"Those girls are posting this on social media right now."

"So?" He pulled her chin up and kissed her. "You need groceries. I need to deal with this, my life. Let's go back inside."

"Are you sure?"

"Yes. Don't leave my side."

"I won't." She smiled at him, and they went back inside.

***

The three girls followed them around the store. Soon, two, then three, then four more girls were with them, until a group of at least fifteen teenage girls were following them around the store.

Sarah was getting annoyed with their giggling and whispering. Her blood was boiling.

"Can I ask you girls a question?" She had stopped the cart in the middle of the aisle. The girls stopped short and stared at Sarah. "Have you ever seen a man and a woman grocery shop? Or do you spend all your time texting your little friends instead of paying attention to what's going on around you?"

Andrew stared at her in disbelief.

"But he's Andrew Collier," one girl announced. The others chattered in agreement.

"So? He's still a human being, and he's allowed to buy groceries without being followed. Now, if you want an autograph, stand in a freaking line, then leave us alone."

The girls formed a line with pen and paper in hand.

"Wow, Andrew, your mom's mean," one girl told him as he signed his name for her.

"I... am... not... his... mother," Sarah growled through gritted teeth.

Everyone, including Andrew, stared at her. "That's right, girls, she's my girlfriend," Andrew told them.

The girls were upset by this news, but the cameras on their cell phones went off. "Sorry, but I'm off the market."

The girls were crying as the last of them got their autographs and left them alone.

"That was dumb, Andrew. The press will be all over that."

He shrugged it off. "I've been through worse. I told you; I'm used to it." He pulled her into his arms and kissed her. "But I didn't know you were so aggressive. I think I like it." He grinned and kissed her again.

"Yeah?"

"Oh, yeah." He gave her a little kiss and pulled her closer to him.

"Andrew, we're in public."

"So? Let them take all the photos they want."

The rest of their shopping trip was uneventful. Except for the occasional stare and a few of the girls occasionally taking random pictures, no one dared come near them. After Sarah's outburst, Andrew was sure everyone was too afraid of her wrath. He was a little turned on by that side of her. His first impression of her had been that of a shy and quiet woman, but now he realized if she were upset enough, she wouldn't take rubbish from anyone.

They paid for their groceries and headed for the exit. "Crap," Andrew exclaimed, spotting a half a dozen photographers waiting outside. "That was fast." Sarah hadn't seen them yet.

"What's the matter?" she asked. She peered toward the door. "Are you kidding me? I told you this would happen."

"Don't worry about it. Hurry." Andrew took her by the elbow and guided her toward the door. The cart was hard to maneuver because one wheel was unbalanced.

Flashbulbs went off. People were calling Andrew's name, asking him for a picture. "Keep your head down."

"I can deal with this, Andrew. Go to the car," Sarah told him.

"I'm not leaving you alone here. They want you now, too."

Sarah stood her ground and lifted her head. The flashbulbs were almost blinding. "What is wrong with you people?"

"Sarah, what are you doing?" Andrew whispered.

"Let me handle this," she whispered. "Why can't you leave Andrew alone while he shops? Jesus Christ! It's one thing to take pictures when he's on the red carpet or something, but is it necessary to invade a person's privacy while he's minding his own business? You people make me sick. It's about the money, isn't it? How much are you going to be paid for your pictures of Andrew Collier and his mystery woman?

"Leave him alone once in a while. You stand outside his house and his hotel rooms waiting for a picture. It's almost obsessive."

The photographers were quiet, but the flashes were still going off, and a crowd had gathered behind them. Andrew glanced around, then back at Sarah. She surprised him more every second, and he liked it.

"You've gotten your pictures. Now leave him the hell alone," she demanded.

The crowd behind them clapped and cheered, but it was short-lived. The paparazzi began hounding Andrew again.

"Andrew, who's your girlfriend... how did you meet her... what are you doing in Denver... are you moving here?" They followed Andrew and Sarah to her car.

"I swear, you people are either deaf or stupid. And, so help me God, if any of you come near my house, I will call the police," Sarah shouted to the photographers as she loaded her trunk with the groceries. "And don't think I will hesitate to run your asses over if you don't move away from my car."

***

"You never cease to amaze me," Andrew told Sarah when they were in her car and on the road headed back to her house.

"I've never understood why they do that. I mean, if you're at some premiere or press conference, sure, take all the pictures you want. But to stand outside stores and restaurants waiting for a photo opportunity is bordering on stalking. I'm sorry for you. It's so sad."

"I'm used to it. It sort of comes with the territory; I suppose."

"Are you mad at me for doing that?"

"Not at all." He chuckled. "I'm impressed. I don't think I could do what you did back there."

"Sometimes you have to stand up for yourself, and others. I can't tolerate that kind of crap. Just because you're a celebrity doesn't mean you don't deserve your privacy."

"I completely agree with you."

"I wasn't kidding, though. If they show up at my house, I'll call the cops."

"Good for you." He squeezed her hand. "You realize by tomorrow you'll be in the paper and on Celebrity Insider, or in some tabloid?"

"I hope they got my good side." They both laughed as Sarah pulled into her driveway. The street around her house was empty, and Sarah calmed down.

***

With the groceries put away, Andrew and Sarah got comfortable on the couch. Andrew had his arm around Sarah's shoulder as they watched television. Sarah had called Chris to tell him she was home. He was in the area and would be at her house within the hour.

"Will you be able to handle all of this now?" Andrew asked.

Sarah shrugged. "It is what it is," she shrugged. "I guess I'll have to, right? As long as you and I are friends, it's something I'm going to have to deal with."

"It won't be easy."

"I want to be your friend, and it comes with the territory, right?"

"If you keep up that spunky attitude with the press, you'll be fine." He kissed her forehead, and she smiled up at him.

"I'll keep that in mind." There was a knock on the door. "That would be Chris." She got up and answered the door. "Hey you." A smile formed on her lips.

"Hi, beautiful." Chris greeted her by lifting her up off the ground and planting a big kiss on her mouth.

Chris's display appalled Andrew, but he refused to make a scene. It would hurt Sarah. He couldn't bring himself to do that to her. After all, Chris had been in her life a lot longer than he had. He had also promised Sarah he wouldn't intrude.

"Hey, man," Chris said. "I'm sorry about yesterday." He extended his hand to Andrew. "I got a little jealous. I thought you were after my girl."

"All is forgiven." Andrew stood and shook Chris's hand. "Don't worry about it. I would act the same way if the roles were reversed."

Chris smiled, then looked at Sarah. "I got the fuse," he told her as he held it up to her.

"Yay! I won't freeze to death," she giggled.

"If you'll excuse me, I need to make a phone call," Andrew said and headed outside. "Hello, mum," he said when his mother answered on the other end.

"Oh, Andrew. I am so glad to hear your voice. I was so worried when I didn't hear from you."

"I thought Susan would have phoned you to complain."

"I haven't heard from her. What's going on?"

"I'm staying with Sarah."

"Andrew, no."

"Relax, mum. Everything is wonderful, except for Sarah's... boyfriend." His tone was contemptuous. He didn't like Chris, more so now than before. The more time Andrew spent with Sarah and the more he learned about her, the more he wanted her for himself.

"Boyfriend? She has a boyfriend?"

"It's complicated. I'll explain it when I'm home."

"I don't think I like the sound of that."

"She's amazing, mum. She's smart and funny and sweet and stunning. I think I'm falling for her."

"Already? Andrew, please remember yourself. She's an ordinary woman, and you're..."

"But she isn't ordinary. She isn't even close to ordinary. You should have seen her with these fanatical teenage girls this morning at the store. *And* with the paparazzi."

"The paparazzi? Andrew, please think about what you're doing to this poor girl's life."

"She handled it well, mum," Andrew told her with a smile. "A few days ago, you were worried about her hacking me up into a million pieces. Now you're concerned about the upheaval I've caused in her life. What gives?"

"You're used to this kind of life, Andrew. She isn't. Think about that."

"She'll adjust. I think she'll be fine with me."

"What about this boyfriend of hers? Do you think she will leave him and her life there to follow you around the world? Think about it, Andrew. Don't do this to her. Don't make her choose."

"I'm not forcing anything on her, mother. I'm letting her make up her own mind. I am only my charming self."

"I think you may manipulate her heart without knowing it. Slow down."

"I need to go, mum. I'll try to call you tomorrow. I love you."

"I love you, too."

"Bye, mum." Andrew hung up and went back inside. "How is everything going with that furnace?" he asked. He walked to the laundry room where the heater was located.

"It's going fine, thanks," Chris told him without emotion as he crammed himself into the tiny space where the furnace sat.

"Give me a shout if you need help."

"Yup." He waved Andrew off.

Sarah smiled at Andrew and followed him to the living room. "Is everything okay?"

"Sure. I needed to call my mum. She worries."

"Aww, how sweet," Sarah grinned at him and giggled.

"She and Susan, my agent, thought you were going to murder me while I was here." Sarah laughed.

"You're kidding?"

"No. Susan and my mum thought you were some psycho stalker."

She couldn't control her laughter. "That's too funny for words. But I called myself a crazy old lady, so I can understand where they're coming from."

"What's so funny in here?" Chris asked as he came into the living room.

"Oh." Sarah was still giggling. "Andrew's mom thinks I'm going to hack him up into little pieces."

Chris fought a chuckle. "You're the most even-tempered person I've ever met."

"You should have seen her in the store this morning," Andrew piped in. "She went off on some teenagers and photographers."

Chris glanced from Andrew to Sarah. "Photographers?"

"Oh, yeah," Sarah began. "These teenage girls were following us around in the store, and I told them to get their autographs and go away." She recounted the run-in with the paparazzi outside the store, and Chris smiled.

"I didn't think you had it in you."

"Neither did I, but you do what you've got to do."

"She'll probably be on the news by Monday," Andrew told him. Chris glared at him. He wasn't happy.

"*You* put her in this situation. She's a regular person, and you come along and turn her life upside-down like this? Who the hell do you think you are?"

"Chris, calm down," Sarah told him. "It's not as bad as it seems."

"Not yet. Give it time. You'll never have a moment of peace because of this jerk. Why would you do this to her?"

Andrew stepped up to him. He would not fight him, but he wouldn't let Chris talk to him this way, either.

"How dare you? Sarah is the one who told them off. I didn't put her in any situation."

"You being here is putting her in this position. She'll never be free of it now... because of *you*." Chris pointed his finger at Andrew, but Andrew stood his ground.

"Both of you... stop it," Sarah shouted. "And stop talking about me like I'm not here. Chris, I'm the one who told them off. It felt amazing. I have wanted to do that for so long. I can't stand to watch those idiots following celebrities around like a pack of wild, rabid animals. It makes me sick because even stars deserve some privacy." She took a breath and continued. "And Andrew, Chris is only looking out for me. He knows I'm a regular person who isn't used to the life you live. I'm not used to it, and I probably won't be for a long time, but I'm willing to try as long as you and I are friends." She shook her head. "God. The two of you are acting like a couple of infants. Quit." She stormed off and went outside.

Both Andrew and Chris raced out behind her.

"Leave me alone."

"I'm worried about you," Chris told her.

"Are you really?" She smirked at Chris and turned away from both.

"This is your fault," Chris told Andrew. He walked down the steps and tried to put his arms around her, but she shrugged him off.

"I should go back to the hotel," Andrew told them. Guilt was setting in.

"You should," Chris agreed.

"Don't you dare," Sarah demanded.

"You don't know what you're saying, Sarah." Chris asked.

"Yes, I do."

"You want me to stay?"

"Of course, I do." She turned around. "Neither one of you is making this easy for me. Why do I even have to choose?"

"You shouldn't have to," Chris told her. "I love you, Sarah."

"No, you don't. Don't say things you don't mean. It only makes things worse."

"I understand, Sarah," Andrew told her, walking down the steps. "You have a tough decision to make, and you shouldn't have to."

"You're right," Chris told him. "If you left, she wouldn't have to choose."

"I care about her, too, mate."

"You just met her, *mate*."

"Perhaps not as well as you do, but we spent several hours talking last night."

"And I've been her friend for over a year."

"Stop it. You're doing it again," Sarah told them. They both stared at her. "I'm standing right here. God, stop fighting over me. I'm not worth it."

"Bullshit," both Chris and Andrew said in unison.

Sarah laughed. "That's the first thing the two of you have agreed on since you met."

"Yeah, I guess it is," Chris smiled and peered at Andrew. Andrew was smiling, too.

"You *are* worth it, Sarah," Andrew told her. "You don't see what we do, but you're more than worth it."

"I don't want the two of you vying for me. I'm not a prize. We aren't contestants on 'The Bachelorette' or something. We're real people with actual feelings, and those actual feelings are sometimes hurt. Someone is going to get hurt. I don't want it to be either of you. I would rather it be me."

"That isn't acceptable, either," Andrew said.

"What are we supposed to do? There shouldn't be a prospect of romance for any of us." She was looking at Chris. "We should all cut our losses now."

"No," Chris told her. "I'm not giving up. Not now."

"Neither am I," Andrew said.

"I won't be a part of your silly game," she told them.

"You're the reason for this game. You're the goal. The prize," Chris told her.

Sarah sighed and stormed off past them. "Whatever. I will have nothing to do with this. I'm finished with this entire mess." She stomped up the steps and went inside.

"This is your fault. You shouldn't have come here," Chris seethed.

"Don't be such a wanker, Chris. You can't look beyond your own ego to understand how difficult this is for her. She needs to be handled carefully. Her heart is in terrible shape, or don't you comprehend that?"

"I am aware of what shape her heart is in. I've been with her all along. Our hearts are in the same shape. She's a good friend, and I'm not about to let some punk come into her life and sweep her off her feet, then take off. That would break her heart more than anything else that has ever happened to her."

"I won't hurt her."

"Don't you dare make her fall for you, then disappear into your Hollywood lifestyle. You act all sweet and sensitive, then when you think you're getting too attached, you take off, and who's here to pick up the pieces? Me, and I will, but by then, she won't trust anyone again... because of you."

"You have no clue what my intentions are, so don't even pretend you understand anything. You would be very wrong."

"What *are* your intentions?" Chris asked, calming down a little.

"I want to be her friend, that's all."

"That's all?" Chris wasn't convinced.

"Yes, if that's all it's meant to be," Andrew sighed in frustration. "You haven't been paying attention at all, have you?" He sat down on the hood of Sarah's car. "Have you seen this house?"

"Of course. Why do you think I'm here all the time?"

"Alright, you are aware how much work needs to be done?"

"Yeah. I fix as much as I can when I can afford it."

"I can afford it, Chris. Right here, right now."

"So, it's about you flaunting your money?"

"No, it's about helping someone who needs and deserves it."

"So, she's a charity case? No, I know. A tax write-off."

"You son-of-a-bitch." Andrew raged. "How dare you? I care about Sarah. I want to be her friend. I want to help her."

"And you think I don't? I want to help her, too. So how do we do that?" Chris was sorry for what he had said. It seemed Andrew *did* care for Sarah. Chris could see that. He would do what he could to help Andrew help Sarah. He didn't want to fight him anymore. He couldn't and wouldn't hurt Sarah anymore. In time, she would see he was trying to get along with her new friend, as long as that's all Andrew wanted to be to her. Perhaps she would perceive that as a point in his favor. He would have to spend more time with her when Andrew was gone. Chris knew this was turning into a competition, and he was going to win with honesty. But he made a vow to himself that he would not fight Andrew Collier anymore. May the best man win.

"What else do you do for her around here, besides install furnace fuses?"

"Well, I've snaked her drain."

"Pardon me?"

"Her pipes, you dolt. I cleaned the pipes under the house."

"Oh," Andrew chuckled. "American slang. What else?"

"I've helped her move a bunch of stuff out to her storage shed out back and hauled out a bunch of wood and crap from her yard. My next project is to insulate the pipes, so they quit freezing."

"And what are your plans for her roof and the windows?"

"I haven't thought about that."

"I'll tell you what... you get estimates for this stuff, and I'll pay you for it. You fix what you can yourself, but I'll take care of the cost of the big things. Does that sound like a deal?"

"I guess, but I don't want it to look like you're doing it all. That's not fair."

"Would you like to split the cost?"

"I can't afford that much, Andrew."

"We don't have to figure it all out right now. Why don't you go inside and check on Sarah? I'm going to sit out here and think for a few minutes."

"Good idea." Chris went inside and found Sarah in her bedroom. She was crying. "Are you okay?"

"No. Go away."

"I can't do that. Tell me why you're crying." He rubbed her back.

"This was a mistake. All of it."

"What was a mistake?"

"You. Me. Andrew. All of it. The two of you will never stop fighting, and I can't have that."

"We're not fighting anymore. We came to an agreement."

"You did?" She turned over on her back. Chris wiped her tears and lay next to her on the bed. He faced her and propped his head up on his hand.

"Yes."

"What kind of agreement?"

"We're both going to help you fix your house."

"No, Chris. I already told you and him. I can't let you do that."

"You don't have to *let* us. We're going to do it whether or not you like it."

"No," she tried to protest, but he stopped her with a kiss.

"He only wants to be your friend and help you out with the stuff I can't." Chris thought he had won by telling her Andrew only wanted to be her friend.

"I have to talk to him about this." She tried to stand up, but Chris stopped her with another kiss.

"In a minute. I want to talk to you." He closed his eyes and sighed. "How do you feel about me?"

"You've always known how I feel about you. Nothing has changed."

"And what about Andrew?"

"I care about him. I think he could be a wonderful friend."

"That's all? A friend?"

"Yes, of course. There's no way it will ever go any further than that. It's not like I'm going to be with him all the time. He travels all the time. He lives in England, for Pete's sake."

"I hadn't thought about that."

"Of course you didn't. You were too busy being stubborn."

"I suppose I was."

She traced his jaw with her finger and frowned. "This jealous side of you is not attractive."

"I'm sorry, Sarah. I feel like I'm losing you already."

"I told you nothing is going to happen. Please believe me. And now that Andrew has told me he only wants to be my friend, I'm certain nothing's going to happen."

"If you thought he had stronger feelings for you, would you let something happen?"

"No. Andrew is too young for me." She lay back on the bed. "Those girls today thought I was his mother."

Chris tried to suppress a chuckle. "Are you kidding?"

"No. I was offended. I work hard to keep from looking old."

"You don't have to."

"Yes, I do. I don't want to look old."

"You don't look old."

"Yeah, I do. That's another reason I won't pursue this."

"I'm glad you're not." He kissed the tip of her nose. "Have you calmed down?"

"Yeah."

"Let's leave this stuffy bedroom."

***

While Chris and Sarah talked in the house, Andrew took a walk around the block to clear his head.

He was falling for Sarah, and he knew he had to take things slow with her. She was fragile. Her heart had been broken too many times. He wouldn't do that to her. He was going to show her she could love again, and everything would be okay.

He wouldn't fight with Chris anymore. They were going to work together to make Sarah's life better. They were going to fix her house and make her happy.

Andrew searched his mind for the best way to make her understand he was the one she should be with without manipulating her. Sure, Chris had her best interests at heart, but so did he. Andrew couldn't be there as much as Chris would be. That would be his disadvantage, but there were telephone calls and video chatting, and he would visit from time to time. He would pay for her to visit him, too. It was perfect. He would be a constant presence in her life. He would send her presents, or would that be pushing it? She wasn't used to being treated the way he wanted to treat her; the way she deserved to be treated. The last thing he wanted was to push her away.

He would keep himself in the front of her mind. He would be her friend. He would help her, and Chris would help him.

Andrew already knew she was reluctant to let him buy her things or let him pay to fix the things that needed to be fixed in her house. With Chris's help, all the things that needed to be done would be done, and she would have a home that was worth living in. She would be so grateful she would have no other choice but to pick him.

The thought made him smile, and as he rounded the corner back to her street, it satisfied him to not leave or give up. It would be a fair fight between Chris and himself, and the best man would win, with sincerity and love for a beautiful, deserving woman.

Sarah was leaning against the car when Andrew walked up. "Where did you run off to?" she asked him.

"I went for a walk around the block. I thought I would give you and Chris some privacy."

"That was very sweet of you. Thank you." She hugged him and kissed his cheek.

"Don't mention it." He smiled. 'Be patient,' he told himself.

"Sarah," Chris called as he trotted out to the end of the driveway.

"Yeah?" She glanced up at him.

"I need to go pick my boys up in Windsor. I have to go, but I'll call you tomorrow."

"Okay." They kissed, and Chris took off in his beat-up old truck. She gazed at Andrew and smiled. "Do you want to go inside?"

"Would you mind if we walked?"

"Not at all." She stuffed her hands in the pockets of her jeans and walked beside him down the quiet street. "What's on your mind?"

"Are you happy?"

"Yes," she told him.

"I mean, truly happy?"

"I have no clue, but things are looking up. Are *you* happy?"

"Not entirely." He stared down at his feet as he walked.

"Why not?"

He stopped and peered at her.

"I won't lie to you, Sarah. I don't want to hurt you. I want to be with you. All the time."

"I thought you wanted to be friends?"

"I do." They started walking again. Sarah tucked her hands into the crook of his arm.

"What's the problem?"

"I believe you have to be friends before you can be anything else, like what you have with Chris. I want what you have with him... with you."

"I don't think I follow."

"You two have been friends for a long time, now you're..."

"Ah, now I understand." She smiled at him.

"Do you?"

"Yes. You want that with me, too."

"Yes." He smiled back at her.

"We can have that. Are you afraid we can't?"

"No, no. That's not it. I want to be so much to you. I want to be your friend *and* your lover. I want you all to myself." She stiffened a little. "Don't be mad, please."

"I'm not mad, Andrew. This is a lot to take in. I'm not used to having two men wanting to be with me at the same time." She chuckled. "I've never had one man wanting me like this." She looked up at him and grinned. "I think we should take things one day at a time and let things happen naturally."

"I think we should, too." He put his arm around her shoulder, and they walked back to the house.

***

"Are you getting hungry?" Andrew asked a few hours later. They had been sitting on the couch, flipping channels on the television and chatting about random issues.

"Yeah, a little. I can fix something."

"No. I thought we'd go out to eat."

"No way. I don't want another fiasco like we had this morning," she protested. "Besides, there's a ton of food here."

"Right. Grocery shopping." He grinned at her.

She sat up and glanced at him. "I can make chicken Caesar salad."

"Is that difficult to make?"

"Not at all." She got up and went to the kitchen. Andrew followed her.

"Would you like some help?"

"Sure, if you want to."

"What do you want me to do?" He looked at the ingredients on the counter in front of him.

"Um... can you chop some lettuce and cut up some tomatoes?" She started cooking the chicken in olive oil. "Do you want some garlic bread?"

"Sure." He was busy getting the lettuce and tomatoes cut when he glanced over at her. She was putting the bread on a cooking sheet and into the oven, and when she stood up, he walked up behind her and wrapped his arms around her waist.

"This is wonderful," he told her quietly. "You and me making dinner together."

"It is," she agreed, leaning into him. The chicken popped. "I need to stir this chicken." Andrew backed off for a moment until she turned around to face him. He put his arms around her again.

"I want to be with you, Sarah," he whispered.

"I know, but..."

"Be with me."

"It's not that easy, Andrew."

"Because of Chris?"

"Not just him. It's because of you, too." He backed away, and she turned around to finish the chicken. When it was cooked, she turned off the burner and checked the bread. It was cooked, too, so she turned the oven off and pulled the sheet out to let it cool.

"Me," he asked.

"Your lifestyle. You travel all the time. You live on another continent. We'll never be together. You can't be here all the time, and I can't afford to come to you at all."

"I can pay for your plane tickets."

"No, Andrew. Stop it. I told you I can't let you do that."

"Why are you worrying about it?"

"I'm not comfortable with you paying for things for me. It was hard enough for me to let you pay for the pizza last night. And I can't even imagine how much those flowers cost. And I know about your little scheme with Chris to fix my house." She glared at him with judgement.

Andrew smiled. "You can't stop us."

"It's my house. I *can* stop you."

"Please don't. We want to help you."

"I feel guilty about it."

"Why?"

"I don't want to take advantage of anyone. It bothers me when people do things for me and buy me things. I don't have the means to repay them. I have no way to pay you back."

"Are we friends?"

"Yes, of course we are."

"What did I tell you last night?"

"I know what you said. And now you have Chris in on it."

"We care about you, and you need our help."

"Yes, my house needs to be fixed, and it will be, in time, when I can afford to fix it. Not you. Not Chris. Please don't push this. I won't let you."

Andrew pulled her toward him again, pulling her body against his. As their lips met, a fire ignited in her. Was the heat emanating from his body or the hot oven making her heart race? She could feel his breath on her skin as he whispered, "I won't give up on you, Sarah." His words were like a promise, one that she couldn't resist. Their mouths moved in sync, their tongues dancing together in passion. She wrapped her arms around his neck. She didn't want to let go. He didn't stop kissing her; she didn't want him to. Every inch of her body was on fire, sensations she hadn't felt in years. She realized she had never felt this way with Chris. He never made her feel the sparks that were coursing through her now. He never made her knees weak just by walking into a room. With Andrew, every touch, every kiss, was electric. She pressed closer to him, wanting to feel more of him. This was something she had been missing for a long time.

Her head turned as he grasped her hair, his mouth exploring her neck. She traced his spine, feeling the tension in his muscles under his shirt. As his hands moved over her, every touch sent electric sparks coursing, igniting a fire within her. She yearned for his touch, her body aching for more. She could feel the heat of his breath against her skin, her senses overwhelmed by his presence. The setting was a blur, her focus on the sensations he evoked. His deep, raspy voice, whispering words of desire punctuated their passionate exchange. The intensity of their connection was palpable, radiating from their bodies like a magnetic force. Every moment with him was like a dream she never wanted to end.

Andrew's body pulsed with electricity as he gazed at her. The thought of being with her sent a heat coursing through him. Every inch of his skin tingled where she touched him, igniting a desperate desire within him. "I want you," he groaned, unable to contain his longing. He silenced her with another passionate kiss, his need to feel her skin pressed against his consuming him. His body ached to be inside her, to lose himself in the intense heat that radiated from her. The setting was tense as the two gave in to their desires.

There was a knock on the door. Both Sarah and Andrew groaned, frustrated. "Whoever it is will go away," Andrew grumbled.

"I'd better answer the door." Sarah tried to smooth her messy hair as she walked toward the front door. "Mary," Sarah chirped when she saw her best friend. She had a bottle of wine with her. "Come in. What are you doing here?"

"You've been a little down, so I thought I'd bring some wine and have a girl's night." Mary put the wine on the coffee table. "Wow, where did these flowers come from? They're beautiful."

"Hi," Andrew announced his presence as he stepped around the corner from the kitchen.

Mary peered up and almost fell over on the flowers. "You're... Andrew Collier." She eyed Sarah. "Okay, what's going on?"

Andrew stepped further into the living room. "It's lovely to meet you." He held his hand out to shake hers.

"Uh... yeah. You, too. I'm Mary... Sarah's best friend." She was stunned, staring in awe at him as she shook his hand. He had that impact on people, women mostly.

Mary Cole, Sarah's best friend, was a voluptuous woman with long brown hair and hazel eyes. She was only a few inches taller than Sarah, but she carried herself as if she were six feet tall. She had a powerful personality that commanded respect. Mary's friendship with Sarah was a unique one. The two of them acted more like frenemies than best friends. The sarcasm emanating from the two of them would cause anyone who didn't know them to think they were not friends.

"Sarah, what is this?" Mary plopped down on the couch, still stunned.

Andrew went to the bedroom to let Sarah and Mary catch up.

Sarah recounted the details of the last two days: about Chris finally confessing his feelings for her, about Andrew showing up out of nowhere. Sarah showed her friend a copy of the letter she had written to Andrew the day she mailed it. Mary had thought she was crazy. Sarah did, too.

"Now the two of them are plotting behind my back to fix the house. They're both insane if they think I'm going to allow that."

"What are you going to do? They both want to be with you. I swear I'm still in shock. I can't believe Andrew Collier is staying with you. Have you two...?"

"No."

"What about you and Chris?"

"No. That's the strange thing. When Chris kisses me, I don't get that spark. There's no electricity, no excitement. And you know how long I've liked him." Mary nodded. "I thought there would be something, but it's not there. But when Andrew kisses me, it's..."

"He kissed you? Oh, man." Again, Mary was in shock. She hadn't seen or talked to Sarah in a week, so she was out of the loop of her best friend's life. "This happens to you when I leave you alone for a week." Mary smirked.

"Funny," Sarah said with a sarcastic tone. "It's like these electric currents race through me when he kisses me." She sighed with a smile on her lips.

"Gross. I don't want to hear that."

Sarah laughed. "Sorry."

***

Later that evening, Sarah, Andrew, and Mary ate dinner together in the living room and talked about the incident at the store that morning. It didn't matter that Andrew was a mega celebrity; Mary was comfortable talking about her decade's long friendship with Sarah. "You're easy to talk to, Andrew."

"Thank you, Mary," his smile was genuine.

"I guess you were right. Movie stars *are* regular people." Mary winked at Sarah.

"I told you." She grinned at her friend.

"I'm impressed by the way you handled those teenagers and the photographers."

"I was, too," Andrew admitted.

"Did any of them show up here?"

"No. I think they're afraid of Sarah," he laughed.

Mary excused herself and went to the bathroom.

"Mary is wonderful," Andrew told Sarah once they were alone.

"Yes. Are you upset we didn't have time alone?"

"Absolutely not." He smiled and brushed her hair off her face, and he kissed her.

"Gross," Mary exclaimed with sarcasm as she came back into the living room.

***

It wasn't long before everyone was yawning. "I think I'm going to head off to bed. You two girls chat it up," Andrew said with a yawn. He gave Sarah a quick kiss, then went to the bedroom.

"I think I'm going to head off to bed, too," Mary said a few minutes later. "It's been a long day, and I've had too much wine." Mary hugged her friend and went to the guest room.

Sarah sat on the couch alone for a little while before she put her pajamas on. She didn't want to wake Andrew when she went into the bedroom.

It was amazing what he did to her. How could she have these feelings for a man she had only met a little over twenty-four hours ago?

She had been pining over Chris for a year, certain he was finally the one who would make her happy. Yes, he was sweet and thoughtful, and he made her laugh, but the spark wasn't there. She tried so hard to bring that excitement to the surface but sit never emerged. The feelings could have ebbed after a year. It was possible too much time passed, and it was too late. Sarah wanted to give Chris a chance. She wanted to know that spark with him. Chris was the safe choice. He was here. He had always been here, and he would always be here. She owed it to herself, and to him, to give him a chance.

Choosing Andrew was taking a risk with her heart. Sarah had never been a risk taker. Her choices had always been sensible ones, unless it came to men. All she could have with Andrew was a long-distance relationship. It couldn't be any more than that. He lived in London and Los Angeles. He traveled all over the world. Beautiful women surrounded him all the time. How would Sarah be sure he wouldn't stray? Andrew was twenty-five years old. He had his whole life ahead of him.

What if he wanted to settle down and have children one day? She could never give him that. Why would he want to be with a woman who never wanted children? But he set her on fire. She knew physical attraction was not a good base for a successful relationship. He made her laugh, too, though.

He was sweet and sincere, and he flew thousands of miles, risking being spotted by fans and photographers, to meet her. Who would do that? He had, and she guessed he would do it again.

She wanted to be friends with him, but it might be hard with the sensations he gave her. Again, she owed it to herself, and to Andrew, to find out where it might go.

Sarah was too tired to dwell on it now. She still had a little time to sort out her feelings.

Andrew would be asleep now, so she crept into the bedroom to change into her pajamas.

"Sarah," Andrew whispered when she came in.

"I didn't mean to wake you. I came in to grab my pajamas."

"You didn't wake me. Turn on the light and come here a minute."

She climbed onto the bed next to him, on top of the covers. She couldn't risk something happening with them yet. It might sway her decision, and she would regret it later.

He played with her hair, and she scooted closer to him. "You've seemed so far away all day," he said.

"I'm fine. I have a lot on my mind. I have a huge decision to make here, and I don't want to make the wrong one. I don't want you and Chris fighting over me."

"Too late, love. We both want to be with you. You're afraid of someone getting hurt in all of this, but Chris and I have already made peace with that. It's going to happen, and we're prepared for it."

"It's still not right, and I want you to stop." She sighed and rolled over on her back. "I was thinking about this. I've had a thing for Chris forever. I believed that the first time he kissed me, the sparks would fly, that he would sweep me off my feet. That hasn't happened. Not once. You show up and, wow. I can't even explain what you do to me." She chuckled and rolled back over to face him. "I haven't experienced this in a long time. But I can't be with you because of the sparks. They go away eventually."

"I don't want you to choose me because of those sparks. There is so much more I want to be for you."

"But how can you? Chris has been here all along. He'll always be here, with me. You don't have that option."

"You could come be with me."

"*I* don't have that option. And even if I did, you wouldn't be around all that much. You'll be on location or at press conferences, or other things."

"You could travel with me." He was trying to show her he would give her the life most people only dreamed of.

"As fabulous as that sounds, it isn't me. That isn't my life. You live your life in front of the cameras, at parties and awards shows. I don't know how to live that kind of life."

"I'm still learning how to live this sort of life. We'll learn together."

Sarah sighed, this time frustrated. "I don't think I'm comfortable with that. I'll never be used to that kind of life. It's kind of invasive and I like my privacy."

"You haven't noticed that I do, too?"

"Chris is the safe, stable choice. I always make the safe choice. I need to. That's who I am. I'm safe."

"Take a chance, Sarah. For once, do something unexpected, something unlike you."

"You both have excellent qualities, too."

"And those are?"

"You're both sweet. You both make me laugh. You're both generous and sincere. Neither of you wants me to be sad or in need of anything."

"Because we care about you."

"I care about both of you, too. That's why this is so hard for me."

Andrew scooted closer to her. He played with her hair and kissed her forehead. "I can't make this choice for you. I can't even imagine how hard this must be for you, but I will never hurt you."

"I didn't think you would." She draped her arm over his bare shoulder. "I'm too tired to think about this anymore." She closed her eyes and was asleep in a few quick minutes.

Chapter Four – Sunday

Andrew had slept little the night before. He got out of bed before the sun came up and turned on the news. Sarah was fast asleep, and that gave him time to think about his current situation.

Andrew had meant what he said when he told Sarah he wanted to be with her and wouldn't hurt her. She didn't deserve to hurt anymore. She had had enough pain in her life. It was time for someone to love her with their whole heart. He wanted to do that. It was time for Sarah to give her whole heart to someone without being afraid it would be broken again. He could do that. He could love her and care for her and not hurt like she had been for so many years.

Nothing about her life was safe, no matter what she believed. Her world was in turmoil, and he couldn't bear to let her live in a world filled with so much uncertainty. Her home was the most precarious thing in her life. She wouldn't have to live this way, not as long as there was breath in him.

When he noticed the bright streaks showing through the curtains, he opened them and let the sun light up the living room.

Breakfast.

Sarah would be awake soon, and she would be hungry, so he went to the kitchen to fix the two of them something to eat. He decided on scrambled eggs with cheese and bacon, toast, and orange juice.

Mary emerged from the guest bedroom, dressed and in a rush. "My mom needs help with my grandmother. I have to dash. Tell Sarah I'll call her later." She stole a piece of bacon and left the house.

***

"It smells delicious," Sarah told him as she walked into the kitchen.

"You're awake." He turned around and smiled at her.

She walked toward him and gave him a quick hug. "Bathroom run." She grinned at him and walked off toward the bathroom. She groaned as she looked at herself in the mirror. She couldn't believe she had allowed Andrew to see her looking this way. She splashed water on her face and applied her anti-aging and wrinkle reducing creams then went back to the kitchen.

"Good morning... again, beautiful." He was almost finished cooking. "Mary had to leave, but she said she'd call you later."

Sarah nodded. "What's all this about?" She pointed to the bacon and eggs on plates on the counter.

"I thought I'd surprise you and make breakfast. I hope it's alright?"

"It's more than alright." She gave him a quick kiss and fixed her mocha, then sat down in front of her computer to check her email.

"Is there anything in particular you'd like to do today?" Andrew asked, fixing mocha for himself, and taking it to the couch.

"I don't think we should venture out for now, Andrew."

"You're probably right."

"It won't even to make it to forty degrees today, and I don't like the cold."

"Maybe we could test out your repaired furnace?"

"I like that idea." Sarah went to the laundry room and opened the furnace to make sure the pilot light was lit. "Everything appears to be working," she told Andrew as she flipped the switch. The motor turned over. After two months of freezing and a skyrocketing energy bill because of the power-sucking space heaters, she had her furnace back. "Thank you, Chris," she said out loud, turning the thermostat up to seventy-five. She walked through the house and uncovered all her heater vents, and within a few minutes, her crappy little house was warm.

She went to sit down next to Andrew. "I usually do my laundry on Sunday."

"Do you want help?"

"No thanks. I'm picky about it, but I'd be more than happy to wash your clothes for you."

"I appreciate that." He regarded her, then looked out the window. He seemed far away.

"What's the matter?"

He shook his head. "Nothing. I was thinking about how much I've enjoyed being with you this weekend."

"So have I." She put her hand on his, and he squeezed it.

"Everything about you is incredible. You have such a beautiful soul."

"But?" She took her hand away and sipped her coffee. Sarah had a feeling this moment would come. She was aware on Friday night when he first stepped foot in her house. Even after all the beautiful things he had said to her, and how he wanted to help her and be here for her, she knew she would be gone forever after this weekend.

"But nothing, Sarah." He smiled at her. "There is no but, no however, no negativity at all. I love being with you. I wish I could stay with you. I want to be with you."

"I can't help but think this is the end."

"Far from it, love." He took her in his arms and held her for a long time. He kissed her forehead and rocked her. "There is so much more. You can trust me on that."

They sat on the couch, holding each other. There was nothing sexual about it, only two people enjoying each other.

After a few minutes, Sarah said, "I had better start the laundry, then we can eat that delightful breakfast you made." Andrew put his few dirty garments in the laundry room for Sarah to wash.

"You're kind of domestic," Andrew teased as she put the first load in the washing machine.

"It's a girl thing," she giggled. "You're kind of domestic, too. Look at this fantastic breakfast." She washed her hands and began filling her plate.

"My mum taught me to cook. I would have starved a long time ago if she hadn't." He filled his plate, too.

"I'm not big on cooking. It's sad to cook for one."

"Well, if you decide to keep me around," Andrew winked at her, "you'll learn that I love to cook."

***

"Would you like to go walk off all these calories?" Sarah asked Andrew after they had finished breakfast.

"I would love that," he told her with a smile.

They put on their coats and walked out the door and down the street.

"Do you have any family here in Denver?" Andrew started the conversation.

"No. My sister lives in Newport Beach. I'd love to visit her, and you in L.A. or London, but I can't afford that."

"Didn't I tell you I would pay the fare?"

"You did, but I have to say no. I'll save, but it may only be once a year."

"That doesn't work for me. I want to be with you as often as possible."

"I want to spend time with you, too, but it's not something I can do right now."

"Then let me do this."

"No, Andrew. Don't push this. We've already had this conversation, and my answer is the same now as it was then. It won't change."

He stopped walking and turned her by her shoulders to face him. "Damn it, Sarah." He closed his eyes and sighed, calming himself.

"What is the matter with you? You're so stubborn. You won't let anyone do anything to help you. I don't understand. Please explain it to me?"

"I don't want to take advantage."

"You aren't taking advantage if *I'm* offering. You're not seeing that."

"And you're not seeing that if you keep "offering" to do these things for me, I'll expect it."

"So?"

"That's when I take advantage. I don't want to be that kind of person; all greedy and materialistic."

Andrew laughed from deep down. "You aren't greedy or materialistic."

"If you pay to fix my house and buy plane tickets, it will head in that direction."

"You let Chris buy the fuse for your furnace."

"I paid for that fuse."

"That doesn't matter," Andrew insisted.

"It matters to me. If I can't pay for it, I don't need it."

Andrew laughed again. "You need a new roof. You need new windows. You need a lot of things."

"Why is that funny?"

"It isn't *funny*, funny. The point is, you say you can't afford them, but you *do* need them. And you need them soon."

"They are going to have to wait, at least until my tax refund arrives." Sarah started walking again. She peered down at her feet while she walked. "Sorry for the rant. I can't fix the things in my house that need to be fixed. I am barely scraping by as it is."

Andrew allowed her to vent on him.

"I'm so sorry you have to go through this." He stopped her and put his arms around her.

They continued walking around the block. "I'm a lot of drama, aren't I?" Sarah asked as they rounded the corner to her street.

"Huge. It's like a daytime serial." He grinned. "I think I can deal with it, if you'll let me."

"Of course, I'll let you. I'd be crazy not to, considering you're such a willing victim." She grinned back at him.

He took Sarah's hand in his and they walked toward her house as Chris was pulling up in his truck. "What is *he* doing here?" Andrew's forehead creased.

"I don't know. He said he was going to call. But he shows up unannounced, most likely because there's a hot British guy staying with me."

"So, I'm not your first British guy?" They both laughed as they reached the truck.

"Surprise," Chris said as he got out of the cab of his truck.

"Yes, it is," Sarah told him and gave him a hug. "I thought you were going to call?"

"I was, but I was already nearby, and I wanted to make sure the furnace was working."

"It is," Andrew chimed.

"Yeah. I can't thank you enough."

"Any time, sweetheart." Chris put his arm around Sarah.

"Not too bad." He headed for the laundry room. "It *is* warm in here... finally."

"It's perfect." Sarah told him as she started another load of laundry.

"Hey, maybe your pipes won't freeze now." He checked the furnace to make sure everything was working. "That reminds me. I have the insulation in the back of my truck."

"How much?" Sarah asked.

"Don't worry about it. This one's on me."

"No. How much was it?"

"I said don't worry about it."

"I'd tell her if I were you," Andrew told him. "She won't budge. We had a long discussion about it."

Chris eyed Andrew, a little annoyed, but the kid was right. "It was ten bucks."

"Show me the receipt. You can leave it in your truck until next payday. I can't afford to pay you until then."

"Jeez, woman, would you get over it already? My God."

"I told you she's being difficult," Andrew told him with a smile.

"You weren't kidding."

"Would you two quit?" Sarah sighed, exasperated, and walked into the living room and sat on the couch.

Andrew and Chris followed her. "Why are being so difficult about this?" Chris asked her.

"What does it matter? It's my house, it's my money, and I don't have it right now. The insulation is going to have to wait."

"It's only ten dollars."

"That's ten dollars more than I have right now."

"I'm doing it anyway."

"Don't you dare."

"Andrew, would you mind helping me?" Chris ignored her.

"I'd be happy to." Andrew eyed Sarah and pleaded without words as he followed Chris outside.

Sarah groaned, annoyed and helpless. They were going to do what they wanted, no matter how much she protested. "I give up."

Sarah stood and went outside to the side of the house. Both Andrew and Chris were halfway in the crawl space under the house, insulating the pipes.

"How's it going out here?"

"We're almost finished," Andrew said, poking his head out.

She squatted down and tried to look where they were working, but it was too dark under the house. "Listen, you guys. I'm sorry

I've been such a pain about all of this. I need to make you both understand that I have no way of paying you back for any of this."

"We understand, Sarah," Chris said as he crawled out from under the house. Andrew was right behind him.

"No, I don't think you do. You're both so willing to do all of this and expect nothing in return. One of these days you might."

"We won't," Andrew told her.

"For once, I agree with Andrew," Chris agreed.

"I don't know how to make this any clearer. If I let the two of you do this, I can't pay you back. I have no way to pay you back. You really need to understand this."

"You've said it about a million times, sweetheart. I think we're clear." Chris glanced at Andrew. Andrew nodded.

"We don't want you to pay us back. And we won't ask you later," Andrew assured her.

"This isn't realistic, but fine. I'm going to stop fighting the two of you on this."

"It's a miracle," Chris said, looking up at the sky with a grin and clasping his hands.

Andrew smiled and hugged her. "Thank you, love," he whispered.

"Yeah, yeah. I don't want either of you coming back to me with your hands out." She crossed her arms over her chest. "It's freezing out here. I'm going inside." Chris and Andrew followed her into the house. They needed to wash up.

Sarah, Andrew, and Chris sat in the living room making a list of the things in the house that needed immediate attention.

They all had agreed the roof was the priority. It needed to be replaced. Sarah listened to Andrew and Chris discuss the details of hiring a contractor and roofers and when they should begin. Sarah couldn't believe she was letting them go through with this, but she promised them she wouldn't complain anymore.

"I'm thinking we should start in May, when it warms up," Chris told Andrew. "I'll find out the cost and time frame and let you know."

"Excellent. Maybe we can shoot for the second week in May. I'll be in Los Angeles then, and my birthday is on the thirteenth."

Sarah interrupted him. "I am aware." They smiled at each other.

Andrew continued. "Sarah can come for a visit while they're working on it." Andrew watched Sarah with hope.

"You're paying for that, too, I suppose?" Chris appeared annoyed.

"Of course." Andrew smiled.

"I'll try to take some time off," Sarah told him.

"Wonderful. In the meantime, let's replace all the flooring. That includes the crappy linoleum." Andrew glanced at Sarah. "Do you know any carpenters?"

"No," she told him.

"I'm sure we can find one. Do you want hardwood?"

"No. I want carpet." Sarah sighed but said nothing. She promised.

"Spit it out. You're dying to," Andrew insisted.

"Nope. I promised I wouldn't."

"Tell me what you're thinking." He insisted.

"You realize all of this is going to cost tens of thousands of dollars?"

"I'm well aware of that, love," Andrew told her.

Sarah passed a glance at Chris. He was gritting his teeth. "As long as you realize the cost."

He nodded and smiled. "Alright, Chris, now for the master bathroom."

Chris leaned forward. Plumbing was his area of expertise. "What are you thinking?"

"Do you think you can handle the electrical?"

"I think the light in the bathroom only needs a fuse. I'll have to do some research on where to find it. It's an old house. I'll take care of the cost for that."

Sarah fell back on the couch, hard, and exhaled. The others in the room watched her.

"Everything alright," Andrew asked.

"Peachy," she said with a smirk. She stood up and went outside.

Andrew started after her.

"Let her be. She needs to cool off," Chris told him.

Sarah leaned on the hood of her car and took in a deep breath. Why couldn't she keep it together? She wasn't used to letting people do things for her like this. If she had any brains at all, she would never have agreed to this. She had never given in so fast before, not with something like this. This was huge. This was major. This was expensive. She was having a very hard time dealing with all of this.

Sarah thought to herself, 'I almost wish Andrew never showed up. I almost wish Chris never told me how he felt about me. Everything was going fine before all of this. My life was quiet and drama-free. Before this weekend, I could go to the grocery store without causing a scene.'

What if she accepted the change? It could be exciting. She'd be able to visit all the places she'd always wanted to visit, and with someone who cared about her.

And what about Chris? 'He's been my friend for a long time. Why does that need to change now? Wouldn't becoming more than friends complicate things?'

***

"Better," Andrew asked when Sarah came back inside.

She nodded and walked past him and went to the laundry room.

Chris stood up and followed her. "You sure you'll be okay?"

"Yep." She forced a smile.

Chris sighed. "I have to go. Walk me out?"

"Yeah. Give me a minute, okay? I need to put the clothes in the dryer."

"Okay." He shoved his hands in his pockets and walked back to the living room. "I don't think she's very comfortable with this," he told Andrew.

"She'll be fine. She needs time to let it sink in. She isn't used to letting people do things for her. It's going to take a little time for her to let it go."

"Yeah, you're right."

"I'm finished. Do you still want me to walk you out?" Sarah appeared from the laundry room.

Chris put on his coat. "Yeah."

Andrew stood up and extended his hand to Chris. "It was good to meet you, mate."

"You, too, Andrew." Chris shook his hand. He thought he could tolerate him once Andrew was back in England.

"You have my number. Please call when you have those estimates."

"I will." Chris and Sarah went outside then. "What's going on with you?" he asked when they were next to the truck.

"You're kidding?"

"Not about what's bothering you, Sarah. I'm talking about you and your boy toy."

"Stop it, Chris. Nothing is going on. Don't ask stupid questions."

"Have you slept with him?"

"Jeez." She swung her arms in the air and rolled her eyes. "Yes, Chris. Is that what you want to hear? We had wild, unbridled sex. God, give me a break." She turned and walked away.

He grabbed her arm and turned her to face him. "I mean it." The look in his eyes was serious.

"Fine. We have not had sex. We fell asleep in the bed when we were talking last night, but we did nothing." She turned and walked away.

"Sarah."

"What?" She stopped and turned around.

"Tell me the truth."

"Sure, Chris." She stepped toward him. "I don't like this jealous part of you."

"I don't want to lose you, Sarah. You've spent an entire weekend with this guy."

"So? Nothing has happened."

"Where do we stand? It's like he's taking over."

"Taking over what?"

"You, dammit. He wants to be with you. I want to be with you. You need to make a choice."

"Don't you think I know that?"

"He has all the money to pay for all the stuff that needs to be done around here. He has all this money to whisk you off to anywhere in the world. I can't do any of that for you."

"Do you think I care about the money? And, as far as him "whisking me off," I have no intention of doing that. I can't handle that life; parties and awards and the media in my business twenty-four hours a day. That isn't who I am. That isn't who I want to be. You don't know me at all."

"That's not what I meant." Chris grabbed Sarah by her waist and pressed his lips hard on hers. She put her hands on his arms and sobbed as he kissed her. He could taste her tears as they fell down her cheeks. "Sarah," he whispered. She peered up at him, her eyes red from the tears. "I know this is hard for you."

She nodded.

"I'm so sorry. I don't want to make this harder for you."

"You have a funny way of showing it."

"I'll do whatever you want," Chris told her and held her closer. "I'll help with whatever you need."

"Thank you." She hugged him tighter. He lifted her mouth to his and kissed her, then he dried her eyes.

"Go inside now. You're shaking." She nodded and backed away as he got in his truck. "I'll see you tomorrow. Get some sleep."

"Okay. Bye, Chris." She waved as he drove away, then she went into the house. She plopped down on the couch and shook her head.

Andrew was on the couch next to her, leaning over the coffee table, looking at the list he and Chris had made. "What happened?"

Without a word, Sarah leaned over and kissed him hard.

"Whoa," he exclaimed, smiling. "What was that for?"

"How do you do it?"

"What?"

"The spark? The tingle? Why does it feel like there's lightning coursing through my veins every time we kiss? I still don't get that with Chris."

"You don't?"

"Not at all. But every time I kiss you..."

"It's happening to me, too."

"Why? What is it? Is it because this is new?"

"I don't know why it's happening, but I like it, and I won't fight it."

"I don't want to fight it anymore, either," she told him, certain of what she wanted to do now.

"What does this mean?" Andrew asked.

"I'm not sure. I want to be with you. I'm sure of that. But Chris..."

"Yes, that presents a problem."

"I have to tell him, Andrew."

Andrew glanced at her. "Wait a minute." He backed away a few inches.

"What's wrong?"

"What made you change your mind?"

"His persistent jealousy. I can't deal with it anymore. I'm wondering if his ex-wife was right all along. She said he was jealous. I can't be with another jealous person."

Andrew sighed. "Don't tell him now. It's not the right time."

"Excuse me?"

"Don't decide now." Yes, he wanted to be with her, but he needed Chris around for a while. He needed Chris's help and if Sarah put him off now, Chris wouldn't help. "I need to be a little selfish and selfless at the same time."

"You're confusing me again, Andrew."

"We need his help right now."

"I can't string him along."

"You're not. Nothing has happened between you and me and it's going to stay that way... for now."

"It still feels like I'm taking advantage of him... this is what I wanted to avoid. I won't lie to him, and I won't use him."

"Let's forget this conversation happened, alright," Andrew suggested.

"It changes nothing. He'll figure it out when our relationship isn't going anywhere."

"How else can we be sure he'll help?"

Sarah shook her head. "I don't like this."

"Ultimately, the decision is up to you," Andrew told her.

She glanced at him. He was right; the only way most of these things would be done would be with Chris's help. "Fine, but I don't like it," she said finally. "I'm only doing it for his help. I still hate the thought of using him."

"It will work out. I promise," Andrew said.

"Can we all forget this for now and have some dinner? I'm hungry," Sarah asked.

Andrew agreed. It was nearly five o'clock.

"What are you hungry for?" Andrew asked.

"There's plenty of food in the fridge," Sarah told them.

"I think Chinese," he shrugged.

"Didn't you buy dinner on Friday?" Sarah asked.

"So? It's my last night here. Humour me, please."

"I give up. Fine. You get your way... again." Sarah laughed and pushed his arm.

About twenty minutes later, the food arrived, and Sarah fixed their plates, and they ate.

***

After dinner, Andrew and Sarah sat together on the couch for a little while, enjoying each other's company. Andrew was glad he had come to the states and met this wonderful woman. Now that she wanted to be with him, he was more certain than ever that he had made the right choice by coming here. He was going to help her. He was going to be here for her, even when he couldn't be with her. She was one of the most amazing women he had ever met. He found it very easy to care about her, and it would be even easier to fall in love with her.

They both felt that spark when they were together. This couldn't last forever, but neither of them had ever felt that with anyone else. It was clear there was something deeper between them than either of them had ever known before.

"Sarah, love?"

"Yeah?"

"Are you getting tired?"

"No. I'm enjoying being here with you."

"I'm enjoying it, too. I wish it wasn't my last night. The weekend went by too fast."

"It's not fair." She turned to face him.

"We have plenty of time to talk to each other. You'll be going to L.A. soon. We'll be okay. And when we're together again, it will be that much better."

"Of course." She smiled and studied her hands.

"What is it?"

"I don't like having to keep this from Chris. I never wanted to hurt him. I never wanted to hurt you. I had a feeling this would happen, but I didn't realize how sad I would be about it."

"You can't help your feelings. I think both Chris and I figured it would happen. I don't think either of us wanted it to happen to ourselves, but there was a possibility."

"Sure, but I would have preferred it to happen to me."

"Why would you want that for yourself?"

"I'm used to it. I can handle it. It hurts that I have to cause either of you this kind of pain."

"It's who you are. You care so much for other people's feelings. That's a wonderful trait, love. You should be proud that you are the way you are."

"I am, but it doesn't make any easier. I do care for Chris. I have for a long time, and I never believed the things his ex-wife said about him, about his jealousy. It's scary."

"You didn't know. He never showed that side of himself."

"Not until you showed up. I guess when he thought he could lose me, he couldn't control his jealousy. Even when I tried to assure him that there was no competition, he would act like he was fine with all of this, but he wasn't. He showed up and watched you and every time you touched me or smiled at me or anything, he appeared to want to rip your head off."

"I saw that on Friday when I first arrived. It was almost frightening."

"I'm not afraid he'll hit me now, but jealousy progresses into abuse at some point."

"I understand. He'll be sorry if he hurts you."

"He won't hurt me. I would leave the situation before it ever got that far."

"I couldn't bear it if anything were to happen to you."

"Don't worry. I'll be fine." She smiled at him again.

"And how is your heart right now?"

"There's a minor fracture, but it's healing."

"Is it?"

"Yes, thanks to you."

"I won't hurt you, Sarah," he reassured her. She could feel the heat of his breath on her lips as he leaned in closer. Slowly, he pressed his lips to hers, leaving her heart racing. The intensity grew with each kiss. His hands caressed her face as she ran her fingers through his hair. Andrew pulled her closer, their bodies pressed together as they lost themselves in the moment. Without breaking the kiss, he wrapped his arms around her, pulling her closer. Sarah felt the softness of his lips, the strength of his embrace, and the warmth of his body against hers. At that moment, nothing else mattered, nothing but the two of them lost in each other's embrace.

Sarah and Andrew were locked in a passionate embrace, their bodies pressed together. But Sarah felt like she wasn't close enough to him. With a determined look in her eye, she climbed onto his lap, her hands gripping his shoulders as she pressed herself against him with even more force. His lips met hers with a hungry intensity, and his hands moved down to her hips, pulling her closer to him. She let out a soft moan, and as she sat up to give him even more access, she thought about how badly she wanted him. The room was filled with the sound of their heavy breathing and the scent of their desire hung in the air. Sarah's skin tingled with every touch, and her heart raced. She knew she was where she wanted to be, in his arms, lost in the heat of their passion.

Andrew's arms wrapped around her, lifting her into his arms. He stood up, his body pressed against hers and carried her down the hall to her bathroom. He didn't need to say anything; how he held her showed his desire. He set her down, allowing her to turn on the water. He wanted to be close to her, to feel her skin against his as they showered together. "Are you sure you want to do this?" he asked, his eyes searching hers for any sign of hesitation. He wouldn't pressure her; he wanted her to be sure.

"I've never been surer," she told him and put her mouth back on his.

As the water temperature rose, Andrew and Sarah's passionate embrace intensified. They couldn't resist each other, their lips locked in a fierce dance as they shed their clothes. Their laughter echoed in the steamy bathroom, unbothered by any inhibitions. The heat of the shower only added to the intensity of their desire.

As they entered the shower, their lips collided with a passionate kiss. The hot water cascaded down their bodies, heating their skin. They were lost in each other's embrace, pushing and pulling as they explored each other's bodies. Sarah's head tilted back in pleasure as Andrew's lips and fingers trailed down her neck and over her breasts. With each touch, she felt a surge of desire course through her. The steam from the hot water enveloped them, adding to the intensity of their intimate moment.

"You have a beautiful body," he groaned, pleased with the view.

As Sarah's eyes met Andrew's, she saw the anticipation in his body. He stood tall and confident, his muscular frame radiating with desire. She smiled, her gaze lingering on his hardened member. She couldn't resist the urge to touch him, to feel the heat emanating from his body. She ran her fingers along his skin, feeling every ridge, curve, and muscle. "You are so sexy," she whispered, her voice filled with desire. She wanted him, and he knew it. Every touch, every look, was a testament to their unspoken desire.

"Do you still want to make love to me?"

Sarah sighed, wanting him more than ever. "Yes. I want you inside me."

Sarah's back arched as Andrew's lips crashed onto hers, their bodies colliding against the cool shower wall. A guttural moan escaped her lips as he pressed against her, their skin slick with water. She could feel the force of his desire, his need for her clear in every touch. "You want this?" Andrew whispered huskily, his voice dripping with desire. Sarah could only nod, her mind consumed by the overwhelming sensations taking over her body. She could feel every inch of him, his hands roaming over her skin, igniting a fire within her. She wanted him, needed him, and he knew it.

After a long while, Andrew carried her to the bedroom.

They made love for several hours.

As Sarah's body quivered with ecstasy, she and Andrew exchanged knowing smiles, their lips locking in a slow, passionate kiss. Without a word, they gazed into each other's eyes and traced their fingers over each other's skin, their movements in sync. It was as if their bodies were made for this moment, moving together in a harmonious dance. The room was filled with the intoxicating scent of their desire, and the only sound was the soft rustling of sheets as they surrendered to each other's touch.

Andrew's lips traced every curve of Sarah's body, eliciting a deep moan from her. She reciprocated, her touch igniting a fire within him. At that moment, he was in awe of her, her beauty and passion captivating him. Lost in each other's embrace, they savored every moment, their bodies entwined in a symphony of desire. He couldn't resist holding her close, his lips never wanting to leave hers. With every kiss, he felt himself falling deeper in love with her.

When he was spent, they were panting. He slid off her and lay on his back, smiling and breathing heavy. Sarah rolled on her side to look at him.

"I don't want to leave you," he told her as they lay intertwined under the covers.

"I want you to stay, too, but you can't." She cuddled closer to him, holding him tight and playing with the soft hairs on his chest.

He rubbed her shoulder as he held her. "Will you listen to me on the radio tomorrow?"

"Yes. I'm going to record the entire show on my computer."

"You can do that?"

"Yeah. It's not that hard."

"Brilliant. I'm going to make an announcement, and I want to be sure you'll hear it."

"I won't miss a single word." She closed her eyes and continued to rub his chest. Andrew held her tighter.

"Are you tired yet?"

"Exhausted," she chuckled.

"Go to sleep, love." He ran his fingers through her hair.

"I can't hide this from him," she whispered as she drifted off to sleep.

"Then don't." He kissed her head and let her sleep.

Chapter Five – What Happens Now?
SARAH

I woke with a start on Monday morning. I had forgotten to set the alarm after Andrew and I made love. Now it was almost seven. We both were going to be late. "Andrew, wake up." I shook him and he stirred.

"What's wrong, love?" He sat up and rubbed his eyes. I sprang from the bed and went to the closet.

"We overslept. Come on. It's seven o'clock."

"Dammit." He jumped out of bed and pulled on a pair of boxers, then headed for the bathroom.

When he came out, I went in, did my business, splashed cold water on my face to wake up, then got dressed and put my make-up on. I wouldn't even have time for my mocha before I got to the office.

Andrew wore a pair of jeans and an Oxford University sweatshirt. He was gorgeous, and I wanted to forget work today and stay in bed with him, but I couldn't, so I grabbed him and kissed him instead.

"I wish I didn't have to leave today," he told me as he held me. We were both prolonging the inevitable.

"Me, too. I wish we had one more day."

"We would say the same thing tomorrow, love."

"You're right." I sighed and held him tighter.

"We'll be together again soon," he told me as he pushed me away.

"Promise?"

"Of course." He gave me a quick kiss. "We had better go."

"Okay." I wanted more time with him this morning. I wanted to lie in bed with him and snuggle up against his warm body until it was absolutely necessary to get up. I hadn't wanted to rush this way.

I grabbed my coat and my purse, and he grabbed his bag, and we headed out the door together.

We stood by my car for a long while, kissing and hugging. I was fighting tears. "Don't cry, love. I'll ring you every day."

"I can call you, too. I'm being silly. It's just that I'll miss you."

"I'll miss you, too." He gave me a long, soft kiss. "We need to go."

I nodded and got in my car. I watched him walk to his car as I let my car warm up. He was so amazing, but I was sure this relationship wouldn't work out. I tried to deny it. I tried to fight it, but his life was so different from mine. Andrew lived in a different world than I, and there was no changing it.

I drove to work that morning, a depressed and lonely again. Andrew would be on his way to the radio station, thinking about his interview and promoting his new movie. He didn't have time to think about me now. His life would be back to its own routine soon and mine would be, too.

As I drove to work, the DJs were talking non-stop about their interview with Andrew. He was all around me now. I could smell him, and see him, and hear his voice. It was getting harder and harder to fight off the tears that were threatening to surface, but I stopped them as I walked into the office.

I sucked in a breath and walked to the kitchen. Even the office reminded me of Andrew Collier. I hadn't even thought about Chris until he snuck up behind me while I was making my mocha.

"Crap," I hissed under my breath. My body stiffened at his touch. I couldn't bring myself to look at him. My guilt was flowing because of the part I was about to play in this game of deceiving him. I wanted to tell him about last night. Just thinking about that made me tingle.

"Good morning, beautiful," he greeted me, putting his arms around my waist.

"Uh, morning, Chris." I didn't turn around.

He sensed I wasn't comfortable. "You okay?"

"Tired. I overslept, and I'm not feeling very well this morning." This much was true. Maybe I wouldn't have to lie to him after all. Maybe withholding the truth would work.

"Stayed up late with your boy toy last night?" He pulled away.

I groaned, annoyed and frustrated with his jealousy. Suddenly, everything about Chris Keller annoyed me. "I don't have time for this, Chris. I'm not in the mood and I have a lot of work to catch up on from Friday." I walked away from him and went to my desk. I couldn't talk to him, or anyone else, today.

At my desk, I turned my computer and radio on. They were still talking about Andrew's interview. Only an hour away. This was going to be the longest day in history. There was no doubt about it.

ANDREW

I drove to the radio station after I left Sarah's house, thinking hard about her. She was in my head. Last night had been amazing, and I wished I had more time with her.

I had a message for her during my interview, and I hoped I had enough time afterwards to surprise her at work.

I wanted to spend my life with her, and I wanted the entire world to know it. It had been only a few days, but I had never known such an immediate connection with anyone, ever, and I was certain it was the same for her. We were kindred spirits. It would be too difficult to explain it to anyone to make them understand. All I cared about was that Sarah and I understood and accepted it.

I was surprised by how light the traffic had been during my commute. It was either a light traffic day or I had been too deep in thought to notice the other cars. I parked in the garage at the station and my cell phone rang. Susan.

"I'm glad you're still alive," she told me, aggravated, when I answered. "Did you forget how to dial a telephone?"

"Give it a rest, Susan. I'm alive and well."

"Are you at the station?"

"Yes, Susan. And I'm fine and happy."

"Oh, God. What happened?"

"Don't worry about it. We'll talk tomorrow and I'll tell you everything."

"I'm afraid." She sounded almost frightened.

"Don't do this. I'm happy." I was. I hadn't ever experienced this before. It was wonderful, but also scary. I loved the feeling, and I didn't want it to end. "I have to go now. I'll ring you later."

"Make sure you do." She hung up.

I went inside the building and checked in at the desk. "Good morning," I said to the young woman at the desk. "I'm Andrew Collier."

"Ah, yes, Mr. Collier. They're expecting you. Take the elevator up to the tenth floor," she told me as she handed me a pass.

"Thank you so much."

I was getting nervous as the lift ascended. My stomach was doing flips, and I was sure it wasn't from the ride up or the interview. It was the announcement to Sarah I was planning to make. I was afraid she would put me off after she heard it. She had to be close to feeling it, too, if she didn't already.

Before the interview, I met with the DJs while they were on a commercial break. I was nervous as hell. My palms were sweating. I was pacing in the hall as I waited to go on air. It was almost time. The producer was calling me into the booth and directing me to a chair across from the DJs. I put headphones on and waited. I thought I might be sick, but the nausea ebbed as quickly as it came.

It was time.

"Well, we've been talking about today's guest all last week. In the studio right now, we have 'Two Hearts' and 'One Life' star, Andrew Collier. Good morning, Andrew." The morning show interview with Brian, Harry, and Erin had begun. I was on air, and I wasn't sick anymore.

"Good morning," I said. I was calm, much calmer than I had been five minutes earlier. It was going to be alright.

SARAH

Everyone had gathered around my desk to listen to the interview. Work was on the back burner. Valerie, Anita, Marie, and even Kelly were standing around my cubicle, listening. I had told them Andrew was going to make an announcement, and they all wanted to hear it. I had told none of them what had happened this weekend, especially about the events of last night. The only one I trusted with that secret with was Marie. She was the only one I had planned to tell.

The interview itself was standard as far as interviews went. Andrew talked about 'Two Hearts' and 'One Life' and when filming would begin on 'Silence'. They would film in Los Angeles and Portland.

"No wonder he wanted me there in May," I mumbled.

"What?" Marie and Kelly asked at the same time.

"Nothing." I waved it off. "I'll tell you later."

Near the end of the interview, I was sure he had forgotten the all-important announcement he wanted to make. I had to stand up and stretch my legs.

"I have something I'd like to say before I say goodbye to Denver. Would that be alright?" Andrew asked the DJs. He *didn't* forget. I listened closely and so did everyone who crammed themself in my tiny cubicle.

"Of course. Go ahead," Brian said.

"I had two reasons for coming to Denver. One was for this interview today, and I want to say thank you so much for having me on your show this morning. The other reason is for the woman in my life. Her name is Sarah. I wanted to make an announcement to her."

Everyone around me leaned in to hear him better.

"Sarah, I'm crazy about you." I smiled and my heart did a flip. Marie patted me on my shoulder. "No, that's not right. I'm in love with you and I want to spend my life with you. Will you marry me?"

119

I thought he was still talking, but my ears were ringing and everything went black, and I my legs gave out under me. Suddenly, I heard people above me asking me if I was okay.

"Can you open your eyes?" someone asked. I thought it was Valerie.

I opened my eyes, and everyone was kneeling above me.

"What happened?" I asked, sitting up. I was dizzy.

"You fainted," Marie told me.

"Do you need a doctor?" Anita asked. I shook my head. It was spinning, but I stood up. "Are you sure?" she asked again.

"No, no. I'm okay," I told her, but not sure I was.

"Do you need to go home?" Valerie asked.

"I think I just need some air. I can't breathe." Everyone backed away from me. I glanced around. Chris was nowhere to be found. I prayed he hadn't been listening to the radio.

"Kelly, why don't you take Sarah outside for a few minutes and let her walk around?" Valerie suggested. "Marie, can you cover the front desk for a few minutes?"

"Sure." Marie eyed me and smiled. "Are you okay?" I nodded. "We'll talk later." I nodded again, and Kelly took me by the arm and led me toward the front office.

When we got outside, the cold air hit me. "This weekend has been... I can't even explain it... stressful." Kelly and I sat down on the cement ledge next to the building. "Did that happen?" I asked her. "Did he ask me to marry him over the radio?"

"Yeah. What the hell happened between you two this weekend?" I grinned. Kelly gasped and grinned back. "No?"

I nodded. "Last night."

"Oh, my God, Sarah. Does Chris...?"

"No, and don't you dare tell him."

"I won't. I swear," she promised as she crossed her heart.

"What was he thinking?"

Kelly shook her head. "I don't know, but it was kind of romantic."

"Romantic? No, no. We spent one weekend together. There's no way he's in love with me. There's no way he wants to marry me."

"Why not? What else happened this weekend? Besides last night?"

"It's way too soon," I told her, and then explained the events of the weekend, I told her about how Andrew and I spent all night on Saturday talking, how he made breakfast on Sunday morning, and how he invited me to visit him in L.A. in May while a new roof, that he was paying for, was being installed on my house. I explained how Chris's jealousy was teetering on dangerous behavior. "I had to make a choice. It wasn't easy, Kelly." We headed back toward the office. "I care about both of them, but Chris's jealousy is taking its toll on me."

"That's not healthy."

"No, it's not. So, I chose Andrew. Stupid, huh? I mean, he's twenty-five, he's a movie star. We'll never see each other. What do we have in common?"

"There has to be something there. Why else would you pick him? And why else would he profess his love for you to all of Denver?"

I shrugged. I didn't have an answer. I prayed with my whole heart that he didn't mean it; that his proposal had just slipped out.

It hadn't. He meant it.

ANDREW

I sped along the highway to Sarah's office after the interview. I had little time before I had to be at the airport, but I had to talk to her again before I left.

I reached the car park just as Sarah and Kelly were going into the building. "Sarah," I yelled as I got out of the car and ran up to her. Kelly had gone inside to give us privacy.

I put my hands on her face and kissed her. She put her arms around my neck and kissed me back. Was she saying yes?

"Marry me, please," I asked her when our lips parted. "I love you."

She stepped away from me and stared at the ground. "How? How can you be in love with me already?"

"I can't explain it, love, but I do."

"I do, too," she told me. She gazed at me and smiled. "I'm so crazy about you."

I took her in my arms and held her close. "Will you marry me?"

"If I say yes, can we take this slow?"

"We can do anything you want. I love you so much." I took her face in my hands again and kissed her with passion.

"Then, yes, I'll marry you," she told me with a smile. Tears were running down her cheeks. I wiped them away with my thumbs.

"I have to go to the airport."

"I wish you didn't."

"Me, too. But I'll call you as soon as I land. The moment I step foot off the plane." I hugged her again. "I need to go. I love you." I kissed her again and sprinted back to the car. I hated leaving her. I didn't want to, but I had to... for now.

SARAH

"Well," Kelly asked, impatient for my answer. Marie was standing next to her in the front office.

"I said yes," I told her. "With conditions."

"Conditions? You put conditions on a proposal?"

"We're going to take it slow. I'm not rushing into anything." Marie came around the desk and hugged me.

"Congratulations buddy. I'm taking you to lunch today and you're going to tell me everything."

"Sure." I smiled at her. I wasn't ready for this. My stomach was in knots, but I had never been this happy before. Andrew thrilled me and scared me at the same time. This was a lot to take in. I had a lot to think about, but I didn't have time now. I was so far behind at work. "We'll talk at lunch."

Chris was standing in his office doorway. "You slept with him, didn't you?" He sounded more hurt than angry.

I followed him into his office and shut the door behind me. I shouldn't have taken this route back to my desk. I sat down and faced him. I was going to have to lie to him and I didn't want to. I took a deep breath and began my deception. "No."

"Then why did he propose to you on the radio?"

I gave a short laugh. "You heard that, did you?"

"All of Denver heard it, Sarah. So, if you didn't sleep with him, why did he ask you to marry him?"

"Well, you weren't around to see my reaction, were you?"

He stared at me. The anger was building in him.

"I fainted. I was just as stunned as you are."

"Answer the damn question, Sarah," he shouted.

"I don't know," I shouted back and stood to leave. He blocked the door. "Move, Chris." I didn't meet his stare.

"He was here. I saw him. He came for an answer. Did you say yes?"

"No." Another lie. I still couldn't look him in the eyes.

"You're lying... about everything. He asked you to marry him because you screwed him, and you said yes because you want to hurt me."

I was livid. "So, the only reason he would want to be with me is because I had sex with him?"

"So, you admit it?"

"I'm not admitting anything, you ass." I tried to push him out of the way, but he was much stronger than I was. "Get the hell out of my way, Chris. I'm done with..."

Before I could finish, his mouth was hard on mine. It was a furious, emotion-filled kiss. There was no love in the way his mouth pressed on mine. "Let me go," I pleaded.

"No," he whispered. "Never. I love you. I want to be with you. He doesn't even know you."

"You don't love me, either."

He sighed and stepped away from the door. "Except that I do, Sarah. For a long time now. And now I guess I've waited too long to tell you because you're going to run off and marry some twenty-five-year-old boy."

"I'm not marrying anyone, Chris." Yet another lie. I couldn't keep this up. He wasn't stupid. At some point, he was going to figure out I was lying. When I wouldn't kiss him. When I wouldn't make love to him. He was going to put the pieces together and realize I had already chosen Andrew. "You keep jumping to conclusions about everything, and you're so jealous. I can't take it anymore." I cried.

"God, don't start bawling." He was being rude and insensitive.

"I can't take this from either of you. You're both idiots." I meant it. "He promised not to push me, but he turns around and proposes to me on the radio. And you... your jealousy just makes me angry. It's childish. I would rather spend the rest of my life alone than put up with either of your crap." I opened the door and walked out.

"Sarah, wait."

"I'm done, Chris, with both of you." I wouldn't let either of them bully me this way. My emotions couldn't take it. I couldn't be pulled at this way.

ANDREW

I sat on the plane, thinking about what I had done. I didn't regret it. I wasn't sorry. I took Sarah's picture out of my coat pocket and stared at it.

I loved her so much and there was no reasonable explanation for how it was possible this soon, but I was in love with her, and I wanted to be with her.

I wanted to call her that minute. I needed to hear her voice, but the flight crew had already made me turn my phone off.

I closed my eyes and took in a deep breath. Mixed with the stale air of the first-class cabin was the faint scent of her skin. I didn't want to lose that. I never wanted to forget one minute detail of her; from the shape of her deep green eyes to the length of her fingernails.

As I drifted off to sleep, I remembered the night before, when I memorized every inch of her body. Her skin was so soft. I could still sense her skin on mine and her legs wrapped around mine as we moved together. She excited me. She gave me goosebumps. I envisioned her smiling up at me right before I kissed her. Everything about Sarah Miller was beautiful and pure. The way her hair fanned out on the pillow, the way her eyes closed and the sounds she made when I moved in her were all things I never wanted to forget.

It wasn't just the lovemaking. I was in love with all of her. My memories took me back to Friday night. We laughed together and talked all night. She was so open, yet cautious at the same time. She wanted to let go, but it frightened her. She allowed me into her world, and I was grateful.

I had opened up to her, as well. I could be my real self with her. She didn't treat me like a star. I was "just Andrew," and I loved being "just Andrew." This was how she perceived me.

My memories then took me to Saturday and how she handled the entire situation with the teenage girls and the paparazzi with such class and control. She never failed to surprise me. These were all things that made me fall for her this soon.

My only obstacle was Chris. I think I may have grimaced then. He was a thorn in my side, but I needed his help for now. Once he had served his purpose, he was gone. I was being selfish now.

Sarah had said yes. She said she would marry me, and I could afford to be a little selfish, but I would never be like him. I would never hurt her the way he did.

I trusted her with my whole heart. She wouldn't betray me because of how hard she resisted in deceiving Chris. This would not be easy for her, but I trusted her.

SARAH

It was one o'clock. Marie was taking me away from what little work I had gotten done. I couldn't wrap my head around any of it. Maybe I should have gone home? No, that would have made things even worse, and I would have even more work stacked on my desk when I came back.

"Let's go," she rushed me.

"I'm coming." I grabbed my coat and purse and followed her out. "Where are we going?"

"Is Olive Garden okay?"

"That's fine." I would have a salad. I wasn't hungry, and I didn't want to talk about this or think about it anymore. Marie had insisted, and I could tell her anything without her judging me.

Marie let me be while she drove to the restaurant. I was thankful for that. I needed to clear my head. I couldn't think. My head was cloudy, and everything was a blur in my mind. I thought I might be having a stroke or something.

When the hostess seated us at our table, Marie pounced. "Okay, start from the beginning."

"You're already aware of Friday. And you heard the proposal today."

"Yeah, well, there are two days missing. And besides, you promised you'd tell me."

"Yes, I did. Alright." I smiled and began with Friday night. She was leaning on her elbow, listening close, until the waitress came to take our order.

"You're going to order more than salad, aren't you?" Marie asked.

"No. My stomach is giving me a fit right now."

She glanced at me but recovered and continued grilling me when the waitress walked away. "Go on."

I continued with Saturday and our infamous shopping trip. The whole thing seemed to amuse her. "No way," she laughed. "I can't believe you told them off. The girls, yeah, but photographers? Amazing. Did any of them show up at your house?"

"No way. I wasn't kidding. I would have called the cops. I'm sure my picture is in the paper or on TV or something. I haven't checked any of them."

"The first thing I'm going to do when I'm home is check the gossip blogs," she told me.

"Tell me what you find. I don't even want to look at them."

"I'm sure it's not all that bad. Keep going."

It was getting easier to tell the story again. Marie was easy to talk to. She always had been. That's why I trusted her so much, and why she was one of my most trusted friends.

I continued my story with the events of Saturday night and how Andrew and Chris got into it over me.

"I've got to say, he sounds amazing so far."

"Just wait. It gets better." The waitress brought our food then, and when she disappeared, I continued with my story. "Chris showed up on Sunday. I think it was to check up on us. I swear, his jealousy has become so unnerving. You didn't hear us yelling in his office this morning, did you?"

"No. What happened?"

"He kept accusing me of sleeping with Andrew. I can't deal with his jealousy, so I went off on him." I ate as much of my salad as possible and pushed my plate aside. My stomach was still doing flips. "The two of them put their contempt for one another aside long enough to bully me into letting them fix my house. Andrew insisted on paying for all of it and Chris doing most of the work. I told them I would agree if they promised not to come back to me later and ask to be paid back. I told them I can't afford to."

"Yeah, I guess so. What happened last night that caused him to propose to you on the radio?"

"Well, I'm not sure if it *caused* him to, but I'm sure it contributed to his decision to go ahead with it. I'm sure he was thinking about it before."

"Before what?" she asked in excited anticipation.

"Things sort of got... out of control, I guess. After Chris left, I realized I never got that spark or tingle, or whatever you call it, with him. When Andrew kisses me, it's like lightning or electricity. So, Andrew and I started kissing, and the kissing led to the shower and then the shower led to the bedroom."

"Oh, jeez. You slept with him."

"Shh." Marie had blurted that out a little too loud.

"Sorry. Details. How was it?"

"It was amazing. He's amazing." I smiled and closed my eyes. Just thinking about it was sending currents through me. "He knows exactly how to touch me. I can't describe it any other way than amazing."

"I cannot believe you slept with Andrew Collier. He's every tween girl's fantasy and you're living it."

"Yeah, well." I smiled. I couldn't do anything but smile. "We had better get back to the office. I still have to catch up on some files."

"Fine." She wanted to hear more, but there wasn't any more to tell. My fantasy weekend had ended, and I was alone again.

"You cannot tell Chris about this. Swear to me you won't say a word."

"I won't. What are you going to do about him now? Did you tell him you accepted Andrew's proposal?"

"No. He knows Andrew proposed. I don't want to lie to him, but we still kind of need his help with this house stuff. I can't do it anymore, though. I can't hurt him. I care too much about him."

"Of course, you do." We left the restaurant and got in her car, and Marie drove back to the office. "He has had a thing for you about as long as you've had a thing for him."

"That's why I don't want to hurt him."

***

By five o'clock, I had finally gotten caught up on my work. I was more than ready to go home, so I grabbed my coat and purse and went out to my car. I peered up at the sky toward the east and thought about Andrew. Would he be landing at Heathrow yet? I didn't know how long it took to fly from Denver to London. I would have to look that up.

"What are you looking at?" Chris's voice broke into my thoughts.

"Nothing." I got in my car and started the engine and put the window down. "I have to go."

"Can we talk?"

I shrugged. "I guess, if you want to follow me home."

"Sure. I need to stop at the store, so I'll meet you there."

"Fine." I left him standing in the parking lot. I had to stop being so mean to him. It hurt me to do it.

The house was dark and quiet when I got home, but it was warm, and I still smelled Andrew's scent everywhere. I missed him so much; I ached.

The flowers were wilting, so I pressed some of them. I ran a finger over each petal and wanted to cry. When would I see him again? When would I hear his voice again? "Okay, woman. Stop obsessing. He's yours," I said aloud as I put the flowers in a press and seal bag. I threw the stems away and took the vase to the sink. I would wash it later. Then I went to the bedroom to change into my pajamas before Chris showed up. My heart raced and my body tingled when I saw Andrew's t-shirt on the bed. It was the t-shirt he had worn last night.

I smelled it. His cologne was strong, so I put it on. I wanted his scent on me. My house would never again be the same to me. Everything would remind me of my wonderful weekend with Andrew Collier.

Chris knocked on the door, ruining my wonderful memories. "Come in," I called from the couch.

Chris let himself in and sat down next to me. "Hey."

"Hey." I didn't know what to say to him and he appeared nervous and uncomfortable being here. He should, after the way he treated me earlier.

"It's warm in here."

"Yeah. Thank you again."

"Sure. No problem."

"You wanted to talk?" I asked, impatient. If I didn't push him, we would have made small talk all night.

"Uh, yeah. Where do I start?"

I looked at him. "I assumed you had an idea what you wanted to say."

"No." He appeared nervous and flustered. I felt sorry for him. He was looking around. "Where is Andrew?"

"He's on his way back to London."

"Ah. Okay." He was panting and sweating.

"Are you okay? You look like you're going to be sick or something."

"I'm trying to calm down. I'm kind of pissed. I have been mad all day."

"All day?"

"Uh-huh."

He was watching me. "Holding a grudge like a child. What's wrong with you?"

"This isn't easy for me, Sarah, knowing I'm about to lose you to some kid you met two days ago; listening to you lie to me about not sleeping with him."

"What makes you think I slept with him?"

"I'm not stupid. Why the hell else would he ask you to marry him?"

"Didn't we already do this?" I looked at him.

"You're his girlfriend, aren't you?"

"What the hell are you talking about?"

He pulled a newspaper out of his coat. I grabbed the newspaper and read the headline. On the front page of the entertainment section was a picture of me giving the press a piece of my mind. The caption below the photo read:

'Andrew Collier's New Girlfriend Tells Off Press.'

"Wow, what a crappy picture. I look like I've been sucking a lemon." I pretended I didn't see the headline.

"Cut the crap, Sarah."

"Jeez, Chris. He told the teenagers I was his girlfriend so they would leave us alone. The press must have gotten wind of it. Give me a break. I'm not his girlfriend." Not a lie.

"But he proposed to you."

"It was a publicity stunt." I stood up and paced. I couldn't look him in the eye and lie to him.

"What?"

"It was a publicity stunt. The press won't leave him alone about his co-star, Karen Steele, so he staged this proposal to throw them off."

"So, the proposal was fake?"

"Yeah." God, this was killing me. How much longer was I going to carry on with this charade?

"None of it's true?"

"No. None of it. I'm not his girlfriend. I'm not marrying him, and we didn't sleep together." I sat back down next to him and took his hands in mine. "I wish you would stop being jealous. I don't like it. It scares me. I already told you this."

"I don't want to lose you, but I can see I am, and it scares the hell out of me." He kissed my cheek. I let him. "I hate that this punk just shows up and sweeps you off your feet. I can't do all the things for you he can and that bugs me."

"Are you talking about all the work on my house?"

"Not just that. He can pay for plane tickets to L.A. and anywhere else in the world for you to go. I can't do that."

"What difference does it make who pays for it? I'm still not crazy about this whole idea, but I promised to keep my mouth shut."

He nodded and stood up and pulled me up with him. "I'm scared. I'm terrified."

"Don't be." I put my arms around his waist and hugged him. He took a breath.

"I have to go."

"Okay." I walked him to the door, and he kissed me softly. "Good night."

I went back to the couch and sat down and cried.

ANDREW

"Hi, love." I called the second I got off the plane.

"Andrew. I am so glad to hear your voice. I miss you so much." She sounded like she had been crying.

"I miss you, too, love. Are you crying?"

"Yeah."

"Why?" I walked out to the terminal. The press was waiting for me like wild animals. "Bloody hell. I've been spotted. Hold on, love, alright?"

"Okay."

I walked past them. They were shouting at me, asking me questions I had no intention of answering.

"How was your trip? Where is your girlfriend? Why did you propose to her on the radio? Are you moving to Denver, or is she moving to be with you?"

I made it outside, with my head down, and unscathed, and got in the back of a waiting taxi. I told the driver to take me to my flat, then got back on the phone with Sarah.

"Are you still there?"

"Yes."

"Why are you crying?" I asked.

"Today sucked, and I miss you."

I laughed, but I wasn't laughing at her. "It sucked for me, too. I want to be with you."

"Chris and I got into it at work today." She sounded as if she had stopped crying.

"Oh, no. Did you tell him?"

"We agreed not to."

"It's hurting you not to. Tell him the truth, alright?"

"Are you sure?"

"Yes. We can hire someone to do the work on your house. I don't want you hurting anymore."

"Okay." She was quiet for a minute. "How was your flight?"

"Long, but I slept through most of it. How are you?"

"Aside from my horrible day?"

"Your heart, love?"

"Mending. Did you mean what you said today?"

"About marrying you?" The driver was looking at me in the rear-view mirror. Sell that to the press, I thought as I glimpsed him in the mirror.

We were in front of my building now. I paid the driver and went inside and took the lift to my flat.

"When can we see each other?" I asked. I was lying on my bed, staring at the ceiling.

"I'm not sure. You know I can't afford to come visit."

"Valentine's Day weekend," I told her. "I'll buy the ticket. I can hardly stand the distance between us already. We can spend the weekend in Portland. We film on the fifteenth."

"Andrew, no. I can't let you do that," she protested.

"Did you or did you not promise not to complain about the money I spend on you?"

"That was for the house."

"I recall the mention of plane tickets as well, love," I reminded her.

"Andrew," she protested.

"Sarah, hush. I love you and I miss you and I want to be with you on Valentine's Day."

"It *does* sound wonderful. I miss you, too." She sighed. "Okay. I give in. I can't wait to see you again."

"Wonderful. It's settled... it's one in the morning here and I have to meet with my agent at eight. Sweet dreams, love. And please talk to talk to Chris."

"I will. I miss you, Andrew."
"I miss you, too. Good night, my love."
"Good night."

Chapter Six – The Countdown
ANDREW

It was a long and irritating Tuesday morning. Susan was livid. She had read the papers and watched the entertainment shows all weekend, waiting for me to show up, either in some kind of scandal or dead. After she found out I had proposed to Sarah, I believed she would have preferred I had been murdered.

"What's wrong with you? You *are* joking, right?"

"I'm not joking," I told her. "I met her. I spent the weekend with her. She's smart, and funny, and sweet. I'm in love, Susan." I dropped onto the chair, grinning from ear to ear.

"No, you aren't. You're in lust. I think we need a background check on her and do some damage control."

"Oh, stop it. Sarah and I spent hours talking starting the first night I was there. I have a lot more to learn about her, but she has a lot to learn about me, too."

"You aren't getting it, Andrew." She rubbed her temples. "You proposed marriage to a woman you have only known for two and a half days. What is the matter with you?"

"I'm in love." I groaned, frustrated and unnerved. "I think about her every minute of the day. I dream about her every night. She is unlike any woman I have ever met."

"I'm still having her investigated. I still believe she's a psycho."

"I'll never forgive you if you do. I'm twenty-five years old. I'm not a child. I can date whomever I please. I can propose to whomever I choose. You cannot stop me." I was getting angry, and this conversation was going nowhere.

"How do you know she isn't after your money or is looking to be a part of your lifestyle?"

"When you meet her, you'll understand that's so far from the truth. You'll understand."

"I don't think I want to, Andrew. I think you have lost your mind."

"Once again, you're right. Love does that to a person." I stood up. "I'm finished with this conversation. I'm meeting my mother for tea."

"You're such a terror." Susan was angry, but I didn't care. She would not tell me who I could be with.

SARAH

Tuesday was beginning less hectic than Monday had, but Andrew wasn't waking up next to me. I was missing him so much already. His presence was everywhere, but he was gone, and I wanted to wake up in his arms. Valentine's weekend couldn't come fast enough.

I took a long, hot shower, remembering Sunday night. Thinking about it made me tingle.

Another long day was ahead of me. Another long week. Another long two weeks.

My phone rang a little after seven o'clock. It was Andrew. The day was getting better already.

"Good morning, love," he said. There was a smile in his voice.

"Morning, sweetheart. Oh, I guess it's afternoon for you, isn't it?"

"Yes. I wanted to send you off to work with a smile."

"Thank you, Andrew." I was ecstatic he called. His phone call made my morning. "How is your day going?"

"Oh, well, I got into it with my agent."

"Because of me?" I had guilt because he was getting grief from his friends and family.

"No, not about you. It's more about me and what I did. It's all over the media here in London."

"It is here, too. I'm sorry I put you through this."

"Don't be. I can handle it," he said.

"It's my fault," I told him. It had been me who had gone off on the press.

"No, it isn't. The media is praising you for the way you handled yourself. My only concern is that they will start hounding you soon."

"I'll be fine. I took them on once. I can do it again."

"Are you certain about that?"

"Yes." I couldn't help but smile. Hearing his voice made everything better.

"Alright, love. If you're sure?"

"I am."

"Listen, love. I'm off to have tea with my mum, then I'm getting your tickets to Portland for Valentine's weekend. I will have them couriered to you straight away."

"Sweetie, I don't deserve any of this." I didn't think I did.

"You deserve this, and more," he assured me. "I have to run. I'll ring you tonight. I love you."

"I can't wait for. I'll talk to you tonight."

"Bye, love."

I hung up and smiled and sighed. How was he able to give me feelings like this? Feelings I had never had before? He was everything I had ever dreamed of and more, so why was it so hard for me to tell him I love him?

ANDREW

I drove to my parent's house in Barnes to pick up my mum. I had so much to tell her. She would be about as happy for me as Susan was, but I was bursting at the seams to tell someone, and my mum and I were close. I would make her understand how happy Sarah made me, and she would be happy for me.

"Andrew, I am so glad you're here." She hugged me. "Come in for a minute, will you?"

I followed her into the kitchen. "I'm glad to see you, mum. I told you I would come home safe and sound."

"I had no doubt. Sit for a minute. I want to talk to you."

I sat, but I asked, "Can we talk at the restaurant? I'm hungry."

"We will, but I have a few things to say first." She handed me a copy of 'The London Times.' Sarah's and my pictures were on the front page.

"Oh." I couldn't think of any words.

"Why would you put her in this situation, Andrew? It's obvious you care about her, and you want to be with her, but don't you think you've put her in a difficult position? Can she handle all this?"

"I asked her to marry me," I told my mother. She gasped and put her hand over her mouth.

"Oh, Andrew, no. You didn't?"

"I did. I'm not sorry. I love her."

"I'm at a loss. Please tell me she had sense enough to say no?"

"I can't say that, but she doesn't want to rush into anything."

"That's something." She shook her head and sighed. "What are you trying to do to this poor girl?" She stood and took her coat from the back of the chair. "We can discuss all this another time. Let's go to tea. I want you to tell me about your trip."

I took my mother to Annie's, a quiet little cafe on White Hart Lane in Barnes. It was private, and the press wouldn't bother us.

"Tell me all about your trip," she asked once we had ordered.

"Where would you like me to start?" I thought for a moment, then began with my purchase of the flowers for Sarah and how I had nearly caused her to faint when I appeared in front of her. I explained how I had insisted I have everything fixed in her house. "If you could see her house, mum, you would want to help her." I told her all about Sarah's life, how lonely her childhood was, and her failed relationships.

"You don't suppose she was only trying to play on your sympathies, do you?"

"No, mother, we were both honest with each other."

"Let me show you some photos I took." I took my phone out and showed her the photos I had taken.

"She's beautiful." She viewed at the pictures. "You care about her, don't you?"

"I do, mum. I love her."

"Do you think she can handle the life you're going to be putting her in? It has been a difficult adjustment, especially for you. Do you remember how recluse you became after 'Two Hearts' came out?"

"Mm-hm."

"It will be much worse for her. You realize that? She has spent her life as a regular person. If you care about her and bring her into your world, you need to consider a few things."

"What are those?"

"You will have to be with her every step of the way to guide her and show her the way."

"I have every intention of doing that, mum."

She put her hand up. "Also, you cannot resent her or be angry with her if she isn't able to handle this life. You are going to have to remember that this is your world, not hers."

"I understand all of that. I'll be patient. I would never be angry with her if she can't do it. Of course, it would hurt me if she left, but I only want her to be happy. I'm certain I can make her happy." I smiled at my mother and took her hand. "Anything else?"

"Yes. At the first opportunity, I want you to bring her to London. I want to meet my future daughter-in-law." She shook her head and smiled. "Boy, that sounds so strange."

"It does at first." I smiled at my mum. "And, yes, I will bring her to London to meet the family."

My mother and I continued to discuss my weekend as soon as our meal was served. It was a splendid afternoon. Spending time with my mum was always wonderful. I couldn't wait to bring Sarah to meet her and the rest of the family. The moment they met her, they would fall in love with her, too, although she was an American. My sisters were always on my case because of my preference for red-headed American women. They would soon find out why she was so special.

SARAH

I spent most of my Tuesday keeping to myself. I put off talking to Chris all day, but I had to tell him the truth. I needed to tell him the truth. Lying to him was breaking my heart. Telling him the truth would break him, but if he found out another way, it would hurt him more.

I think it was after three when I went to Chris's office. I had avoided him all day. Every time he had been near me, I found an excuse to go somewhere else. "Hey," I said, giving him a quick smile.

"Hey, what's up?"

"Um, I was wondering if you would come by after work?" I wouldn't do this to him at work.

"Sure." He appeared pleased. That would change before he left my house.

I grinned, then I walked back to my desk.

Five o'clock came too fast. I wasn't sure I was ready to break his heart. It was the last thing I had ever intended to do.

I got home a few minutes before Chris arrived.

Chris knocked on the door. I let him in. "Thanks for coming over. Do you want something to drink?" This was awkward.

"No thanks." He sat down on the couch.

I sat down next to him and rubbed my sweating palms on my pants. "God, this isn't easy for me."

He scooted closer to me and put his arm around my shoulder. Bad idea. I stood up. "What's wrong, sweetie? You've been weird all day."

"Yeah." I sat down next to him again but didn't let him touch me. I tucked my hair behind my ears. "Okay, I should spit it out." I took a deep breath. "I lied to you."

"About?"

"Everything."

"Can you be more specific?" He was becoming irritated.

"Everything. Andrew and I slept together last night. He asked me to marry him, and I said yes. It wasn't a publicity stunt." I cowered and glanced at him out of the corner of my eye. He was calm. Too calm.

"So, everything that came out of your mouth this weekend was a lie?"

"No, only today."

"Ah. Okay. Why didn't you tell me the truth?"

"I didn't want to hurt you. I'm sorry I lied." I cried. "I told you all this would hurt someone."

"Why are you crying? You should be thrilled. You chose your sugar daddy. He can give you whatever you want. He could buy you the world if you asked for it." His voice was getting louder.

"That's not why, and you know it."

"Then why?"

"Because of your constant jealousy. I told you I couldn't deal with it, but you still got so jealous and almost controlling."

"I guess your boy toy never showed that side of him to you, did he? He sure as hell showed it to me when you weren't around."

"You're lying."

"Am I? Think about it, Sarah. We were both vying for you. Don't you think some of that was bound to come out?"

"I guess, but you act as if I asked for this, like I told him to come here and turn my life upside down."

"Well, you kind of did with that stupid letter of yours."

"Excuse me?" I was still crying. I didn't care. I wouldn't let him blame me for this. My only fault was that I lied to him.

"You're crying because you know I'm right."

"You can't blame me because he showed up here. I only asked for a picture, nothing more."

"Sure. I'm sure he's smart enough to read between the lines."

"You don't know what I wrote, and I'm only at fault for lying to you."

"And leading me on."

"I never did that to either of you."

"Sure, you did. Not on purpose, but you did. You kept telling me you weren't going anywhere. Lie. You told me there was no competition between the two of us. Another lie." He was pacing, and it was making me nervous. "I should have known I would lose you the minute he showed up. I was watching the way you two were looking at each other all weekend, and how distant you became with me when he was around. But I believed you would wake up and see him for what he is."

"And what is that?"

"A little boy flaunting his fame and money in front of everyone."

"He never did that."

"Of course he did. He might as well buy you a new house instead of trying to fix this piece of crap you live in now." He stopped and glared at me with a sinister grin on his lips. "Hey, now that's an idea. Why don't you "hint" to him you want to move? I'm sure he'll take that and run with it. You'll be moving into a brand-new house in Cherry Hills Village before the end of February."

"You're horrible, Chris. I would never do that. I don't like people spending money on me. Why are you being so mean?"

"I'm not being mean, sweetheart. I've simply figured out your game. You cry and complain that you can't afford to fix this or buy that, but you need it, and when someone offers to give it to you, you cry some more. 'No, I can't let you do that. I can't pay you back.' Sound familiar?"

"You're mean. I hate you. Get out!" I yelled at him.

He was inches from my face. My body was convulsing from holding my tears in. "Wait. I'm not finished." He moved away and took a breath. "So, you give in and let us help you, but what happens when we can't help you anymore? You find someone who can. You play on our emotions to get what you want, or, in your case, what you need. Brilliant. You're an expert at this game. On to the next, Sarah. For his sake, I hope he doesn't run out of money."

"You're a rotten human being. Haley was right."

"Don't you dare bring my ex-wife into this."

"No, no. Now it's my turn. If you won't leave my house, then you're going to listen to what I have to say, so sit down and shut up." I pushed him down on the couch. "Yeah, she told me all about you. About your jealous streak, about how you have to have control. Isn't that why she left you?"

"You're unbelievable. What did you do? Did you call her?"

"You're trying to take control of this conversation. I didn't believe her. You never acted that way around me, so I gave you a chance. I told you my feelings a long time ago, but you blew me off. I still liked you and you are the one who kept showing up here, wanting to help me. I didn't ask you for anything."

"No, Sarah, you never do."

"Would you shut up?" It was my turn to pace. "I mentioned once that my furnace was broken. Oh, and *you* asked *me* what I was doing the weekend you showed up to move that junk in my yard. That was all you. And when you came by to help me snake the pipes, I was talking to Kelly about it. Not you. Again, you showed up on your own. Now, go ahead, accuse me of playing games." He appeared stunned. "Well? Nothing to say?"

"No. You're right. I'm sorry." I wasn't sure he was.

"I'm sorry I lied to you, Chris." I sat down next to him again. "I swear, the last thing I wanted was for anyone to get hurt."

"I don't believe you," he told me quietly. He stood up and went to the door. "I hope you have a happy life. I mean that."

CHRIS

I got in my truck and sped away from Sarah's house as fast as possible. I didn't want to be anywhere near her anymore, but before I made it two blocks, I had to pull over.

My mind was racing backward, and I started thinking about the times we spent together; the things we did. I helped her, and she never asked for it. I only said those things to hurt her the way he hurt me.

Our friendship, the friendship we had been building for a year, was over. We would never be together. She had made sure of that. Andrew had made sure of that. The relationship we were building was dead.

I wanted to destroy Andrew. I wanted to destroy the two of them. No, I didn't. It wasn't her fault he showed up and swept her off her feet.

But why should she be this happy and leave me miserable and heartbroken? Was I as jealous as she claimed? I thought about that. Yeah, I had been. Every chance I got, I made some snide comment about her boy toy and upset her. No wonder she thought she had to lie to me. I couldn't blame her for that, but I couldn't forgive her for it either. It might have hurt less if she had told me the truth when I asked.

We were finished. I would be around her at work until her boy toy whisked her away to L.A. or London. Then we would never have to be near each other again. Until then, I would avoid her, and she would avoid me. We would never have to speak to each other again. The hard part would be seeing her and her perma-grin every day and having to walk past her desk and see pictures of the two of them or hear her on the phone with him.

Perhaps one day I'd move past this, and we'd try to be friends again. I wasn't betting on it, but I had hope.

It was getting late. I had spent too much time parked on the side of the road thinking about this crap. I put my truck in drive and went home.

Tomorrow would be different.

ANDREW

I had hoped Sarah told Chris everything. She wouldn't let me down, but I was afraid of what might happen to her when she told him. It was two in the morning, and I had a photo shoot at nine, but I had to talk to her.

"Hello, love. I missed you all day."

"Hi. I'm so happy you called."

"Have you been crying again?"

"Yeah. I told him. It didn't go well."

"What happened?" My poor Sarah. I wanted to put my arms around her.

"He was so horrible. The things he said about both of us were cruel. I wanted to hit him."

"He didn't hurt you, did he?"

"No, he never touched me, but the things he said were awful." She gave me a brief run-down of their conversation. I was sad for her.

"I'm so sorry you had to go through that alone. I want to be with you."

"I wish you were here, too, or I was with you."

"On a lighter note, my mother wants to meet you."

"Are you kidding? Why?"

I had to laugh. "What do you mean, 'why?'?"

"I mean, what made her decide she wanted to meet me?"

"I told her we're engaged."

"Oh." She sounded underwhelmed.

"Should I not have told her?"

"I'm not sure. How did she react when you told her?"

"She was shocked, but the more we talked, the more she accepted it. My mother and I are close, Sarah."

"As long as she doesn't hate me. She doesn't still think I'm an ax murderer, does she?"

"No. She's concerned about how you're going to handle life with me."

"Wow!" She seemed surprised.

"Sarah?" She had been quiet for so long; I was afraid she may have hung up.

"Uh, yeah, sorry. I kind of zoned out for a second."

"Everything alright?"

"Yep." She was smiling now. I heard it in her voice.

"Will you be able to sleep?"

"I think so. And I should let *you* go to sleep."

"I'm not ready to hang up," I told her.

"Me, either."

"I got your ticket today. You should have it in your beautiful hands this Friday."

"I can't wait to see you, Andrew."

"I can't wait for you to be here, love. I miss you."

"We'll be together soon. Soon. Go to sleep, please," she insisted.

"You, too. I'll be dreaming of you."

"And I of you."

"I love you. Good night, Sarah."

"Good night, Andrew."

I hung up and closed my eyes, and I realized we had to be the most sickening couple ever. I fell asleep with a smile on my lips as I thought about that.

SARAH

I had planned to talk to Valerie about leaving early on the twelfth and taking the fifteenth off. I needed to talk to her about Chris stuff, too.

As I was getting ready for work that morning, Andrew called like clockwork.

"Good morning, my love."

"How is your day?" I asked.

"Boring. I've been studying my lines most of the morning."

"How's that going?"

"Not well. You're in my head."

"Andrew, concentrate on your job. Don't let me keep you from that."

"You're not. I need a break. I'm flying to L.A. this weekend to rehearse with Karen and Trevor, then I'll stay in Portland until we film."

"Hey, the plus side is we'll be on the same continent." I smiled.

"It won't seem like we're a billion miles apart anymore."

"That will be nice. You're so far away right now."

"Cheer up. I have news."

"What's that?"

"I have a three-hour lay-over before I fly to L.A."

"Here?"

"Yes." I was more than excited. I was ecstatic. "My plane lands in Denver at four-thirty on Friday. Can you meet me at the airport?"

"Of course. I would never miss an opportunity to see you."

"Can you take the afternoon off work?"

"I'll work it out. You'll have to come up to the terminal, though. Passing through security will be difficult since I won't have a ticket."

"I can't wait," he told me. "I had better let you go to work. I'll call you tonight. I love you."

"I miss you." I was so close to telling him I loved him, but I didn't want it to be over the phone.

"Have a wonderful day, love."

"I will now. Goodbye." I hung up and jumped up and down. One more thing to talk to Valerie about.

Come on Friday.

***

"Well, you're cheerful this morning," Kelly told me when I walked into the office.

I was beaming. "I am." I ran to her desk. "Oh, wow, where do I start?" I had to remember to breathe. "Okay, well, Andrew has a three-hour lay-over in Denver on Friday. He's going to L.A. until they film in Portland on the fifteenth. I'm going to meet him in Portland for Valentine's weekend."

"What about Chris? Have you told him?"

I scanned the room. "Is he here?"

"He's been here for hours."

I shrugged. "Oh well. I haven't told him, and it's none of his business, anyway. We're done. I told him the truth last night. Let's say it didn't go well."

"Ooh. What happened?"

"He was mean. He said some awful things. I should have told him the truth when he asked." I was deflated. "It's too late to do anything about it now."

I peered up and Chris was standing in the doorway, staring at me. He didn't say a word.

"What?" I demanded.

"Come here." He was calm. It was more of a request than an order. I followed him to the office, shrugging to Kelly as I walked. He closed the door. Chris took my hands and gazed at me with a smile on his lips. The situation wasn't threatening, but I was still nervous.

I wasn't sure what this was about or what was going to happen next, and it frightened me.

"What's going on, Chris?"

"Be quiet for a minute. I want to look at you."

My forehead creased. I was confused. We didn't end things on a friendly note last night, despite him leaving with kind words. "What is this?"

"I was right," he said.

"About what?"

"I did a lot of thinking last night. I was so angry with you when I left your house last night. I wanted to kill both of you, but then I realized it wasn't all your fault. I mean, it's going to take a long time for me to forgive you for lying to me, and for sleeping with him, but I love you, and you're worth fighting for." He sat down. "Sit, please."

He was too calm, and I was getting scared, but I sat down on the chair closest to the door. I could leave faster from this chair. "What are you talking about?"

"Shh. I have a lot to say." He took a deep breath and continued. "It took all the strength I had not to drive back to your house last night. I'm glad I didn't. I was still pissed, and I wanted to make sure I didn't say something stupid when I talked to you again.

"I love you, Sarah. Nothing you ever do or say is going to change that. Have you told him you love him yet?"

"No."

"Then I stand a chance." He stood and walked toward me. He kneeled in front of me and took my hands.

"I need to go back to work. I need to talk to Valerie and..." He put his lips, soft, on mine, to quiet me. A spark. Where did that come from? No, not now.

"Wait, please. I need to say this."

I nodded. He wasn't going to let me leave yet. As long as he didn't kiss me again, everything would be okay.

"I tried to stay mad at you, Sarah, but I couldn't do it. You waited for me for a year, and you were right. Well, sort of." He stood again and went back to his chair. "You said I blew you off. I guess I did, but it was only because I was too afraid. I wasn't ready. I don't think either of us was ready then. If I hadn't had been so scared, we would be together now."

"Perhaps," I mumbled.

"You wouldn't have written that letter and you and I would be happy. Do you think?"

"Possibly," I said again. "But you didn't, and here we are."

"I'm going to fight for you, Sarah. I'm going to do all the things I promised you I would do. I'm going to be here for you whenever you need me. No questions asked. Promise me you'll give me a chance, okay?"

"Really?"

"Yes." He stood up again and walked toward me and took my hands. He pulled me up and gazed into my eyes. "Please. You never really gave me a chance. You owe me that much."

"I suppose I do, but..." He put his lips on mine again. That spark emanated. Nothing close to the electricity when Andrew kissed me, but it was something. Why now? Why couldn't things stay normal for a while? Why did my life have to be in a constant upheaval?

"Yes, or no?"

I couldn't say yes now, but I couldn't say no, either. Chris was right; I never gave him a chance.

"What about your jealousy? How are you going to control that?" I was sure I had my out. He would always show his jealousy with Andrew, and he was part of my life, much more than Chris was aware at this point. "Andrew is still a big part of this. He's still paying for everything, and, no matter what happens, he will always be my friend, above all else. The same goes for you."

"I can control my jealousy."

"Are you sure about that? You couldn't control it before."

"You're right. I have a right to be cautious and a little suspicious now, though."

"You never asked me to be your girlfriend."

"I told you about my feelings for you. That should have been enough, but it wasn't. I won't make that mistake again. I'll tell you all the time I love you. I'm not giving up on us."

"I don't think Andrew will, either." I sat back down and sighed. "You don't know how difficult all of this has been for me."

"I do."

"You don't. I've never had to make a choice between two men before and, honestly, neither one of you gave me the choice to make. You, with your jealousy and fighting with Andrew every time you were in the same room. Andrew, with his unexpected proposal. *That* came out of nowhere, Chris."

"Sure."

"I told you both in the beginning, someone would get hurt by all of this. I wish now I would have said no to both of you. At least then it would be me who got hurt. *I* can handle that." I stood up and went to the door. "I have work to do." I left his office and went to talk to Valerie.

"What happened to you?" she asked when I walked into her office.

"Chris cornered me."

"Ah. Is everything okay between the two of you?"

"As okay as they're going to get. I didn't realize how jealous he is."

"You didn't expect him to be happy about Andrew showing up and staying with you all weekend, did you?"

"No, but it was that scary jealousy."

"I'm familiar with that," she told me and leaned forward. "He didn't hit you, did he?"

"No. Not at all, but it was still scary."

"What's going to happen now?"

I sighed. How to say this. "Well, that's sort of why I'm here. I need to leave early on Friday. I guess around two."

"What's going on?"

"Andrew has a lay-over here on his way to L.A."

"Not a problem, but please, make sure you're caught up before you leave."

"I will. I've kind of been slacking."

"Well, with everything that has been happening, I can understand."

"Yeah, I guess so. One more request?" I cringed a little.

Valerie wasn't upset or annoyed. "What else?"

"I need the twelfth and the fifteenth off. I'm going to Portland."

"Valentine's weekend? Does this involve Andrew?"

"Yeah."

"Hmm. Chris is aware of this trip?"

"No. I didn't have time to do much talking. I'll talk to him today."

"Promise me you will."

"I won't hurt him again." Her eyes went wide. "Long story. He hurt me, too. I'll have to tell you about it soon." I smiled and stood up. "Thank you, Valerie."

"I haven't said yes yet."

"But you will, right?"

She chuckled. "Yes, of course I will."

"Then, thank you."

"Don't you have work to do?" She was still laughing when I left her office.

ANDREW

Sarah called my phone at seven p.m. What a wonderful surprise! It was her lunch hour, and she wanted to talk to me.

"How are you, my love?" I was happy to talk to her.

"This has been a strange day. Where do I start? In a minute, though. How was your day? What time is it in London?"

She was talking so fast. "Slow down." I laughed. "My day was fine. I'm studying my lines. Now I'm watching the news. We aren't on it."

"Thank goodness. Is that all you did today?"

"Yeah." I was still chuckling. "And what about your strange day?"

"Oh, yeah. Chris asked me to give him another chance. He still wants to help with the house. I explained you are still a huge part of my life. He said he didn't care. He told me he's going to fight for me."

"I hope he has it in him. I'm stronger and younger." I laughed again. I wasn't worried.

"I talked to Valerie. Everything is fine with my time off. I'll meet you at the airport on Friday. I can't wait. I already miss you so much."

"I miss you, too. I want to be with you all the time. I wish we could make that happen." I meant every word.

"I do, too. I want to say something to you, but I don't want to tell you over the phone. It will have to wait until Friday. I can't wait to put my arms around you again." She was still rushing her words.

"Oh, baby. This is killing me. I hate how far apart we are right now." I wanted to hold her so badly, my body ached for her touch.

Sarah became silent. "I need to tell you something, Andrew. It's bad."

"What's the matter, love?"

"He kissed me, twice, and a there was a spark." Now I *was* a little worried. "It wasn't like when you kiss me. Why now? Why did it have to happen now?"

"Did you kiss him back?"

"No. Not really. Do you think it might have been a spark of anger? I mean, I am still mad at him for the things he said last night."

"It could have been. Are you scared?"

"No. I love you..."

She caught herself, and me, off guard and stopped short. "What?" She said what I had been waiting for her to say. "Say it again."

"I love you," she whispered. "I love you. God, I didn't want to say this for the first time over the phone. I was planning to tell you on Friday."

"You can tell me again. I'll let you. I love you."

"I love you, but I need to go back to work. My lunch hour is almost over."

"Alright. I'll call you tonight. I'm glad you called."

"I am, too. I love you," she told me again.

"I love you, too. Goodbye."

CHRIS

I watched Sarah outside while she was on the phone with that punk. I sensed how happy she was when she talked to him, and it made me angry. I needed to put a stop to it. It should have been me she was laughing with and being crazy in love with. Not him.

When she hung up, I sprinted toward her. I was going to ask her to dinner on Valentine's Day.

"Sarah," I called out to her.

She turned. "Chris." It wasn't a happy greeting, but she was talking to me and that's all I hoped for at that point. "I was on my way to talk to you."

"Oh, yeah?"

"Mm-hm. Do you want to sit for a minute?"

"Sure. I want to ask you something." We sat down on the ledge near the building.

"What did you want to ask me?"

"I was wondering if you would have dinner with me on Valentine's Day?" I prayed she would say yes.

She frowned. "That's what I was going to talk to you about. I'm going out of town that weekend, to Portland."

"To be with *him*?" I was having a hard time controlling my anger. The mention of his existence set me off.

"You're doing it again, Chris."

"What?"

"The jealousy. It's in your tone. You aren't trying." She put her head down and chuckled. "Why do you hate him so much?"

"Now that's a stupid question, Sarah."

"I don't think it is. You haven't given me a reason for it, and I think I deserve one." She glanced at me then. She wasn't kidding.

"He walked into your life and took over your attention and your affection. I never had a chance. I was here first, doing these things for

161

you, helping you, trying, in my own way, to tell you how much you mean to me, for over a year. He shows up and three days later he's proposing to you. I don't understand it. How did this happen?"

"I don't understand how it happened, either."

"Is it because of who he is?"

"Yes, on the inside. Not because he's Andrew Collier." She smiled at me. "I felt the same way about you until the green-eyed monster showed up."

"You didn't expect me to be okay with this, did you?" I was far from okay with it, and she knew it.

"No. Not at all, but you also didn't help your case with your incessant jealousy. You were scaring me."

"That wasn't my intention, Sarah."

"I'm sure it wasn't, but you never tried to control it. It was so obvious, and you kept getting so angry." She hopped off the ledge and stood in front of me. "I don't enjoy fighting with you. I don't like it when we're yelling at each other. It hurts me because we've always been friends and I never wanted to lose that, no matter what."

Why did she have to make sense? Why couldn't she be wrong? We were always friends, and my jealousy tore that apart. I had to learn how to control it. I wanted to be with her so much that I lost my head. I *was* going to fight for her.

"Are your plans for Valentine's Day set in stone?" I asked her.

"Yeah. Andrew already bought the tickets."

"Okay. What are you doing on Friday?"

"I'm leaving early."

"Why?"

She sighed. "I am meeting Andrew at the airport. He has a few hours here on his way to L.A."

"Jeez, Sarah. He never goes away. He's always going to be right here all the time, isn't he?"

"Not all the time. I found out about his lay-over this morning."

"So, it's him? He's doing this on purpose to keep us apart?"

"I doubt that. I'm sure you have nothing to do with his filming schedule." She was chuckling.

"I can bet he made sure his lay-over was here instead of Chicago or New York or somewhere else."

"His agent schedules that kind of thing and she doesn't like me, so I'm sure she wouldn't go out of her way to get his lay-over in Denver. It was the least expensive flight."

"I guess that makes sense, but he probably asked for a flight with a Denver lay-over. Did you ever think about that?"

"Why are we talking about this?" She glared at me, frustration in her eyes. Her forehead creased. "I have to go back to work."

"Wait a sec." I grabbed her arm and hopped off the ledge to stand in front of her. "What about Saturday?"

"Saturday is fine." Her smile was weak and unsure.

"You're not blowing me off?"

"I have never blown you off."

"This is wonderful." I was happy. I was going to show her I was the one she should be with. "Just you and me?"

"Just you and me," she agreed.

"No, Andrew?"

"No. It will be fun." She smiled and hugged me, a friendly hug, but it was a start. "We should go back to work now."

We walked back to the office together. I was so happy I wanted to pick her up and hug her.

SARAH

It finally was Friday. I didn't sleep the night before. After I had hung up with Andrew, I lay awake. Hearing his voice usually calmed me down.

I told him about my "date" with Chris on Saturday. "He sounded so pitiful. I couldn't say no," I had told him.

"It's only dinner, love. I wouldn't stress too much over it."

"What happens if he expects more than dinner?" I had been nervous about it since I agreed to go out with him.

"I trust you. Everything will be fine. Don't worry," he assured me.

"You're right," I said with a sigh.

"Try to sleep, alright? I won't be able to call you in the morning."

That was disappointing, but I knew he'd be at the airport, getting on a plane to the states. "Okay, sweetheart. I can't wait for tomorrow. You try to sleep, too."

"I'll try. It won't be easy, though. I'm too excited about seeing you." There was a smile in his voice. "Good night. I love you."

"I love you. Good night."

I had hung up and tried to fall asleep, but I only dozed off a few times. No actual sleep, and I knew that would make for a lagging day. I didn't want to be too tired to miss one second with Andrew. I was so pathetic.

***

"Is it true you're leaving early today?" Marie teased on Friday morning.

"Yeah, so," I teased back.

"And what about Valentine's weekend?"

"Where are you getting your information, woman?"

"Don't worry about that."

I turned around and glanced at her. "You never told me what you found online the other day."

"Eh. Nothing exciting. Everything was what I already knew."

"I haven't turned my computer on in days. And I'm surprised I don't have hordes of photographers following me everywhere."

"I wouldn't be surprised if you became headline news after Valentine's Day."

"Oh, joy. I'm so looking forward to that. Not." We both laughed.

Marie chuckled. "Are you sure you know what you're doing with these guys?"

"No, but what choice do I have? They both want to be with me, and I owe them both so much, for my house, their feelings, my feelings. I care about them both."

"Of course you do, but take care of *your* feelings, too. None of you should get hurt."

"I agree with you, but before all of this is over, someone will be."

"I don't envy you, buddy. Take care of yourself, too, okay?"

"I will."

"Have fun this afternoon. You can tell me all about it on Monday." She hugged me.

"I will." I smiled at her, and we both went back to work.

I got caught up with my work earlier than I had expected; one o'clock. I was all nerves, and I had to go outside for some air. I was so nervous. I may have been having a caffeine rush. I drank five cups of coffee to wake myself up.

I paced up and down the sidewalk, trying to calm down. It wasn't working. In a few brief hours, I would be in the arms of the man I loved, and I was too anxious. I didn't want to wait anymore.

Chris walked toward me, his cell phone to his ear. He smiled and started walking more quickly toward me. He hung up with whoever he had been talking to. "I thought you were leaving?"

"At two. I finished my work and needed some air. I'm hyped up on caffeine."

"I made reservations for tomorrow night. Brittany Hill. It's their grand re-opening."

"I wondered when that place would open again. It's been closed forever."

"Is six o'clock okay?"

"Yeah, that's fine," I told him with an unconvincing smile.

"Are you okay?"

"I've been stressed."

"I caused part of that. I promise I'll do my best not to from now on."

"Are you sure that's a promise you can keep?" I started walking toward the office. Chris walked with me.

"I promised I would try."

"That's all I can ask for." I smiled at him. I hoped he *would* try to behave.

"I'll pick you up around five-thirty then?"

"Why don't we meet at the restaurant? It's close to my house."

"Sarah, I want to do this right."

"Okay," I sighed. "Whatever makes you happy."

Five minutes to two, I shut my computer down, grabbed my coat and purse, and told everyone goodbye for the weekend. I needed to stop at an ATM for some cash for parking. I would be at the airport for a while because I wanted to be early enough to make sure I was waiting for him when he showed up.

I stopped at the gas station and put gas in my car and got a bag of chips and a soda. I needed to put something in my stomach. I had eaten almost nothing all day.

The drive out to DIA was smooth. Not much traffic at two o'clock and I made it in less than forty-five minutes. I had a long wait. I would find something to do while I waited, even if it was nothing more than browsing the shops. That place was like a mall in the middle of nowhere.

I found a parking space in the garage near the entrance. Lucky me. That never happened. I locked my car and behind it for twenty minutes. I was getting nervous again. Why? It wasn't as if I hadn't seen him a week ago. It would be the only way I'd be able to be with him for a long while. This would be my life for a while: airport meetings and the occasional weekend getaway.

What kind of life was that? I thought to myself as I checked the time on my cell phone for the millionth time. I didn't care what kind of life it was. I loved him and I wanted to be with him. Sometimes you had to sacrifice certain things when you loved someone. And it wouldn't be this way forever. At some point, we would be together all the time. Once we were married, if that ever happened.

It was after three-thirty, and I was still hanging out in the parking garage. What was wrong with me? I shouldn't be stressing about seeing Andrew.

I forced myself to go inside the terminal and found myself face-to-face with photographers. It was starting already. Did they hang out at airports day and night, waiting for someone to pass through on their way somewhere else?

The Celebrity Insider cameras and several other paparazzi bombarded me right away. "Sarah. Sarah," a cameraman yelled. "Are you here to meet Andrew?"

"Nah, I like spending eighty dollars for parking to hang out at the airport." I smirked at him, and they all laughed. "Can we have some privacy? We only have a couple of hours together." I was quite happy with myself for being so polite to them. They backed off and left me alone while I waited for Andrew.

Four-thirty. It would take at least another twenty minutes before he came up the escalator. I stood behind the ropes, up front, scanning each set of moving stairs. I watched every face that appeared.

Anxious impatience was growing. My nerves were going crazy. It was then he came up the escalator on the left. He wasn't trying to hide himself.

He stopped and dropped his bag and put his arms out, and a huge smile on his beautiful lips. I slid under the ropes and ran to him and jumped in his arms, kissing him all over his face.

"I love you. I love you. I love you," I repeated over and over between kisses. He was doing the same and holding me. Neither of us cared we were being filmed and photographed.

With hesitation, he put me down and held my hand as he picked up his bag. We walked toward the exit, ignoring the paparazzi.

"Andrew, how was your flight? How long are you here? Is Sarah going with you?" They were like vultures.

"Didn't I ask you guys to leave us alone when I came in? Go away. God." I rolled my eyes and pulled Andrew outside.

"That was mellow for you, love. I was expecting a blowout." He laughed.

"I'm going to chill out with them a little. It's something I'm going to have to deal with now." I stopped him and started playing with his coat collar. We were secluded where we were standing. "I don't want to waste what little time we have together talking about the paparazzi." I peered up at him and gave him a seductive smile. He dropped his bag and put his arms around me and kissed me long and hard.

"God, I missed you," he breathed between kisses.

"I missed you, too. I love you so much." I continued to kiss him and told him I loved him until I couldn't breathe. I put my arms tight around him and buried my face in his coat.

"I won't be able to wait two weeks to be with you again."

"We'll be closer now."

"Not close enough. I need to be with you, Sarah. I need to fall asleep holding you. I need to wake up next to you."

"I need you, too. I'm not sure how to make that happen yet." I gazed up at him. He was so much taller than I that I had to stand on my toes to be face-to-face with him.

"We'll work it out, love. Let's go up to the lounge. I'm thirsty. No paparazzi allowed." He picked up his bag and held my hand as we walked back inside the terminal and upstairs to the VIP lounge.

The lounge was quiet and dimly lit. I was allowed access because I was with Andrew, otherwise I never would have seen the inside of this place. A dozen computer screens hung on the wall announcing the arrivals and departures.

"My flight leaves at seven-forty," he said, checking his flight to L.A. "I wonder how difficult it would be to get you through security so you can go to the concourse with me."

"I'm sure we'll run into red tape."

"I want you at the gate when I board the plane," he told me.

We found a semi-secluded couch in the back of the room. I ordered a soda, and Andrew ordered a scotch when the waitress showed up. When she left, he scooted closer to me, and we kissed again.

"I can't believe how much I have missed you. It seems like I haven't seen you in months. What is it about you, woman?" He smiled at me, keeping his nose pressed against mine. Our lips were inches apart.

"I'm the same me I've been my whole life."

"Don't you dare change that."

"I hadn't planned on it." I smiled at him, and he began kissing me slow and deep.

The waitress was clearing her throat. "Eight-fifty," she said, annoyance in her voice. Andrew gave her a twenty and waved her off, then started kissing me again. We were like teenagers the way we were making out.

"When are we going to be together all the time? This is killing me." He sounded almost desperate.

"It won't be long, but I don't know when. We're moving so fast, Andrew. I want to enjoy every moment we have together."

"We don't have that many moments right now. Weekends and phone calls will not satisfy me much longer. I need to be with you every day." He put his arms around me and held me tight. I swore he was crying, but I wouldn't embarrass him by pointing it out.

"What do you want me to do?"

"I'll figure it out. I just know I need to be with you. It's going to break me to leave you tonight."

"Me, too. I'll have to sit in my car and cry for an hour before I can leave." I chuckled.

"You feel it, too."

I glanced up and turned to face him. "Of course, I do. You're everything to me. I never want you out of my life."

"You mean that?" He sounded unsure of our relationship all of a sudden.

"Of course, I do." I put his face in my hands. "Does this have anything to do with this pity date with Chris tomorrow?"

He closed his eyes, and a tear fell down his cheek. He only nodded.

"Oh, Andrew. No. Please don't worry about any of that, please. I want *you*. I love you."

"I need to be certain he won't try to take you away from me."

"I will never let that happen. You are who I want to be with. I want to spend the rest of my life with *you*." I kissed him, and he pulled me in with a deep, passionate kiss. I didn't want to let go of him... ever.

We spent some time sipping our drinks, holding each other, and not talking. I loved how we could be near each other without speaking. With anyone else, I would have the silence would have been uncomfortable, but not with Andrew. We could sit like this for hours without the silence being awkward.

"We should try to get you downstairs with me," he suggested.

"Is it that time already?"

"We still have time but getting you on the concourse is going to take up much of it."

I sighed. I wasn't ready for this moment to end.

We went downstairs to security. The entire process took less than an hour. I wasn't on any watch lists, so the whole thing was smooth sailing.

It was almost seven when we got on the train to Concourse C. Andrew's flight was on time. I was hoping it would be late. We stood near the back, in the last car, and held hands and stared into each other's eyes as the train turned and jerked. We were pressed together, and I didn't care. The closer, the better. His scent engulfed me, and I wanted that scent to stay with me forever.

"You left your t-shirt at my house," I told him.

He smiled down at me. "I left it for you."

"You did? I didn't give you anything."

"Oh, but you did." He was smiling at me.

"What did I give you?"

"You," he whispered, then kissed me.

The automated voice on the speakers announced our arrival at Concourse C. It was getting closer to his departure, and I wanted to cry already. It seemed like we had only been together for a few minutes, not a few hours.

"What's your opinion on diamonds?" he asked me as we rode the escalator up to the concourse.

I wrinkled my nose. "Ew. They look like pieces of glass."

"Alright, no diamonds," he responded with a laugh. "What *do* you like?"

"What is this about?"

"Answer the question, my love." He was still chuckling.

"You aren't buying me an engagement ring," I protested.

"I am so. Now tell me, please, otherwise I may pick something you don't like, and it will be your fault."

"You're impossible."

"You're not the first person to tell me that." He laughed again. "So, are you going to tell me?"

"Fine." We sat down on the chairs next to the window at his gate. "Emeralds, Opals, and Pearls."

"That's it?"

"I'm not big on jewelry."

"I noticed you don't wear any." He put his arm around me, and we held each other for a long time. His arms around me were wonderful. I didn't want to let go, but our time together was getting shorter. "I don't want to leave."

"I don't want you to leave."

"I don't have to."

"Yes, you do. You need to rehearse with Karen and Trevor."

"All it takes is a quick phone call."

"Yeah, to the mean lady who hates me."

Susan doesn't hate you; she's concerned for me. I'll pay for the extra fare with my own money."

"Andrew, no."

He stood up and walked away. He was on his phone for less than five minutes. "It's a done deal," he said when he came back.

"You didn't."

"I did. Now I need to call Trevor and ask him to pick up my bags at LAX."

"Now she hates me more than she did before."

"She doesn't hate you." He was laughing at me again. He called Trevor and asked him to hold on to his bags until Monday. He was spending the weekend in Denver. "It's settled," he told me. "Now, let's go."

CHRIS

It made me sick to imagine the two of them together. What were they doing? Had they gone to a hotel together? I couldn't stand to think about them having sex.

I needed to talk to her, to find out what she was up to without sounding like I was checking up on her. I called her cell phone. "Hey you, what's up?" I asked when she answered.

"I'm leaving the airport. What are you doing?"

"I got bored, so I thought I'd call," I lied.

"Oh, well, thanks for that."

"How was your visit with... Andrew?"

"Wonderful, thank you." There was a smile in her voice. I knew why. Disgusting.

"Perfect." I knew my tone was sarcastic, and I didn't care. "Did he leave?"

"Um...no."

"What do you mean, no? What does that mean?"

"It means he didn't leave. He's staying until Monday. Sort of spur of the moment."

"I'll bet," I said under my breath.

"I'm sorry?"

"Nothing. Nothing at all," I said.

"Chris, I'm driving and it's dark. Can I call you when I'm home?"

"Sure. I'll talk to you later." I hung up on her. I was livid.

This was not spur of the moment. That punk had planned this before he ever got on the plane in London. I was going to show her how sneaky he was. I wondered if she had told him about our date tomorrow night. Was she going to blow me off now because he was here? I would never forgive her if she did.

At this rate, I would never win her heart. His sneaky maneuvers were making it impossible for me. I had to show her that her perfect man/boy was manipulative. I would show her he had this whole thing planned. She would never believe that. Even if she believed he had already planned to stay this weekend, she would think it was sweet and she would fall more in love with him.

I was sick to my stomach thinking about it. I poured a drink and swallowed it, then collapsed on my couch and passed out.

Chapter Seven – The Accident

When Andrew and Sarah reached her house, they ran inside, giggling and kissing.

Andrew picked Sarah up and carried her to the bedroom.

Sarah and Andrew made love for several hours. It was slow and passionate, much the same way it had been the previous weekend. The heat and electricity were intense. When they had finished, they were panting and sweating and giggling.

"God, that was amazing," Andrew panted.

"Incredible," Sarah agreed. "Wow." She was still fighting the giggles.

He rolled over to face her and smiled. "I love you so much, Sarah."

She looked at him and kissed him. "I love you, too," she whispered.

"I am so happy I decided not to go straight to L.A. tonight."

"I am, too, but I can't believe you ditched everyone like that. Won't your director give you grief for missing filming?"

"Not. It's mostly tech set up at this point. You can help me study my lines and I can run lines on FaceTime with Trevor and Karen tomorrow night while you're on your date with Chris."

"Oh, God, I almost forgot about that." She rolled over on her back. "What am I going to do about that? Should I cancel?"

"No, love. I told you it's alright. It's only dinner."

"He insisted on picking me up here."

"So? He knows I'm here." He put his arms around her and held her tight. "You're worrying for nothing."

"You're right."

They began kissing with passion again but were interrupted by a knock on the front door. Sarah looked at the clock.

"It's after eleven. Who the hell would come over here this late?" she wondered aloud as she put on a pair of sweats and a t-shirt.

"Chris," they said together.

Sarah answered the door. Sure enough, it was Chris. "What are you doing here so late?"

"I couldn't sleep and wanted to talk to you," he said. He was talking very loudly and slurring his words.

"Are you drunk?" She pulled him into the house. "Come inside."

Chris stumbled inside. Andrew stood in the bedroom doorway. He wore only his boxers. "What the hell is this?" he asked, glaring at Andrew.

"I told you he was here, Chris."

"You weren't kidding?"

"No, I wasn't kidding. What are you doing here so late?"

"You never called back. I thought you might have been in an accident." He was still watching Andrew, but he was laughing.

"So, you drove forty miles, while drunk, to make sure I was okay? I find that hard to believe, Chris. You were checking up on me."

Andrew had gone into the bedroom to put his clothes on. "I thought we had all of this worked out, mate," Andrew asked when he came back out. He stood next to Sarah.

"You planned this, didn't you, you little punk?" He stumbled forward.

"What are you talking about?"

"You set this whole thing up. You had planned all along to stay here this weekend because you found out Sarah and I had a date."

Andrew laughed. "You are mad."

"You're damn right I'm mad! You did, didn't you?"

"No, I didn't. Once I was with her at the airport, I didn't want to leave. My being here is none of your business, anyway."

"Chris, you promised," Sarah pleaded. "Don't do this."

He shot an angry look at her. "I figured you'd blow me off for him."

"I haven't blown you off, Chris. I forgot to call."

Chris stumbled as he tried to walk toward Sarah. He almost fell twice.

"Chris, sit down. You can't even stand up straight," Sarah told him.

"Not until I have a word with this little punk."

"Chris, please." Sarah took his arm and tried to take him to the couch, but he pushed her off, hard, and she fell on the stone tiles in front of the door, hitting her head.

Andrew ran to her side. "Sarah, are you alright? You're bleeding."

Andrew shot up and lunged at Chris.

"Andrew, no," Sarah yelled, and groaned in pain. "I'm fine."

"You're *not* fine. You're bleeding." Andrew looked up and Chris. "She needs to go to the emergency room."

Chris stood above them, stunned. Did he do this to her? He would never hurt her on purpose. "Sarah, I'm sorry. I didn't mean to..."

"You bloody hell stay away from her. You've done enough." Andrew scooped her up. "She needs a towel for her head. Go," he barked at Chris.

Chris stumbled to the bathroom and came back with a towel and handed it to Andrew. Sarah was fading in and out of consciousness now.

Andrew was having a hard time driving and keeping Sarah from falling asleep at the same time. "Sarah, love, don't fall asleep, please." He was scared and crying.

He looked over at Sarah, who had lost consciousness again. "Sarah," he shouted. Sarah stirred.

"I'm fine," she whispered.

He drove to the emergency entrance and parked at the door. He carried Sarah inside. "My fiancée hit her head," he told the nurse. "She's bleeding pretty badly."

"Follow me," she ordered and led him to an exam room.

"She keeps fading in and out of consciousness."

The nurse hooked Sarah up to machines. "What's her name?"

"Sarah... Miller," Andrew told the nurse, panic in his voice.

"Sarah, honey, you're going to have to keep your eyes open," the nurse told her, as she took Sarah's blood pressure.

"I'm so tired," she whispered and closed her eyes again.

"Is she going to be okay?" Andrew asked, panicked.

"She may have a concussion. I'll have the doctor come in. Please try to keep her awake."

Andrew nodded. He was still crying as he leaned over Sarah, talking to her to keep her awake.

"I'm going to end that son-of-a-bitch." He looked at Sarah, tears streaming down his cheeks. "If anything happens to you." He shook his head. He kissed Sarah's forehead.

The doctor came in and scanned Sarah's chart. "I'm Doctor Morgan," he told them. "What happened?" The doctor was an older man, late fifties, with salt and pepper hair and deep blue eyes. He was tall and muscular and had a commanding air to him that demanded respect.

"She fell on some stone tiles," Andrew told him. "I can't keep her awake. Is she going to be alright?"

Doctor Morgan checked her pupils. "Her pupils are dilating. That's a good sign, but I want to take a CT scan and an MRI before I can rule out a concussion." He tapped Sarah's face with his palm, and she stirred. "Sarah, stay with me. I'm Doctor Morgan. I need to ask you some questions."

"Mm-hm."

"Can you keep your eyes open for me?"

Sarah opened her eyes, but her eyelids were heavy. "I'm tired," she groaned. "Where's Chris?" Andrew grimaced.

"Sarah, can you tell me the date?"

"January twenty-first."

The doctor looked at Andrew. "What year is it?"

"Twenty twenty-three. What kinds of questions are these?"

"You may have a concussion," Doctor Morgan told her.

"I don't. I'm exhausted and my head hurts. Can I have some ibuprofen?" Sarah tried to sit up, but she was too weak and dizzy.

"I can't give you anything yet. I need to take you to radiology for a CT scan and an MRI."

"I'm okay."

"Sarah, you lost a lot of blood when you hit your head. Please let the doctor do what he needs to do," Andrew told her.

Sarah looked at him. "Hey, I sent you a letter." Her forehead creased. "You're Andrew... Collier. Yeah." She smiled at her revelation.

Andrew frowned. "Not good," he whispered.

"Why are you here?"

Tears streamed from his eyes. "You don't remember me?"

"Yeah, you're in 'Two Hearts' and 'One Life.' Oh, I have the biggest crush on you." Sarah giggled.

Andrew nodded and walked out of the room. Doctor Morgan followed him.

"It's temporary, Mr. Collier. It happens often with head injuries. It's only short-term memory that's affected."

Andrew nodded again.

"Let me take her to radiology and make sure she doesn't have a concussion or any permanent trauma. Why don't you have a seat in the waiting room?"

"Alright."

Andrew walked into the waiting room where Chris was sitting. He seemed forlorn but stood when he saw Andrew approach. Andrew ran toward him and punched him square in the jaw. "You bastard."

Chris rubbed his jaw. He lunged at Andrew and shoved him. A security officer came out to break up the fight. "I'm going to call the police if you two don't stop right now," the guard demanded.

Andrew stood still, panting. "Get the hell out of here. You've done enough damage."

"It was an accident." Chris was rubbing his jaw. "Do you think I'd hurt her on purpose?"

"Yes. You're drunk." Andrew paced. "Because of you, she may have a concussion, and she has short-term memory loss." He stopped and glared at Chris. "Because of you, she doesn't know she and I ever met."

Chris smirked. "Outstanding!"

Andrew stared at Chris. He was seething. "You son-of-a-bitch. This isn't funny. I should kill you for this."

Chris laughed. "This is awesome. She doesn't remember meeting you. I have a right to make sure she's okay," he told Andrew.

"You don't have any rights. I should have assault charges pressed on you," Andrew growled.

"Hey, you hit me."

"For Sarah, you idiot."

"I'll press charges on you," Chris told Andrew.

Andrew walked away and sat down. Chris sat down on the other side of the room, keeping his eyes on Andrew.

'This is *my* fault,' Andrew thought to himself. 'If I would have gotten on the plane...' He put his face in his hands. 'She doesn't even remember meeting me.'

Andrew looked over at Chris. He was staring at Andrew. It wasn't an angry stare. He looked like he was plotting.

Chris noticed Andrew's suffering and was thrilled. With Sarah's memory of that punk gone, he could take care of her. He wouldn't have to compete to win her heart. If Sarah never remembered meeting Andrew, she and Chris would continue where they had left off before he showed up and ruined everything.

Another hour passed before the doctor came out with Sarah's results. Andrew stood when the doctor came out. Chris followed Andrew's lead and walked toward Doctor Morgan. "Sarah is going to be fine. She doesn't have a concussion."

"Thank God," Andrew sighed, relieved.

"We didn't find any fluid or swelling, but she has a nasty gash on her head. She needed stitches, but otherwise, she's going to be fine." Doctor Morgan smiled at them.

"When can she go home?" Andrew asked.

"In a few hours. I want to monitor her, as a precaution."

Andrew nodded and smiled. "And her memory?"

"With no trauma to her brain, she should recover her memories in a couple of days. She asked for you," he told Andrew.

He followed the doctor back to Sarah's room and went inside.

"How are you?" Andrew asked her.

"Better. My head still hurts, though." She touched the back of her head where the bandages covered her stitches and cringed.

"You shouldn't do that," he told her and pulled a chair up next to the bed.

"Can I ask you something?"

"Yes." He smiled at her. He wanted to hold her hand, but it wasn't a good idea yet. She still didn't remember being with him.

"How did we meet?"

"You wrote me a letter a couple of months ago and I came here to meet you last weekend."

"I remember the letter. Have you been here this whole time?"

She remembered writing to him. That was something. It might help jog her memory. "No," he told her. "I was on my way to Los Angeles this weekend, but we couldn't stay away from each other, so I decided to stay until Monday."

"Are we dating or something?"

"No, love, we're engaged."

"What?" Sarah laughed. She looked at her left hand and held it up. "No ring?" She was still giggling.

Andrew was a little hurt by her laughter, but he couldn't blame her. If it were him in her place, he wouldn't have believed it, either. "Not yet. I was going to give it to you on Valentine's Day."

She cocked her head and smiled and took his hand. There was a spark, and she pulled away. "What was that?" she asked.

Andrew nodded and smiled. "That spark? It happens every time."

"Have we... slept together?"

He smiled and nodded again.

"I wish I could remember." She was frustrated now.

"I do, too, but you'll remember."

"Why do I remember everything except meeting you? I've had this huge crush on you since I went to see 'Two Hearts.' How do I not remember something like meeting the star of the movie?"

Andrew chuckled. "You hit your head, but the doctor says it's temporary memory loss. I'm glad you're alright. I have been so worried about you."

"How did this happen?"

Of course, she wouldn't remember that part, either. Andrew cleared his throat and began. "Well, Chris showed up about eleven, after you and I had finished... um..."

"Chris." She smiled and sighed. "How is he?"

Andrew frowned. "Alright, I guess. Who cares?"

"What happened?" Sarah asked. She was frowning, too.

"He came over, drunk, starting his rubbish."

"He isn't supposed to be drinking. He's an alcoholic. That doesn't sound like him. Why was he at my house?"

"Jealousy, I suppose. He was yelling and being obnoxious. You tried to make him to sit down, but he shoved you off him and you hit your head on the stone tiles in front of your door."

"He's jealous of you and me? Why? We're only friends. We've been friends for a long time. I don't understand why he would snap like that." She shook her head, but she had to put her hands on the side of her head. "Ooh, bad idea. That gave me the spins." She grimaced at Andrew. He glanced at her.

"How much do you remember?"

She thought about it for a minute. "I got home from work today and woke up here.

"It's January thirtieth. You remember nothing after last Thursday?"

"No. Why?"

He looked at her solemnly. "That explains it."

"Explains what?"

"The doctor says your memory loss is stressed induced. I think when you hit your head, your brain was protecting itself from trauma by blocking out all the stress."

"I'm not following you." She seemed confused about everything that was going on.

"Last Thursday night, Chris came to your house to express his feelings for you. I showed up the next day and you have been stressed out every day since."

She looked at him with a blank expression.

"I want to try something." He said, standing up and leaning forward. Sarah gazed at him as he moved closer. He was staring into her eyes.

He closed his eyes and put his lips on hers. Electricity coursed through both of them. Sarah backed off with a start.

"Did I hurt you?"

"No. What is that spark? It was like a powerful surge of electricity."

"I told you it happens every time."

"Kiss me again." She smiled at him. "I liked it."

He leaned in and kissed her again, a little deeper. Heat rushed through Sarah's body, starting with her toes and moving up to her face. Her cheeks flushed. Something like a light switch turned on in her head and she remembered. She pulled Andrew closer and kissed him deep and passionate.

He pulled away and looked at her with soft, loving eyes. "I love you, Andrew," she whispered. "I remember and I love you."

He put his arms around her and rocked her. "I love you."

"Oh, don't do that. It's making me sick."

"Sorry," he chuckled, and let go. "You remember everything?"

"Everything," she grinned, then frowned at him as she remembered the Chris issue. "I need to take care of a problem."

"Chris?"

"Yeah. Is he here?"

"Yeah."

"Would you ask him to come in here, please? And ask the doctor when I can leave?"

"I will, love." He smiled at her and gave her a quick kiss. He walked toward the door.

"Hey, Andrew." He turned and looked at her, the smile still on his lips. "I love you."

"I love you." He left the room and went to the waiting room. "She wants to talk to you," he told Chris. Chris smiled and went to her room. It didn't bother Andrew at all because Sarah had her memory back and she loved him.

She didn't remember that punk. That's what Chris thought about as he walked to Sarah's room. He had his chance now. The boy toy was out of the picture. She would send Andrew packing, and they would be together. "Hey, sweetheart," he greeted her as he walked in.

"Come here," she said. It wasn't a happy greeting. He walked toward her. Sarah slapped him on the same jaw where Andrew had punched him. "How dare you," she growled.

Chris was taken aback. Why was she so angry? She couldn't have her memory back already. "Why did you do that?"

"You're an asshole. Are you still drunk?"

"No. Andrew punched me. That sobered me up damn quick."

"I'm glad he punched you. You deserve a lot worse. I have eighteen stitches in my head because of you. Andrew told me everything."

"All lies, I'm sure."

"Why don't you tell me *your* side of the story? Did you or did you not show up at my house, drunk off your ass, and start a fight with him?"

"Yes, I was drunk, but I never intended to fight with him."

"No, if my memory is correct, and I remember everything, your lame excuse for showing up was that I didn't call when I got home from the airport. Am I right?"

"You remember that?"

"Oh, yeah."

"When did that happen?"

"A little while ago. Right after Andrew kissed me."

"Dammit."

"Yeah, when I hit my head, my brain was trying to protect itself by forgetting certain events that caused me stress. I forgot everything after last Thursday, before you told me how you felt about me. Funny, huh?" She let out a quick laugh.

"Hilarious." Chris sat down, defeated... again. "I can't believe this. I can't believe I caused all your suffering."

"I tried to warn you about your jealousy, Chris. You wouldn't listen to me. I can't do this anymore."

"I don't blame you." He couldn't look at her. "My jealousy put you in the hospital. You got hurt because of me."

Tears were falling from Sarah's eyes. "I'm sorry, Chris."

"I understand. But I still want to be your friend."

"I don't think that's a good idea. You and Andrew have too much bad blood between you."

"You *do* care about him, don't you?"

"I love him, Chris. I can't explain how or why so soon, but I love him."

"Okay, Sarah." He stood up and looked at her, finally. "I won't bother you again. I promise." He kissed her forehead and left, walking straight out the doors and outside.

Andrew watched him leave. Chris looked sad, like he was about to cry. Once Chris left, Andrew went back to Sarah's room.

"Hey love," he greeted Sarah.

"Hey. Can I go home now?"

"Soon."

"Did Chris leave?"

Andrew nodded. "He looked like he was going to cry when he walked out. What did you say to him?"

"I told him it was over. I can't even be friends with him. He ruined everything."

"Yeah, he kind of did." He sat down on the chair next to the bed. "How's your head?"

"It hurts."

"I should talk to the doctor," Andrew told her.

"Thank you. I want to go home."

Andrew patted her hand and left the room. In a few minutes, he returned.

"The doctor says he's going to come in and check on you."

"I'm fine. Nothing ibuprofen won't cure." She smirked.

"You're going to have to take it easy, love. You hit your head hard and lost a lot of blood."

"Yeah, but I don't want to be here anymore. I want to go home and sleep in my bed, next to you."

Andrew sat down on the bed next to Sarah. He caressed her face. "You had me terrified for a while."

"I'm sorry about that. Do you forgive me?"

"Always." He smiled at her, and leaned in to give her a long, soft kiss.

The doctor's entrance interrupted them. "I understand you got your memory back?"

"Yes." She smiled up at Andrew and squeezed his hand. He smiled down at her.

"Let me check your vitals and find out if we can release you."

"Good. I want to go home."

"I'm sure you do." Andrew stepped out of the way to let the doctor check on her. He was so thankful Sarah was alright. He would have gone mad if he lost her. He kept his eyes, and a big smile, on her while the doctor examined her one last time.

"Everything looks fine. How is your head?"

"It's sore where the stitches are."

"No headache?"

"Not anymore. Can I please go home?"

Doctor Morgan chuckled. "Yes. Let me get your discharge paperwork ready for your signature. Once you sign them, you're free to go." He removed the wires that monitored her pulse, her heart rate, and oxygen.

"Thank you."

"You're welcome. The nurse will be in soon."

Sarah scooted off the bed. "I'm going to go to the bathroom and get dressed." She was still weak and a little dizzy. Andrew rushed to her side. "I'm fine. What time is it?"

Andrew looked at his watch. "Four-thirty."

"God, what a waste of a Friday night." She rolled her eyes and picked up her clothes and went to the bathroom to change. She came back out a few minutes later, laughing.

"What's so funny?" Andrew asked.

"I looked in the mirror. I look like crap and you're still here."

"You don't look like crap. You're beautiful." He smiled at her and gave her a quick kiss. "You are not crappy, my love."

"Ah, you're full of it, but thank you."

The nurse brought in Sarah's paperwork. She signed where she needed to and asked the nurse, "Can I go to work on Monday?"

"If you're feeling up to it, sure."

"What about my stitches?"

"The doctor wants you to come back in two weeks to take them out."

"Can I come in on the eleventh?"

"I'll check Doctor Morgan's schedule. Would you prefer morning or afternoon?"

"Morning. Before eight, if possible."

"I'll make the appointment for you."

"Thank you." A few minutes passed before the nurse came back and told Sarah her appointment was at seven-thirty on the eleventh. "Great, now let's go home." Sarah told Andrew.

***

Andrew drove back to the house and helped Sarah inside. She saw the blood on the stone tiles. "I need to clean this up."

"No, you don't. You go change your clothes and I'll take care of it."

"Andrew, I can do it. I'm not helpless."

"Right now, you are. Go change and don't argue." He kissed her nose and patted her on her butt.

Sarah didn't protest again. She let Andrew clean up the mess and when she came back out, the blood had been cleaned up and Andrew was sitting on the couch.

Sarah sat down next to him and snuggled up next to him. "How are you, love?" Andrew asked.

"I'm good. I want to sit here with you."

"Are you sure you don't want to sleep?"

"Not yet. Can I sit here with you for a while?"

"Of course, love." He kissed her forehead.

"I'm sorry this started out to be a crappy weekend for you."

"It didn't start crappy. We hit a snag. Everything's alright now."

"Yeah?"

"Yes. Please stop worrying so much."

"Sorry, I didn't want you to have a terrible weekend. I'm sure you weren't planning to spend your Friday night in the emergency room."

"It's not my idea of the perfect date, but we're together and you're fine and everything is alright."

"I'm glad I don't have to go on that date with Chris. It bothered me how much he was pushing the issue. He wouldn't give up after he found out you proposed, which reminds me." She sat up and looked up at him. "You were going to give me the ring when I got to Portland?"

"When you got off the plane, yes, but I wanted it to be a surprise."

"I ruined that, didn't I?"

"No, and this doesn't mean I'm not still going to give it to you. You still haven't seen it." He gave her a playful grin.

"Remember, I said no diamonds."

"I remember."

***

Andrew lay with Sarah on the bed, running his fingers through her hair. They were face-to-face, smiling at each other. "How did I get so lucky?" Sarah asked.

"How did *I*?"

Sarah laughed.

"I have never fallen this hard for anyone," he told her.

"Neither have I. It's wonderful and frightening. I never want to lose it."

"I'm always going to love you, Sarah. I'm not sure how all of this happened. You brought something to life in me I've never experienced before. I'm afraid it's all going to disappear, like it isn't real."

"I keep thinking if this is a dream, I don't want to wake up."

"It's not a dream, love. It's very real. I love you and you love me. It seems so odd how soon I fell in love with you. This isn't supposed to happen this fast. Love is supposed to take time, but it's like I've known you for years. It's like I'm under some kind of spell. It's difficult to explain."

"It's like sparks and the electricity and the heat. Where did that come from?" Sarah sighed and closed her eyes for a moment. "Before I met you, I used to have fantasies about meeting you and being with you, but we had this regular life. It wasn't anything like this. I'm not sorry about the way things are. I love you for what's in here," she said, touching his chest. "I don't understand how all of this happened so fast. All I did was write a letter. It's weird how things work out." She smiled at him. "Do you ever think we're moving too fast?"

"Yes, but I don't care. I want to be with you. I can't live without you. Perhaps the proposal was sudden, but..."

"You can take it back."

"No way. I'm not sure how I'm so deeply in love with you already, but I am. I looked at it like this: Why fight something that's right in front of you? Do you agree?"

"I agree, but I've never been very good with this kind of thing. I've always made the wrong choices in love. I don't want to do that this time."

"I won't hurt you, Sarah."

"I never thought you would. That's not what I meant. I'm saying I'm the one who always picked the losers; the ones I shouldn't have been with but stayed with. The difference here is that *you* chose me. *You* came to Denver. If it had been left to me, I would be with Chris right now. I would never have been able to come to you, and we never would have met. I never would have been able to meet you. You're Andrew Collier."

"If you would have been able to go to London, would you have tried to find me?"

"Of course. I mean, I would have loved to have met you, but that's a fantasy. I'm glad it happened the way it did."

"I am, too. I couldn't wait to board that plane to meet you. I remember when I first read your letter and saw your picture. I couldn't get here fast enough. Everyone, especially Susan, was so against it.

"She still thinks you're going to kill me or something," he chuckled.

"She hates me." Sarah smiled and gave him a quick kiss. "I don't care, though. One of these days she'll meet me, and she'll find I'm an ordinary person."

"Baby, you are far from ordinary." He kissed her and held her a little tighter. "Are you even tired?"

"I'm not. I bet you are, though."

"No."

The sun was streaming through the curtains. "It's morning already?"

"It has been morning for hours, love."

"You know what I mean," she giggled and snuggled closer to him.

"Yes."

Sarah heard him breathing. She felt his heart beating and the warmth of his body. Being in his arms was safety to her. She never wanted it to end. He would be gone soon... again, and she would be left to deal with the tragedy that Chris would become because of what had happened. She didn't want to think about him right now, but he kept popping up in her head.

"I hurt him, didn't I?" she asked.

"What?"

"Chris. I hurt him and I promised I wouldn't. I've done it twice now."

"He hurt you worse than you ever hurt him. You had to have stitches, and I lost you for a while."

"He never would have done that if he were sober."

"But he wasn't sober, and he *did* do it. Honestly, love, your heart is far too pure. You care too much about everyone, no matter what they have done to you."

"I can't help that, Andrew. Unless someone hurts me on purpose, I try to be kind to everyone."

"You are an amazing woman, Sarah. Do you want to call him to find out how he's doing?"

"Would that upset you?"

"Not in the least." He smiled and kissed her forehead.

"This is another reason I love you so much. You let me be me."

"I don't want you to change anything about who you are, and if that means letting you call the one person who causes you the most pain, I need to let you. It only proves how special you are."

"I love you." She grinned at him. "I'm not ready to leave you yet. I'll call him later."

"Do you think you'll still go to dinner with him?"

"I want to make sure he hasn't hurt himself."

Andrew squeezed her. "God, you have such a pure heart."

***

Chris sat on his couch drinking his fourth scotch. He knew he shouldn't. He wasn't supposed to be drinking. His drinking got him into this mess in the first place.

What possessed him to do something so horrible to the woman he was supposed to be in love with? No wonder she hated him now. No wonder she never wanted to be near him again. He deserved it after what he did to her. He hurt her badly, and it was all because of the alcohol and his jealousy.

He threw his glass across the room. It shattered against the wall. He didn't care. His phone rang. "Hello," he answered in a rough tone.

"Chris?" It was Sarah. Why was she calling him and torturing him?

"Are you calling to rub it in?"

"I called to find out how you're doing."

"I'm drunk. That's how I'm doing. Why do you care? I thought you wanted nothing to do with me?"

"I did say that, but Andrew told me how terrible you looked when you left the hospital. How is your jaw?"

"It's fine. It's not broken. Your boy toy is lucky. I could press charges on him."

"But you won't."

"No. It would hurt you too much."

"Yeah, it would. And why are you drinking again? Didn't you learn your lesson?"

"I don't think you should lecture me."

"Look, just because we can't be together doesn't mean I don't still care what happens to you."

"You don't even want to be my friend, Sarah. Why should you care what happens to me?"

"Because I do, okay?"

"I don't want you to. I don't want to talk to you anymore."

Sarah sighed. "Fine, Chris. I won't talk to you again."

"Sarah?"

"What?"

"I deserve this. I don't deserve to be your friend. I hurt you, but hearing your voice is hurting me."

"I understand. I won't call again. Goodbye, Chris." She hung up. He was left sitting on his couch, staring at his phone.

He wanted to call her back; to apologize, but that wouldn't do any good. What would that solve? Talking to her made him miserable. Hearing her voice only made him want to drink more.

That damn Andrew Collier ruined everything. Where did this jerk come from? He was the source of all their problems. If he would have stayed away and let them be, everything would have been fine. He should have gotten on that plane to L.A. instead of staying here and ruining everything.

Why was he blaming Andrew for his drunken rage? Sure, he hated the boy toy with every fiber of his being, but Andrew didn't tell him to show up drunk at Sarah's house and put her in the hospital. He did that on his own. Why couldn't he control his jealousy? What was it about Sarah Miller that made him so crazy? He loved her for a long time and never said a word. Suddenly, someone else swooped in and took her away from him before she was ever his. He didn't make his move soon enough. The boy toy stole her heart in one weekend. How was that even possible?

This whole situation was impossible. It was impossible that they were in love with each other already. It doesn't happen that fast. He would never find out. He was going to avoid her. He wouldn't talk to her unless it was work related. Of course, she wouldn't be at the company much longer. The punk would have her flying all over the world with him in no time. She would love that. She could go to Egypt and Australia like she always wanted to. He should be happy for her. She would end up having the perfect life. One day, he would have to tell her he was happy for her new life, but not now.

***

"How is he doing?" Andrew asked.

"Not good. He's still drunk or drunk *again*. It doesn't matter. I won't be talking to him again."

"How are you going to avoid him at work now?"

"It won't be hard. We work at opposite ends of the office. I'm not too worried about it. What I *am* worried about is getting some food in my stomach. I'm so hungry."

"What would you like? I'll fix you anything you want. I'll go pick something up." Andrew would take care of her. She was still weak and, although she tried not to show it, she was still in pain.

"I'll find something. You sit."

"Not on your life, love. I'm going to take care of you."

"Andrew," she protested.

"No. You're still in pain. It's in your eyes when you move."

"I'm sore. I fell on my back, too, but I'm okay. I'll take an ibuprofen. I can't heal and get stronger if I don't move around."

"I don't want you to push yourself and make things worse."

"Making myself something to eat isn't 'pushing it,' honey." She laughed at him.

"Would you let me take care of you, please? Stop fighting me on everything I try to do to help you."

She groaned, frustrated. "Fine. You win... again."

"Thank you." He kissed her and got up and went to the kitchen. A minute later, he came back with a couple of ibuprofens and a glass of water. "What do you want to eat?"

"I'm not sure. That's kind of why I was going to go in and look for something." She smirked at him.

"Never mind. I know what I'll fix for you." He gave her a sweet smile and went back into the kitchen.

Sarah pulled the blanket over her and started flipping channels on the television and stopped on Celebrity Insider. Sarah didn't watch celebrity gossip shows, but now that she was with Andrew, she was interested. She almost hoped to see Andrew on the show. She was with him right now, but when she couldn't be, it was nice to see his face. He didn't show up on these shows very often because he was so private, but the two of them seemed to be all over the place now that they were a couple. It was as if the press were looking for something, anything.

Sure enough. It was right on the TV. Andrew was carrying her into the emergency room.

"We're on TV," she called out.

"Are you kidding?" Andrew rushed into the living room and sat down next to her. "I didn't see a single photographer."

"Were you looking for them?" She asked.

"No, who told them we were at the hospital?" He was stunned.

"Do you think they're watching the house?"

"I hope not. God, what does this mean?"

Sarah shook her head. The media couldn't have any details. Neither Andrew nor Sarah had told the doctor the whole truth about what had happened. "They were knew you're here in Denver. Maybe they started asking questions."

"They aren't supposed to give out that information. It's private, but anyone can be bought."

"Beautiful." Sarah forced a laugh. "Is this what you have to put up with all the time?"

"Mm-hm."

"Well, we'll deal with it together." She smiled at him and put his face in her hands. She kissed him. "I think the eggs are burning."

"Crap." He shot up and ran back to the kitchen.

Sarah got comfortable under the blanket and closed her eyes. She was asleep in minutes.

As Andrew finished cooking Sarah's breakfast, he started thinking about how much happier his life had become since he met her. Even with the paparazzi on their tails every time they left the house, he didn't even want to picture what his life would be like if he hadn't made that first trip to meet her. He would be alone, and the rumours about Karen and him being an item would still fly all over Hollywood.

Sarah was everything to him, and he didn't want to imagine his life without her. His heart belonged to her forever.

He smiled at that as he took Sarah's plate to her. She was asleep, so he put the plate on the table and picked her up and carried her to the bedroom. She stirred and buried her head in his neck. "I love you so much," she whispered in her sleep.

"I love you, too," he whispered back and lay her down, being mindful of her stitches. He kissed her cheek and left the room to let her sleep.

He sat on the couch and ate the food he had made for Sarah and dialed his parent's number. His dad answered.

"Hey, son, how is Los Angeles? The news says it has been raining."

"I'm not in L.A., dad. I'm in Denver."

"You're staying with Sarah?"

"Yes." He started crying.

"What's the matter, son? Is everything alright with you two?"

"Yes, we're fine, but she had an accident last night."

"Oh my. Is she alright? What happened, Andrew?"

"Remember that boyfriend I told you about? He's not actually her boyfriend. Anyhow, he showed up here last night, pissed off his arse. He was angry and yelling. When Sarah tried to calm him down, he shoved her, and she hit her head."

"Is she still in hospital?"

"No, she's home now."

"Why the tears, then, son?"

"She had to have eighteen stitches in her head," Andrew explained everything that had happened. "I thought I was going to lose her, dad, and it scared the bloody hell out of me."

"I'm so sorry. Stay with her as long as you need to. I'll ring Susan and tell her what's happened. Your mum isn't home, but I will tell her and your sisters as well. You do what you need to and take care of her."

"I will. Thank you, dad."

"You're welcome, son. Take care of yourself, too."

"I will. Goodbye."

"Goodbye. Call me if you need anything."

"I will." Andrew hung up and wiped his eyes. The mere thought of losing Sarah at the hands of that drunken psycho, or for any other reason, had his emotions bouncing around. He couldn't control them.

***

Chris knew he shouldn't be driving. He was still drunk, but he was driving with caution. He didn't care. He had done it before, and he was still alive. He hadn't killed anyone, either.

He wasn't sure why he was going to her house. She didn't want to be near him, and he told her he didn't want to have anything to do with her. He didn't mean it. He never meant it. No matter what happened between them, he always loved her, and he always would. The boy toy wouldn't stop him. Andrew couldn't keep him away from her. The little punk couldn't be with her all the time. He didn't even live on this continent.

Andrew had to leave for L.A. on Monday. Once he was gone, Sarah was free to be herself, away from the hype of Andrew Collier and the media circus that was finding its way into her quiet world. Chris was going to put a stop to this nonsense and give her the life she needed to have.

Chris was going to make up for what he had done to her. He owed her that. He had to do it. He never meant to hurt her. He meant to hurt the man-boy. And he would still do it if he thought it wouldn't hurt Sarah, but he and Andrew had been hurting each other too much, which hurt Sarah. He would do his best to control his temper. He would do his best to control his jealousy. She needed to give him the chance to prove he could. He would not go off on her boy toy again. Andrew would break her heart, or it would be too much for her to live in his world. Either way, Chris would be around to pick up the pieces when her heart broke. No matter what he said to her, he would always love her as much as Andrew *claimed* to love her.

Chris pulled up in front of Sarah's house. He sucked in a deep breath and got out of his truck. Andrew would be hovering over her like a vulture. Andrew needed to go away and leave her alone; to give Sarah her life back. Andrew's life wasn't Sarah's life. Andrew needed to let her be.

He was getting angry again. He needed to calm down before he did something stupid again. He took another deep breath and knocked on the door. Andrew answered.

"What the hell are you doing here?" Andrew asked, grinding his perfect white teeth.

"I need to talk to her," Chris told him. Saying calm wasn't hard.

"She's sleeping, and she doesn't want to see you."

"Can I please come in? I didn't come here to fight. I came to talk." He was doing well keeping his temper in check.

Andrew opened the door for him. "Didn't you tell her you didn't want to anything more to do with her?"

"I can't stay away from her any more than you can."

Andrew chuckled. "She has that effect on us, doesn't she?"

"Yeah, she does." Chris smiled and sat down in the chair. Andrew sat on the couch, not in the least bit relaxed. "I'm tired of fighting, man. It's obvious we don't like each other, but for her benefit, we need to be civil. We're supposed to be helping her, not hurting her."

"I'm not hurting her, Chris."

"I don't want to hurt her anymore, either. I love her, no matter what I say."

"Where did this revelation come from?" Andrew was less threatened. He draped his arm over the back of the couch and crossed his right leg over his left.

"A drunken hallucination." Chris laughed. "I don't know, man." He looked at Andrew with sincerity. "I guess it doesn't matter where it came from. What matters is that I don't want to fight with you anymore. I don't have to like you, but we both love her, and we have to do what's best for her."

"I agree. No more outbursts?"

"No. And I'm torn up about what I did to her."

"It's not up to me to forgive you, mate. Sarah has to do that."

"Yeah." Chris sat back and sighed. "So, I was thinking, since we're going to tolerate each other, why don't we concentrate on the details of fixing this place until she wakes up and I can talk to her?"

"I think that's a brilliant idea," Andrew agreed. "Let me ask you something."

"Go ahead."

"You aren't still planning to take Sarah to dinner tonight, are you?"

"Oh, God, no. I'm sure she's still in pain and exhausted."

"Alright. She isn't in any shape to go anywhere."

"I didn't think so. Maybe next weekend if she hasn't beaten me to death." Chris laughed again.

"She's very forgiving if you hadn't already noticed. She insisted on calling to make sure you were alright, even after what happened," Andrew said.

"Maybe that's why we can't help but love her."

"You may be right." Andrew grinned at him, and Chris realized Andrew wasn't *that* bad. He was only competition, not a bad person. If the roles were reversed, he would have put his foot down against Sarah calling Andrew. Andrew supported her and encouraged her; it was what she needed most. Chris was determined to show her he would support and encourage her, too.

For an hour, the two of them discussed fixing the master bathroom before Sarah emerged from the bedroom. She rubbed her eyes and yawned. "Hey."

"Hello, love," Andrew laughed.

She hadn't seen Chris until she came out of the bathroom. "What are you doing here?" she asked with anger in her voice. She was staring at Chris.

"Please don't be mad, Sarah. I came to talk."

"What is this?" She was looking at Andrew.

"He's sincere. We've been talking for an hour," he told her.

Chris stood and walked toward her. "Don't come near me," she demanded as she cowered.

"I'm sorry, Sarah. I never meant to hurt you. I can't expect you to forgive me, and you can throw me out of your house if you want to. I won't blame you if you do, but please listen to me."

"I should call the police. Say what you need to say, then leave."

Chris took another step forward. Sarah stepped backward. "Sorry."

"Uh-huh. Talk." She crossed her arms over her chest and cocked her head.

"God, you are so beautiful," Chris told her and smiled at her.

When Chris smiled at her, she couldn't help but smile, too. Not this time. She rolled her eyes and snorted.

Chris began telling her what he had told Andrew. He hoped it would help her realize he meant what he was saying. He didn't want them to hurt each other again. "We will never have a romantic relationship now, but I do still love you. I always will. Nothing will change that. Please, let me be your friend. Let me do what I promised to do. Let me help Andrew fix your house. Let me be your friend again, please."

Sarah eyed Andrew. He was smiling at her, assuring her he believed Chris was sincere. "Sit down," she told him, still not totally convinced. He sat back down. She sat down, too, next to Andrew. "I don't understand any of this, Chris. You've said all this before but look what happened."

"You're right, but because that happened, it made me wake up and realize that this isn't healthy for any of us. I don't want to hurt you anymore. Like I told you before, I love you and I want you to be happy."

"How can I be sure of that? You hate Andrew. You have proven how much you hate him. He's part of my life. He's always going to be part of my life. You've told me to go to hell. So, how do I trust what you're saying?"

"You said the same thing to me."

"You put me in the hospital. Come on, Chris."

"You're right. I don't know how else to tell you I'm sorry. I can only ask you to give me another chance. I'm not even going to ask you to forgive me. Please, give me a chance to prove it to you. I mean it this time."

Sarah sighed, frustrated, unsure of which direction to go with this. This wouldn't be easy to forgive, and she would never forget what he had done. This was something she would have to think long and hard about. His brief yet tumultuous history with Andrew was a huge issue for her. She couldn't handle the jealousy and outbursts and fighting. It was draining. She put her face in her hands and breathed hard. "I need to think about this, Chris." She looked over at him. "With everything that has happened, you understand, right?"

He nodded. There was nothing else he'd be able to do or say. He would wait, no matter how long it took. He loved her and he would not give up. "I understand," he whispered.

She took a deep breath and looked at the paper on the coffee table in front of Andrew. "What are you working on?"

"We have been working on plans for the master bathroom," Andrew told her.

"We?"

"I told you I'm sincere," Chris spoke up.

"You did this once before, too," she reminded him.

"I did."

Sarah grabbed the paper and looked at it. These plans were all wrong. "I only wanted a shower. No tub. And I wanted tile, not panels."

"This isn't set in stone, love. Things can change." Andrew took the paper from her and made corrections.

"Can I have a window in the bathroom? It's so dark."

"Of course. What else?"

"I'll paint the walls once everything else is done. And I want new white cabinets. I hate how dark that bathroom is. It's depressing."

"Without electricity in the bathroom, it's so much darker than it should be," Chris said.

"Is the bathroom the first project after the roof?" She asked.

"Yes. One thing at a time," Chris told her with a smile.

"What about all of that hardwood for the floors?" She asked.

"You're going to have to call a wood floor installer. Can you do that this week?" Andrew asked.

"Sure. I'll do it on Monday and find out how much they charge. I'll give you the estimates once I have them."

"You're being cooperative about all of this," Andrew said.

"I guess I'm not the only one who can try to keep their word." Sarah glanced up at Chris. "You can't do that again, Chris. I mean it. I can't do drama. I like my life drama free."

"You're with the wrong person," Andrew chuckled under his breath. Sarah punched his arm and smiled.

"Does this mean you're giving me another chance?"

"One day at a time, okay?"

"That's all I can ask. Thank you."

She smiled at him, and the three of them went back to talking about her house.

Chapter Eight – I Will Possess Your Heart

"I didn't eat anything earlier," Sarah said as she stood up. She felt dizzy.

"Sit down," Andrew told her. "I'll fix you something."

"I'm fine," she told him.

"Do we have to do this again?" he glanced at her with a smile.

"No," she said and squinted. Her head was hurting again. It was most likely from lack of food and sleep.

"Are you okay, Sarah?" Chris asked.

"Fine. I need an ibuprofen." She stood up.

"Sit," Andrew called from the kitchen, and brought her two pills and some water. "Your lunch will be ready in a minute." He kissed Sarah's forehead and went back to the kitchen.

Sarah ate as if she hadn't eaten in months and wanted more. Andrew obliged her request and made her another sandwich. She inhaled that one, too.

"Jeez, Sarah, I've never seen you eat like that before. Are you pregnant?" Chris was half joking.

Sarah laughed. "Yeah, right." She glanced at Andrew. He tilted his head, as if he were questioning Chris's statement in his mind. "Come on, you two. Be serious. I haven't eaten anything in almost two days. I'm hungry."

Andrew and Chris stared at her with suspicion.

"This is ridiculous," she chuckled and stood up. "I'm getting dressed. I'm going to check the mail. I have plane tickets to Portland waiting for me."

Andrew's eyes lit up. "That's right. I'll go with you."

Chris let out a deep sigh. "I had better go." He sounded tired and frustrated.

"Let me get dressed and we'll walk you out," Sarah told him. She changed into a pair of jeans and a sweatshirt and came back out and walked to the door. She locked it behind her.

Andrew waited at the end of the driveway, letting Sarah say goodbye to Chris. Andrew was sure this wouldn't be the last time he would have to deal with Chris, but he hoped Chris would keep his word and stop fighting and stop drinking. It was only hurting Sarah. If he loved her, he would stop causing her pain.

"Are you okay?" Sarah asked Chris.

He sighed. "Do you think you're...?"

Sarah chuckled. "For real? Come on."

"Yeah, you're not. You're too old."

Sarah punched his arm and smirked at him. "You're a jerk."

"I was kidding," he chuckled as he rubbed his arm.

"We'll talk later?"

"Sure."

"Are you going to behave yourself?"

"Yes. I can't stand the thought of hurting you again."

"I hope you mean it this time."

"I do, Sarah." He gazed at her with sincerity and kissed her cheek.

"I hope so. Drive careful."

"That's no fun." He smiled and winked at her and got in his truck.

Things were still awkward. Sarah sensed Chris's tension, but he appeared to be trying. How long that lasted remained to be seen.

He drove away, and she turned and looked at Andrew and gave him a weak smile.

"Everything alright," he asked as she walked up to him.

She shrugged and put her arms around him. "Do you think everything will be alright?"

"I hope so, love." He held her.

"What about the other thing?" She didn't want to think that she might be pregnant.

Andrew chuckled and kissed her forehead. "What about it, love?"

"Do you think it's possible?"

"Do *you*?" They walked toward the mailbox. "I'm sure they did a test at the hospital, but what is your body telling you?"

"It's telling me no. First, it would be too soon to tell. Second, I'm too old. Third, I only ate so much because I hadn't eaten anything since Thursday. It's not possible."

"May I correct one thing?"

"What?"

"You are not old, so please stop saying you are."

"Whatever. I'm thirty-five. I'm too old to have a baby. How do you feel about that?"

"About having a baby? I never gave it much thought."

"You'll never be able to have one with me."

"I don't care."

"You will one day."

"Let's not worry about that, alright?"

They turned the corner where the mailboxes lined the street. On the other corner stood waiting photographers. As soon as they spotted Andrew and Sarah, the flashes went off and the paparazzi surrounded them.

"Lay off, guys," Andrew told them. "She just got out of the hospital."

Sarah opened her mailbox and grabbed her mail. Andrew took her hand and led her away from the photographers.

"Sarah, what happened? How did you end up in the emergency room last night?" One photographer asked.

"How are you?" Another reporter asked.

Any other time, Sarah would be all over them to leave her alone, but she wasn't in the mood. She was tired and the camera flashes were giving her another headache.

They hurried back to the house. The paparazzi followed them halfway up the street. Sarah's neighbors were looking out their windows and stepping out onto their porches to see what was going on outside.

***

Sarah sat down on the couch and went through the mail. It was junk mail and a card to pick up a registered letter from the post office. "Oh great. I have to wait until Monday to pick up my tickets." She was upset.

"It's alright, love." Andrew sat down next to her and put his arm around her shoulder. Sarah started crying. "What's the matter?" He held her close.

"I'm frustrated with everything." She wiped the tears away from her eyes.

"It's going to be okay," Andrew told her, still holding her.

"Yeah, but right now, it's difficult. The media. Chris." She chuckled and shook her head in frustration at the mention of Chris's name. "He's half the reason for my emotional breakdown. What's wrong with him?"

"He loves you," Andrew told her.

"He sure has a sadistic way of showing it." She shook her head again.

"In his own strange way, I think he does," Andrew said. "It's weird, but I think he's trying to show you. I'm sure that's why he acts the way he does. He's jealous and can't figure out how to express his feelings."

Sarah nodded and looked at him. "Yeah, well, he should have said it."

"I don't think he knows how, love."

She gazed up at Andrew. "And none of this bothers you?"

"Of course it does, but what am I going to do about it? I can't stop him from being in love with you. The only thing I can do is love you more."

Sarah smiled and looked up at him. "See? *This* is why I love you."

"I love you more every day," Andrew told her.

"I love you, too, and I don't want to talk about Chris anymore."

"That's fine with me." He kissed her forehead, and they held each other as they leaned back on the couch.

CHRIS

I needed to set some kind of plan in motion. Sarah was too in love with Andrew. It was going to be difficult getting her away from him. It would be harder once she came back from Portland. Every moment she spent with Andrew was a step backward for me.

The only thing I could do was be around when Andrew wasn't. At work. On the phone. At her house.

I had to be near her all the time, in front of her, keeping her safe, and as far away from the memory of Andrew Collier as possible, for as long as possible.

I would not drink anymore. I couldn't plan this if I wasn't sober. I'd go back to AA.

Making amends to Sarah was at the forefront of my agenda. I was very much in love with her, and I would prove it to her... somehow.

A realization hit me as I sat in my living room, flipping channels on the TV. I might be able to stay with her while I was working on her house. I would have to prove that I wouldn't flip out or try anything with her. But if I convinced her it was more economical for both of us with me living with her while I did the work on her house, she might let me stay. She had offered to let me stay with her once before, but that was before Andrew, and before I put her in the hospital.

It was going to be difficult convincing her that this was a good idea, but I was sure I would be able to. I needed to be persistent.

***

It was getting late, but Sarah wasn't close to being tired.

Andrew was fighting yawns as he sat on the couch next to her. She would look over at him, only to find him sitting with his eyes closed.

211

"Sweetie, why don't you go to bed? You're falling asleep," she told him.

"No. I can't sleep until you're asleep," he insisted.

"That's crazy. I'm not tired."

"Why don't we lay here and snuggle and see what's on the telly?"

"Fair deal," she told him with a smile.

They cuddled up under the blanket on the couch, with Andrew behind Sarah, his arms wrapped around her.

"Comfortable," he asked her.

"Mm-hm. You?"

"I'm with you. What do you think?" He kissed her head and Sarah cooed. "How's your head?"

"No pain." She scooted closer to him. "I wish you weren't so tired."

"Hmm. Why, love?" He was fading.

"I want you."

"I would make love to you no matter how tired I am, but I won't take a risk with your stitches. It's barely been twenty-four hours."

"You're right."

"Try to sleep, love." He kissed her head again and pulled her closer to him. Within minutes, Sarah heard his slow breathing, telling her he was sleeping.

She wasn't tired until around two a.m. She didn't remember what was on TV. The last thing she remembered before she fell asleep were thoughts of Chris. How was he doing? And why did she care so much now? He kept hurting her and he would continue to hurt her. She didn't want to keep living her life wondering when he was going to snap again.

**

Andrew woke up early on Sunday morning, before Sarah. He enjoyed being able to sit next to Sarah and gaze at her before she woke up. The only time she seemed at peace was when she was sleeping. Her expression was so serene and calm. He wished she could find that kind of peace when she was awake.

It made him sad that her life wouldn't be private because he was in it. He realized his family and, as much as he hated to admit it, Chris, were right. Sarah had always lived in an average, simple world. How would a life with him be for her? Would she adapt or end up leaving him? He couldn't bear the thought of her not being in his life. She was everything to him. He was certain Sarah loved him, but was their love enough to keep them together? Or would life under the media microscope be more than she could deal with?

He couldn't worry about this now. Right now, they were happy and very much in love. That was all he needed.

Andrew brushed the hair off Sarah's face. He kissed her forehead and whispered, "I love you," before he got up to take a shower. She moaned with happiness and rolled over on her side. He smiled and went to the bathroom.

***

Sarah woke up and heard the shower running. Andrew was nowhere to be found, so she crept into the bathroom and undressed without a sound and slipped in the shower behind Andrew and put her arms around his wet torso.

He jumped and turned around. "Jeez, woman. You scared the bloody hell out of me." He was smiling, despite his being scared out of his skin.

"Sorry. I had to be near you."

"You aren't supposed to get your stitches wet, love. I have a better idea for you." He kissed her and turned the shower off and plugged the tub. He found some bubble bath under the sink. "Now, sit," he told her.

The water was hot. It felt wonderful to her. Sarah sat down and sighed. "This is wonderful. I haven't taken a bath in months."

"Prepare to be pampered, my love." He smiled at her. He rubbed her body with his soapy hands, caressed her breasts and her thighs. Her body tingled up from her toes and she closed her eyes and moaned.

Sarah let him bathe her. It was sensual, but not sexual. It was relaxing. Andrew rubbed her feet, and her legs, and to her fingers and arms. He stepped in the tub behind her and rubbed her back and her shoulders. It was a very loving massage, to relax her, not to seduce her. "Your hands feel so good," she moaned.

"Calm down, love, or I'll stop. We're not making love," he assured her.

"But it's so good."

Andrew kissed her cheek as he poured water from his hands down her arms. "You'll have to return the favour someday," he told her.

"I intend to. Until that time, keep rubbing," she giggled and leaned up against him, so he could rub the front of her body. Andrew laughed with her.

"I love you so much, Sarah," he whispered, kissing her shoulder and neck.

Sarah whispered, "I love you, Andrew," as she brushed her hair away from her neck. She rubbed his legs as he drew her close and kissed her neck. His hands traced over her curves, eliciting a soft moan from her. She leaned back and met his gaze, her eyes filled with desire. As they sat there, Sarah tilted her head against Andrew's chest. He couldn't resist and captured her lips with his own. Their mouths moved in perfect harmony, their bodies fitting together like puzzle pieces. With every touch and kiss, it was as if they were made for each other. Sarah and Andrew explored each other's bodies, their passion growing with each passing moment. It was impossible to distinguish where one ended and the other began. They were meant to be together.

She pivoted her body to face him, her eyes burning with desire. With a fiery kiss, she submerged her hand in the warm water and moved it between his legs, leaving a trail of goosebumps in its wake. His moans echoed throughout the room as he pulled her closer, unable to resist her touch. The surrounding air crackled with electricity as their bodies intertwined, lost in a passionate embrace. She smiled, her fingers dancing over his skin, knowing she had him under her spell. The water lapped at their bodies, the only witness to their intense connection.

"Dammit, woman. What are you doing to me?" he moaned.

"What do you think I'm doing to you?" she whispered with a seductive tone.

Andrew grabbed her hands and opened his eyes. "We are *not* making love," he insisted.

Sarah stood up and got out of the tub. He sensed disappointment.

"Don't do that, love. You understand why we can't right now," he told her, concern in his voice.

"Sure." She wrapped the towel around her and picked up her clothes and left the bathroom. She stomped into the bedroom and sat on the bed.

Andrew wrapped a towel around himself and followed her. "Listen to me." He sat down next to her. She turned away from him. "I want to make love to you. You don't know how bad I want you, but I'm afraid of hurting you right now."

"You won't hurt me." She gazed at him and took his hands. "Don't you think I know what I can handle?"

"Have you ever had eighteen stitches in your head before?"

"Well, no, but..."

"My point, exactly." Andrew pulled her up on his lap. "Listen to me, darling. Not being able to make love to you will not make me love you any less. Is that the only way you think we can express our love for one another?"

"Kind of. I mean, that's the way it has always been before."

"I don't want us to be that way, alright? We can do other things to express our love."

"Such as?"

"Well, for one, I can fix breakfast, and you can do my laundry." He smiled. Sarah couldn't help but giggle.

"Like an old married couple?"

"Well, not old, but yes." He pulled her up and stood next to her and put his arms around her waist and kissed her. "Now, let's get dressed and act like a married couple."

"Okay." Sarah stood on her toes and kissed him with a long, soft kiss. She loved the current that ran through her body when they touched. Andrew's body twitched when they kissed, so she was sure he sensed it, too.

***

"What are you up to today?" Chris asked Sarah when he called her on Sunday afternoon.

"Laundry, like every Sunday," she told him. "What are you up to?" Her attitude toward him was bland. She couldn't let her guard down with him yet.

"I was wondering if it's okay to come by. I wanted to talk to you and Andrew about something."

"Um, sure. I guess so." She looked at Andrew, who was on the couch. "Chris's coming by," she told him.

"Good. I have a few things to discuss with him regarding the house."

Sarah rolled her eyes and turned her attention back to Chris. "Sure, come on over. Andrew wants to talk to you, too."

"Outstanding. I'll be there in about an hour," Chris told her, then hung up.

This would be his chance, and if he had Andrew on his side, Sarah would have no choice but to agree to letting him stay with her while he was fixing the house. The hard part would be convincing Sarah. He was sure Andrew would agree to anything that would benefit Sarah and keep her safe and make her happy. If he could assure Sarah that his presence was both economical and would keep her hidden from the media when Andrew wasn't around, he'd be moving in this week.

It was the perfect plan to stay in Sarah's life, whether or not she wanted him to be right now. He thought she didn't, but this made perfect sense. She would have to see that. Andrew would see it.

He had to first prove he was only moving in to help her out, not moving in on her and take her away from Andrew, which was his actual goal.

He pulled up in front of Sarah's house and she came out to greet him. "What is all of this about, Chris?" She was suspicious.

"I have some things I want to run by the two of you. Don't freak out." He let out a derisive chuckle.

"Are you sober" She was still suspicious.

"Yes. Calm down, would you?" He put his arm around her shoulder and walked with her back to the house. She kept her arms crossed over her chest. She wasn't comfortable being so close to him yet.

"You're not hiding a gun in your coat, are you?" Andrew asked, half joking, when Chris walked in the door.

"Are you kidding?" Chris smirked at Andrew.

"What is all of this about?" Andrew asked.

Chris sat down on the couch. Sarah sat on the coffee table in front of him. "I've been thinking, I live all the way out in Windsor. That's a long drive."

"Yeah, but you make that drive every day to go to work," Sarah reminded him.

"Sure, but I'm going to be helping you with the house, so I'll be here more often."

Sarah's suspicion was growing. She was sure what he was getting at, but she wanted him to confirm it. "What are you trying to say, Chris?"

"Well, since I'm going to be here more often, I thought it would save gas, and you'd be safer with someone else here when Andrew's not here." He stopped and looked at her, a little fearful of her answer.

Sarah stared at him with a blank expression. "No," she told him in a flat tone. He was right about her resisting. He was prepared for that.

Andrew was smiling. "I'd like to hear this." He ran his fingers through his messy hair.

"Thanks." He grinned in Andrew's direction and looked back at Sarah. "I can help with rent and bills; I can be here to fix anything that needs immediate attention. I'll be here to supervise the roofers while you're away."

"Plus, I can keep those annoying photographers away. They have seen your car, and they'll follow you everywhere."

"They have seen your truck, too, Chris. They have been hanging out in the neighborhood, watching the house," Sarah informed him.

"Well, I can keep them from harassing you every time you leave the house."

"I can handle the paparazzi, Chris. I've done it before."

"Hold on, love. He may have an idea here."

"Andrew? No," she protested.

"Thank you, Andrew."

"I'm not sure about this," she resisted. "I mean, you're unstable right now. You're not exactly reliable."

"Sarah, I meant what I said. I want to prove to you I can be your friend and help you without freaking out about your relationship with Andrew."

She shook her head. "I'm don't know." She eyed Andrew, pleading with him to consider this situation before he agreed to anything.

"Well, love, think about this... you wouldn't have to wait for him to drive out here every time something needs to be done. You'll be able to save some money with his help with the bills."

"I can't believe you're considering this, Andrew."

"Consider it for a minute. It's not a horrible idea. It wouldn't have been my first solution, but it works."

"But it's Chris. Let's think about his track record."

"Excuse me," Chris interrupted. Both Andrew and Sarah stopped and looked at him. "Sarah, didn't you offer to let me stay here a few months ago?"

"That was before you turned psycho," she told him, waving her arms over her head.

"You also said you would give me a chance to prove myself to you."

Sarah sighed, frustrated, and stood up and paced. "I swear to God, Chris, if you blow it, that's it."

Chris grinned.

"Chill out. I have major conditions on this." Sarah eyed him. "You'll sleep in the guest room. You'll have to fix that window, or you'll freeze to death. You will not bring any alcohol into my house, and if I find out you've been drinking, you're gone."

"Fair enough."

"Quiet. I'm not finished." She paced again. "Your half of the bills are due on the last day of the month. If you want to pay half on the fifteenth, that's fine, but if any of my bills are behind, you're out. You'll have to buy your own food, too. I do the laundry on Sunday. I'll do yours, but if your dirty clothes aren't in the laundry room on Sunday morning, you'll have to wait until the following Sunday because no one uses my washer and dryer. I'm very picky about it. I'm also picky about the dishes, so I will do them. You can rinse them off, but don't wash them." She took a breath. "And one more thing, you will keep your shit picked up and keep this place tidy. Have I made myself clear?"

"Crystal."

"Good. So, when are you planning on moving in?"

"Whenever is good for you."

"I have one more condition," Andrew said, looking surprised at Sarah. He was pleased, but one important detail out was left out.

"What's that?" Chris didn't mind Sarah's meaningless rules. It was Andrew he was more concerned with.

"Sarah has agreed to let you stay here, but it doesn't give you permission to move in on her when I'm not here."

"I wasn't planning on it," he lied. "I want to make things easier and more convenient for everyone." Chris was sure he had convinced Andrew of his lie. Andrew would be oblivious until it was too late.

"Now that it's settled, I guess you can move your stuff in tomorrow after work," Sarah told him, still frustrated. "I'm hungry. I need to eat before I pass out."

ANDREW

I wanted to hold her forever. I lay in bed that last night with her and I watched her sleep. I hated leaving her, but in the morning, I would have to. It would be another two weeks before I'd be able to see her again; we couldn't get around that. I couldn't come back, and she couldn't come to me for two weeks.

She was at peace. I liked to think I was a part of that peace. She told me she was happy with me, but how long would that last the longer we were together? I wondered if she could adapt to life with a celebrity. I couldn't live my life without her, but she might be able to live her life without me. I never wanted her to have to find out. As I closed my eyes, I decided I would make it my priority to make this transition from a regular life to life in the spotlight easy.

"I love you," I whispered before I fell asleep. She mumbled something resembling 'I love you,' and cuddled closer to me.

SARAH

I was so glad I had remembered to set the alarm. Andrew and I could snuggle in bed for a little while before we had to get up.

"How did you sleep, love?" Andrew asked me as he stretched and yawned.

"Wonderful. I was sleeping next to you." I put my arms around his bare torso and held him tight. "How did you sleep?"

"Great." He smiled down at me and kissed my forehead. "My bladder is going to explode. I have to go to the bathroom." He frowned.

I let him go, and I got up and went to the kitchen to turn the coffee on.

I didn't want him to leave me. The only thing that kept me from trying to keep him here was knowing I would see him again in two weeks and we would be on the same continent. Maybe a time zone away, but still closer than if he was far away in London.

I poured our coffee and put the hot chocolate in the way we both liked it, and I realized I had to use the bathroom, too. He was taking forever.

I ran past him as he came out. While I was washing my hands, I looked in the mirror. My eyes were so puffy, and the dark circles were darker. A great deal of concealer would fix that, but the puffiness would never go away. That was a residual effect of a past medical condition.

I washed my face with cold water and put lotion on my face and went to the couch where Andrew was sitting, watching the news.

"What does the weather look like today?" I asked him. He didn't answer. "Andrew, honey?"

He looked over at me. I glimpsed sadness in his smoky-blue eyes. I could swear tears were forming in the corners.

"Are you okay?"

He nodded.

"No, you're not. What's wrong?"

"I don't want to leave you yet. You had a horrible accident you're recovering from, and I'm having second thoughts about Chris staying here with you. We're both aware of how he feels about you. He's still in love with you."

"My head is fine. The stitches come out on the eleventh. I don't notice them. And the issue with Chris, I can always tell him no."

"I'm worried he'll try something with you."

"I'll tell him I changed my mind. If you recall, I wasn't too keen on the idea to begin with."

" No, no," he insisted and looked at me with a smile on his beautiful, full lips. "It *is* convenient for you to have him here at your beck and call. The financial benefits alone will be a major plus."

"I'll start sleeping in my bedroom with the door locked. You can call me at night, and I can fall asleep talking to you." I smiled at him and took his hands in mine.

"You're right, my love, as usual." He smiled at me again and kissed me. "We should get ready to go."

"Nooo," I whined and held his arm. I wasn't ready for our time together to end.

He chuckled and kissed me again and pulled me off the couch. "Come, love," he insisted in a sweet tone, and we walked to the bedroom to get dressed. "Are you certain your head is fine?" he asked.

"Mm-hm." I looked into his eyes. His expression was seductive, almost lustful. Was he going to make love to me again? I glanced over at the clock. We had little time. So, I would go to work without make-up. I had done it before.

Andrew cocked his head and smiled at me with pure love in his eyes now. A rush of some sensation, I wasn't sure how to describe it, raced through my entire body. My knees went weak, and my heart raced.

He never said a word. He lay me on the bed and undressed me, and we made love for almost an hour.

***

Sarah cried on her way to work that Monday morning. Andrew sat in the back of the Uber on his way to the airport and cried. It hurt to leave each other.

Andrew dialed Sarah's number as the car went at a snail's pace on the highway to Denver International Airport. "Hello, love," he spoke into the phone when Sarah answered.

She had been pacing in front of her car, outside her office building, trying to contain her tears. "Hey, sweetie. Are you at the airport yet?"

"No. The traffic is horrid this morning. I'm still on the motorway." He sighed. "I miss you already."

"I miss you. Only two weeks. That's how we have to think about it."

"It's hard being away from you. I'm worried about you."

"Why? I'm fine." She was having a hard time not crying. He already seemed like he was a million miles away.

"Did I hurt you this morning?"

"The opposite. I'm still tingling." Remembering their wonderful morning together made her smile and ache for him at the same time.

"You aren't in any pain?"

"None. I'm great." She said. "Are *you* okay?"

"Amazing, but I miss you."

"We'll be together soon. Valentine's weekend will be here soon," she said.

"You're right, again." He laughed. "Don't forget to go to the post office and pick up your tickets."

"I'm going during lunch. I'll call you when I have them."

"Alright. You had better go to work. It's almost eight o'clock."

"Okay. I'll talk to you later. I love you."

"I love you, too. Have a good day."

"Have a safe flight."

ANDREW

I hung up and fought the tears that were threatening to surface again. I needed to call Trevor and tell him I was on my way. I couldn't cry while I was on the phone with him, especially when it involved a woman.

I kept the conversation short and my answers shorter. "I'm on my way to the airport now."

"Good. How's Sarah? I saw Celebrity Insider. What happened?"

"She's fine," I told him. "It's a long story. I'll tell you later."

"You wasted a lot of rehearsal time by staying in Denver, but I'm sorry about your girlfriend. I'm glad she's okay."

"Thanks, and I'm sorry." The Uber pulled up to the terminal. "I'm at the airport. I'll give you a ring when I land in L.A." I hung up and got out of the car.

The paparazzi spotted me the moment I exited the cab. "Andrew, how's Sarah?" someone asked.

"She's doing well."

"When are you going to see her again?" someone else asked.

"Soon." I smiled at them and walked quicker. "I have to catch my plane now."

They left me alone after that.

SARAH

I went upstairs to the office as slow as possible, but I had to go to work. Work would keep me busy. I needed to stay focused on something other than Andrew. It wouldn't be easy. Everything in my life reminded me of him: the office, my car, my house. His scent was on my clothes. I saw his smile; he was everywhere around me. Strange as it was, Chris reminded me of Andrew, too.

When I walked into the office, Kelly was all over me. "What are you doing here? How are you? You were on the news."

I had to stop her. Her incessant questions were making my head spin. "I'm fine."

"You should be at home resting."

"I'm okay."

"We didn't think you'd be here today."

I had to laugh. "Please. I'm fine. I should go talk to Valerie." I paused. "Is Chris here?"

"Yeah. Are you two okay?"

"Kind of. We'll talk later."

I needed to avoid Chris for the time being. I was sure he would still be giddy about staying at my house. He would think he'd have a shot at being with me.

"Hey, you," Valerie greeted me when I entered her office. "What are you doing here?"

I sat down opposite her. "I still work here, don't I? I'm fine. I bumped my head, that's all."

"And got eighteen stitches," she reminded me. I touched my head. It didn't hurt anymore.

"How is everyone aware of this?"

"Don't you watch television, girl?" She laughed at me. "Even Chris is aware."

'That's because he's the one who caused me to *have* eighteen stitches,' I thought. "Yeah, he was at my house when it happened." I gazed at her. I could see she had already figured it out.

"Oh. I see." She came around the desk and hugged me. "Are you okay?"

"I'm fine. It was an accident."

"Was it?" She sounded doubtful.

"Yes." It wasn't on purpose. "I don't need a restraining order or anything, if that's what you're hinting at."

"Okay. No bad blood?"

"We're working some stuff out. He's going to stay at my house while he's working on it. He and Andrew concocted a scheme to fix my house. It will help with bills and stuff, too."

"Is Andrew okay with this?"

"Sheesh, he encouraged it. Can you believe that?"

"That man must love you to trust you and Chris that much."

"He does. Chris has made peace with all of it. I think it still stings a little, but we're all okay with everything."

"Well, I'm glad. And I'm glad you're well enough to be here. Tell me if you have any pain."

"Thanks, but I'm great." I wasn't experiencing any pain, and I was still tingling all over.

ANDREW

Rehearsals were maddening. I couldn't concentrate on my lines, and I sensed Karen and Trevor were getting annoyed.

"I'm sorry, guys. I can't keep my head in the game right now," I apologized.

"Why don't you call her, man?" Trevor suggested. "We'll take a break for a little while."

"Yeah, that sounds like a good idea," Karen agreed.

I smiled and thanked them and stepped outside. I didn't need to call Sarah. She was already calling me.

"Hi, love," I greeted her. I was so glad she called.

"How are you?" she asked.

"I'm great now that I'm talking to you. I've had a bit of a horrible day. I can't concentrate."

"Oh, honey, I'm sorry. What's wrong?"

"Missing you, love. That's all."

"Well, stop. Guess what's in my hands right now?" She was ecstatic.

"You have your tickets?" That made me smile. Being with her again was closer than ever.

"I do. I can't wait." She took in a deep breath, and she continued to remind me of why it was important for me to focus on work and not her. "You have this amazing job that makes millions of girls go crazy. You can't let them down because you haven't done your job. Besides, if you're fired because you can't memorize your lines, I can't come see you," she teased. "We can't have that now, can we?"

"No, we can't," I chuckled. Hearing her voice and knowing she was encouraging me gave me back my enthusiasm for my job. I wanted to work harder because of her, because she believed in me. "God, I love you." I smiled into the phone.

"I love you, too. Now, get your gorgeous butt back to work. I have to drive back to the office. I'm still at the post office."

"Alright, love. I'll give you a ring when we're finished here. It might be late. Will you wait up for me?"

"I'll keep the phone by my ear all night."

"I love you, Sarah." I told her again.

"I love you. I'll talk to you tonight."

We hung up, and I went back inside to continue rehearsals.

"Better?" Trevor asked, hopeful.

"Everything is great," I told him. I was beaming.

"Great, now that you're done pissing and moaning over your girlfriend, maybe we can rehearse." Karen's tone was sarcastic.

The rest of rehearsals went better. I was having a fantastic day, and I couldn't wait to talk to Sara later that evening.

SARAH

Chris was waiting for me outside when I got back to the office. I wasn't ready to talk to him yet. I was still high from my Andrew fix and the fact that I had my plane tickets. My trip to Portland was going to happen. With everything that had been happening, I was afraid I wouldn't be able to make it.

A twinge of pain from my stitches caused me to grimace as I got out of my car. I wasn't sure if it was residual or if it was the prospect of having to have a conversation with Chris. I didn't hate him or dislike him. It was that everything about our relationship was awkward and complicated, and for good reason. I hoped one day it would be easier.

"Hey," he greeted me. He was happy.

"How's it going?" I replied in a bland tone.

"Pretty good. I packed some stuff up last night. It's in the back of my truck. How are things with you? Did Andrew make it to L.A. okay?"

"Yeah. He's kind of having a bad day, though." My head was hurting now. I grimaced and touched my head. No blood. I needed ibuprofen. I had some in my desk drawer.

"I'm sorry." He didn't sound sorry. "Are you okay? Is your head hurting?"

"I'm fine. I need to take something. It's a headache," I assured him. It wasn't bad. I got headaches all the time. It was from eyestrain and the fact that I had been bawling this morning. A headache had been threatening me most of the morning.

"Are you sure you're okay?"

"Yes," I told him, annoyed. "Why is everyone treating me like a child? It's a bump on the head. It's not like I had major surgery." I started walking away, toward the front door of the office building.

"Sarah, wait," Chris called after me. I stopped, but I didn't turn around. "I'm worried about you," he told me when he caught up to me. "Everyone cares about you. Stop pushing everybody away."

I turned around. "I'm not pushing anyone away; I want everyone to stop worrying so much. I can take care of myself. I've been doing it since I was sixteen. I think I'm pretty good at it." I looked up at him and smiled. "It's only a headache, Chris. It will go away. I promise." I patted him on his chest and turned and walked into the building.

Chris followed me into the elevator. "Do you still want me to stay at your house?"

"Where did that come from?" I pushed the button for the second floor.

"You're so defensive toward me."

"I kind of have a reason to be, don't you think?" I asked him matter of fact.

"Sort of, but you're taking it to the extreme."

"How so?" The elevator doors opened, and I stepped out with Chris at my heels. He opened the office door for me.

"You're being kind of rude and evasive, and a little mean."

I didn't speak until we were in his office with the door closed. "You almost killed me, Chris. You're lucky I'm speaking to you at all, let alone letting you stay at my house. If you're going to make an issue of this…"

"I'm not." He put his hands up. "I hoped we'd be able to be friends."

"I thought that's what we were trying to do. Where is all of this coming from? Because I'm annoyed with everyone treating me like a baby?"

"I'm not the only one?"

"No, Chris. I'm not singling you out just because you're the reason I have eighteen stitches in my head."

"Please don't remind me. I feel guilty enough."

"You should. Drop it, okay? It's not about you, anyway. I have a lot on my mind and I'm nervous and anxious and excited about Valentine's weekend."

"Oh, Andrew." He sat down, deflated. He and Andrew would never be friends, but the simple fact was that Andrew was a major part of my life and if Chris wanted to be a part of my life, too, he was going to have to accept it. That was a concept that had evaded him for the past two weeks. That's the reason I ended up in the emergency room. It was also the reason I chose Andrew over him.

"Yes, Andrew." I sat down on the chair next to the door. "Are you ever going to let this go?"

"One of these days, maybe, but I promised to behave, and I meant it." He gave me a genuine smile. He sounded sincere, but I was still guarded.

"I hope you're able to keep that promise. Andrew isn't going anywhere and if you're going to be staying with me, you might see and hear things you may not be comfortable with."

"Can we not talk about that?"

"Sorry. I understand it's a sore subject right now." I checked the time on my phone. "I need to go back to work."

"Okay. I'll follow you home after work."

"Sounds good." I gave him a quick hug and left his office.

***

I arrived home close to five-thirty, with Chris following and parking his truck next to my Nissan in the driveway.

"Do you need help with your stuff?" I asked him, walking around to the back of his truck.

"Nah, just hold the door for me."

He followed me into the house and took the boxes he was carrying down the hall to the guest room.

I put my purse and coat on the couch and checked my answering machine. "Hey, bitch, it's your BFF. Call me, dammit."

I realized I hadn't spoken to her since she stayed over that first weekend. I couldn't believe I had neglected her for so long. I grabbed the phone and dialed her number.

She answered on the first ring. "Hey, bitch," she greeted me, laughing.

"I am so sorry, Mary. I have been so busy," I apologized.

"I've seen how busy you have been. I check Celebrity Insider, too."

"Oh, great, so everyone is aware of my love life?"

"Duh," she commented with her usual sarcasm. "Tell me how all of this happened? I have all night, so you had better start from the beginning."

I began at the beginning, as requested, or in Mary's case, demanded with humor, with the day after she stayed over.

"Keep talking."

I continued with every detail I had neglected to keep her apprised of, and with all the insanity with Chris, and on to this last weekend.

"There were pictures of you going to the emergency room," she told me. "How did that happen?"

"Chris was drunk," I began. "I tried to make him sit down and calm down and he threw me off him. I hit my head on the stone tiles and lost my memory for a while. That was interesting," I chuckled. "I ended up with eighteen stitches. I guess that's about it. Oh yeah, Chris's living here now." I waited for her response.

"Excuse me? He what?"

I explained how that came about and how Andrew encouraged it. I almost heard her head shaking.

"Okay, let me make sure I have this right. I'm starting from the *very* beginning.. You write a letter to a smoking hot super-star, and he shows up to meet you right when you and Chris are starting something. Next, you and this gorgeous super-star fall head-over-heels in love with each other in one weekend and he proposes to you over the radio. I'm still shocked at how all of this happened so fast. And didn't you say you were never getting married again?"

"Yes, I'm aware of what I said. I'm not rushing into anything."

"That's not what this sounds like."

"I understand how it appears, but..."

"Hold on. I need to make sure I've got all this right. Chris gets out of control and jealous and freaks you out to where you choose a hot, rich guy over him?"

"I didn't choose Andrew because he's hot and rich. I chose him despite those obvious qualities."

"Sarcastic bitch here. Let me finish. So, Andrew invites you to visit him in Portland on Valentine's weekend. I want details on that, too."

"Sure. I won't forget to call next time."

"Good. So, Chris loses it again when he finds out Andrew skipped out on rehearsals in L.A. and puts you in the hospital. Now he's moving in with you to help you out. Do I have everything correct?"

"Everything. That's all that has happened so far. You're up to speed," I told her.

"This is a lot to take in, Sarah. I wish you hadn't waited so long to tell me all of this."

"I said I'm sorry."

"Yeah, yeah. Whatever. So, are you in love with him?"

"Yeah, I am. He's amazing, Mary. I can't explain how it happened this fast, but from the very first time he touched me, a simple touch, I got this spark of electricity, and it's gotten stronger. He's so fun to be with, he's funny, smart, caring, attentive, and he makes me feel good about myself."

"I can't believe this is happening to you. I mean, you deserve it. You do, but it's almost like a fairy tale. This kind of stuff doesn't happen."

"I keep thinking it's a dream and I'm going to wake up soon and find out none of it's real."

"But it *is* real, Sarah. I am so jealous of you. Who would have thought a simple letter would turn your life into a soap opera?"

"Tell me about it. I'm still kind of in shock. I'm happier than I think I've ever been in my life. I never want this to end."

Chris walked out of the bedroom. "I need a shower. Do you need the bathroom?" he asked. At least he was being courteous.

"I'm good," I told him.

"He's at your house now," Mary asked, surprised. "Do I need to come stay with you, too?"

"No, I'm fine. I told him he might as well move his stuff in now."

"You're a freaking saint."

"No. I'm trying not to hold a grudge. I'm still on the defensive and suspicious. He's not in the clear, but you have to remember, we've been friends for a long time. I do care about him."

"Do you think you guys would be together if Andrew hadn't shown up?"

"Maybe, but I don't think about that anymore. Andrew *did* show up and I am so in love with him. And he's an amazing lover."

"TMI. I'm not interested in your sex life." She was laughing at me.

"But I have to be subjected to yours, in vivid detail? How fair is that?"

"Whatever." She was still laughing. "How are you handling being in the spotlight? I noticed the press is all over you."

"They're a minor annoyance." She already knew about the confrontation at the store. "If I don't want to talk to them, I don't talk to them. It's not that bad."

"Yet," she insisted.

"It can't get much worse than them standing out by the mailbox waiting for a random photo op."

"They are waiting for you near your house?"

"I don't know if they are waiting all the time, but yeah. I think it's because of Andrew. They don't show up at the office. It's only when they think they're going to get a picture of him."

"Trust me, Sarah, as soon as they have more info on you, they're going to hound you, too."

"By then I'll be used to it... I hope." I snorted out a laugh.

We talked for another half hour. She caught me up with her mom's health and her grandmother's latest escapades. The poor old woman was suffering from Alzheimer's. I was sad for her, but the crazy things she did were kind of funny.

"I'm planning a trip to see Jeremy in London in March. You want chocolate, right?"

"Of course," I laughed. I envied her. Mary went to London every year. I had never been out of the United States. I'd never be able to afford a plane ticket anywhere. I hoped that would change now that I was with Andrew. I was going to Portland, and he said his family wanted to meet me, so maybe a trip to London was in my future, too. That thought made me smile. It made me wonder what other surprise trip Andrew may be planning.

"My mom is yelling at me from upstairs," she told me. "It's my turn to take care of grandma."

"Okay, Mary. We should have lunch this weekend."

"Andrew won't be here?"

"No, he's rehearsing with Karen and Trevor for the next two weeks."

"I think it's so funny how you talk about these people like they're average, everyday people."

"Well, I haven't met them in person yet, but they *are* regular people. They have high-profile jobs. That's all. I'd better let you go. I'll keep you updated."

"You had better. Bye."

I hung up the phone and chuckled to myself. I was missing Andrew so much after my conversation with Mary.

CHRIS

"Are you hungry?" Sarah asked when she got off the phone. "I'm sure you haven't been able to pick anything up from the store yet."

"No, but I can go to the store," I told her.

"Don't worry about it. You can make a sandwich. You can pick some stuff up tomorrow."

"Are you sure?"

"Yeah, make something to eat if you're hungry."

"Thanks." I smiled at her and went to the kitchen. She was sitting at her computer, checking her emails. I glanced at her out of the corner of my eye. Sarah and I were alone, and I was trying to think of something to say to her. She took the phone into the living room and sat down on the couch. She was waiting for Andrew to call. "Are you nervous about your trip?" I asked her as I sat down on the chair in the living room.

"A little. I'm more excited, though." She looked up at me and smiled and went back to flipping channels on the TV. "I haven't been out of Colorado in over five years or on a plane for about ten. I can't wait, though. I miss him already."

I had to make a conscious effort not to grind my teeth. "You were together this morning," I chuckled.

She peered at me. "You don't understand, I guess." She went back to flipping channels.

"Maybe not." I shrugged. "What do you do after work?"

"This is about it. I watch TV until I fall asleep. Boring, huh?" She looked over at me and chuckled.

"Kind of, but it's okay." I smiled at her and finished my sandwich.

"You can do whatever you want in that room. It's all yours, but I wouldn't put off getting that window fixed. It's supposed to be cold this weekend."

"I'll measure it tomorrow and go buy a new window."

"Cool. Make sure you give me the receipt so I can have Andrew reimburse you."

"Nah, that's a minor repair."

"Are you sure? Didn't he tell you he'd pay for anything that needed to be fixed?"

"Yeah, but I'll let him handle the bigger stuff, like the roof and the floor. That reminds me, did you ever call the flooring people?"

"No. I think I change my mind about that. I'd rather have carpet throughout the house. This floor gets so cold sometimes."

"You'd better tell Andrew. He will ask."

"Yes, but it's my house, so he has to go along with whatever I decide." She smiled up at me.

It was wonderful to have a pleasant conversation with Sarah again, despite her boy toy being part of it. She was smiling, and I liked to see that. She didn't appear stressed. Only tired.

"Are you okay?" She looked annoyed at my question. I figured it bothered her that everyone kept asking, but I needed to make sure. I promised the boy toy I would take care of her and keep her safe.

"I'm fine. Don't start." She sighed, not annoyed or frustrated, more like she was thinking about something, or wanted to say something, but wasn't sure how to put it into words. It appeared we were going to have a serious conversation. We were. "Are we going to be okay, Chris?"

"Of course."

"Will we? I don't want to be angry anymore. I don't want to be afraid you're going to flip out."

"I'm not going to. Sure, it sucks that we will never be a couple, but I'm learning to live with that. You're happy, and that's all I care about."

"Is it?" She didn't sound convinced by what I was telling her.

"Yeah. I'm always going to love you, but I want you to be happy and if Andrew is who makes you happy, I need to let you go."

"I don't want to stop being your friend, as long as everyone can be civil."

"Trust me, I almost lost you as a friend. I never want to go through that again. It nearly destroyed me because I caused it."

"I need to be certain you won't hurt me again."

"I'm not. Trust me, please." I got up and went to sit on the couch next to her. I took her hands and looked into her eyes. "I never want to hurt you again. I want to be here for you."

She leaned in and hugged me. I breathed her in. I wanted to kiss her so much. I held her close to me for as long as possible; until she was ready to let go.

"I need to put my pajamas on. Andrew is supposed to call soon." She got up and went to her room and came back out a few minutes later wearing a pair of sweats and one of Andrew's shirts. She wouldn't smell like herself anymore. I thought about excusing myself and going to bed, but that might have been a little suspicious, so I sat with her for another hour, until Andrew called. That's when I went to bed.

Chapter Nine – Valentine's Weekend
SARAH

The first week flew by. Work was a great distraction for me. It kept me from thinking too much about not being with Andrew. We talked on the phone every night, so his was the last voice I heard before I went to sleep at night.

I wasn't getting a lot of sleep, but I didn't care. I could see the time I spent talking to Andrew was bothering Chris, but he was behaving himself. He never said a word. When Andrew called, Chris would excuse himself and go to bed. I think it bothered him more because Andrew's called interrupted one of our conversations rather than who was calling.

On Friday, after work, I called Mary as promised. I told her about the week's events.

"How are you?" she asked, concerned about my injury.

"I'm fine. I my head doesn't hurt at all. My stitches come out next week."

"That's good. Any recent developments?"

"Um... yeah, a few."

I reminded her I was going to Portland for Valentine's weekend and Chris living with me. "You used to be this quiet girl with an average life. Now you're engaged to one of the biggest stars in Hollywood and he's flying you to the coast to be with him, and you are letting Chris live with you?"

"I'm still completely baffled by all of it myself."

"You are a lucky bitch."

"I don't think it's luck. A lot of bad crap has happened since I met Andrew."

"I'm sorry. But you're in love. You should be happy about that."

"I *am* happy."

"You deserve it. It is your turn."

Mary and I talked for an hour about the goings-on with her boyfriend, Jeremy, and got caught up on the renovations with her family's rental house. She explained that her previous renters had destroyed the house, so fixing the things they had damaged was costing a fortune. She told me again that she would be in London with Jeremy in March. "So, about this trip to Portland on V-Day?" Mary had to have every bit of info she could about everything that was going on with me. She was so busy all the time, our phone conversations were the only way we stayed in contact most of the time.

I caught her up on everything; that Andrew was getting a swanky hotel room for the weekend, and he was taking me sight-seeing, among other things.

"Again, too much info." I could tell she was mock cringing. "Pictures. I want tons of pictures of the two of you."

"I'll take as many pictures as I can. I'm not sure if we'll leave the room that much," I giggled.

"Okay, that's enough. I'm hanging up. You're making me sick." She laughed hard. "I'll talk to you when you're back from Portland. I'll be gone next weekend."

"Okay, Mary. I'll call you when I'm home. Tell Jeremy I said hello."

"Will do. Bye."

"Bye, Mary." When I hung up, I was still laughing at our conversation. We never ceased to have a phone call where we didn't end up laughing about something. Mary was my best friend, and I was so blessed to have her in my life.

***

On Saturday afternoon, I was making lunch while Chris was outside working in the yard. I was a little afraid to be alone with him at the house. He never tried anything, aside from our normal hugs, but it still worried me.

I could almost trust him again, but I couldn't get past the feeling something was going to happen between us, and how could I live with myself if it did? How would I tell Andrew? How would I ever look him in the eyes? He would never forgive me if anything happened with Chris. I shouldn't have been worrying about it. I wasn't about to let anything ruin the best thing that ever happened to me, but it kept nagging at me. I pushed it aside and called Chris in for lunch. He had to be hungry. He had been outside for over four hours with nothing to eat.

"Hey, goofball," I called from the porch. "Come inside. I made lunch."

He smiled up at me and stood. He was dirty. "I'm starving," he admitted as he took the porch steps two at a time.

"Go clean up. We'll eat in the living room." My dining room table had construction materials stacked on it. Chris had been doing a lot of work around here. I wondered if he ever slept.

When he came out of the bathroom, we sat together on the couch and enjoyed some chicken quesadillas and tortilla chips and queso, and a somewhat upsetting conversation.

"What are you working on outside?" I asked him.

"Pulling weeds."

"After lunch, I'll come out and help. I want to clear out those weeds next to the house so I can plant my gardenias."

"I'd welcome the help," he said and bit into his quesadilla. "Don't you have anything hotter for these things? They're bland as hell." He grinned at me.

"I don't do spicy." I grinned back at him.

"How is Andrew doing?"

Chris's question took me by surprise. He never asked about Andrew. I had to swallow hard. "He's... good. They're rehearsing every minute of the day. He's exhausted by the time he calls, so we don't talk long."

"Are you getting excited about your trip?"

"Yeah. Nervous, too. I'm going to meet Karen and Trevor. I'm a little nervous about it."

"Why? They're regular people, too, aren't they?"

"Sure, I guess. Andrew says they are, but regular to him differs from what it is for me. He hangs out with movie stars all day. That's normal to him. I'm not used to people like that."

"I wouldn't worry too much. I'm sure it will be fine." He finished his quesadilla and started on the chips. "You're not worried about him and that Karen girl? Weren't there rumors about the two of them a while back?"

I eyed him. I didn't like the question. "No, I'm not worried," I said, with a little too stern tone. "They were only rumors. They were always only rumors." I felt defensive.

"Chill out, Sarah. I wasn't implying anything."

"Yeah, but I *am* a little worried about it."

"Don't be. He loves you. That's obvious."

"You think so?" I looked at him and gave him a weak smile and giggled. He had cheese stuck to the corner of his mouth. I wiped it off, and he stared at me with a serious expression. Uh-oh. No way was I going to let this happen. I looked away and took his plate. "Are you finished?" He could take that question any way he wanted. He had to know putting the thought of Andrew and Karen together in my head would cause all kinds of wild ideas.

"Yes. I'm sorry, Sarah. I didn't mean to..."

"Let's forget about it, okay?" I took the dishes to the kitchen and let them soak in the sink. I went to change into some grubby clothes and went outside with Chris to pull weeds and plant my flowers.

ANDREW

It was one week before Sarah would be in my arms, and I was as restless as a caged animal. Rehearsals were going well, and I talked to her every night, but time was going by too slow for my liking.

Both Karen and Trevor could see my frustration all week, and they had cornered me while we were having lunch on Saturday afternoon.

"What is wrong with you this week, bro?" Trevor asked.

"Yeah, you're acting like you're caged or something," Karen agreed. How funny that she would use that phrase. That's exactly how I felt.

"I'm anxious. Sarah will be here in a week."

"She ought to be more nervous than you, man," Trevor said.

"I'm sure she is, but she isn't used to this. I'm not sure if she can handle it."

"Look, Andrew, we're your friends. We'll help her out and make her feel welcome. I'm sure she's a great girl. If she loves you, she must be special. She also probably has a sense of humor if she's dating you." Karen was pretty good at finding the sarcasm in everything.

"Thank you for that." I smirked at her, and she laughed.

"Don't worry about it so much, Andrew," Trevor told me. "We'll take care of her, like Karen said. We won't let the press harass her."

"I'm not worried about that so much. She can handle herself with them."

"Well, what is it?"

"All the screaming fans, the cameras, the lights."

"Don't leave your hotel room." He gave me an impish grin.

"Disgusting," Karen snorted, and stood up and walked away.

"What's her problem?" I asked. Trevor only shrugged. I got up and followed her. "What's the matter with you?" I asked her.

"Nothing," she retorted. She didn't turn around.

"Liar." She spun around, her long, dark hair flying around her face. She had sadness in her dark brown eyes. I could see she was trying not to cry.

"Why, Andrew? Why her? I don't understand it. She's old. That's gross."

"First, she's only ten years older, not old. Second, age is only a number. She's a beautiful person. You're going to love her."

She crossed her arms over her chest and stared at me. I could still see a hint of moisture in her eyes.

I smiled at her, trying to lighten the mood. It didn't work.

"Do you love her?"

"With all my heart. She's the best thing that has ever happened to me."

"I'm worried, Andrew. I'm worried she can't handle this. You're never home. She'll never see you. You'll never see her. Has she ever been to a movie premier or an awards show?"

"No, but why should that matter? I can help her with all those things. I *will* help her with all those things. Are you going to help me?"

"I guess, but I don't think she's up for this. This isn't her world. Try to remember that, would you?"

"That's not it at all, so what is it?"

"Nothing. Not anymore. Drop it. I'll help her out. Trevor will help her out. Don't worry about your precious Sarah, okay?"

"Whatever. If you're going to have that attitude, don't bother." I walked away from her and went to sit back down with Trevor.

"Is everything cool?" he asked me.

"No, but she'll deal. She has no choice." I looked back at her. She was leaning against the wall.

SARAH

The week before Valentine's weekend went by slower than any other time in my life. Each day at work seemed to drag on. Each night was long, until Andrew called, and then the time flew by faster than I would have liked. One night, he told me he had been having issues with Karen, but he wouldn't go into detail. He said she and Trevor were excited to meet me. I had to admit; I was excited to meet them, too, but I was also nervous. I didn't let it bother me too much.

I was left with a lot of alone time with Chris. I still wasn't comfortable with that. We talked every night, until Andrew called, as usual. He was trying to make this situation work. He was my friend again, and I was thankful for that.

I had to wake up early on Thursday morning to have my stitches removed. I was tired. I was staying up too late talking to Andrew every night and the lack of sleep was catching up with me.

Chris wanted to go with me to make sure everything went well.

"You don't have to go with me, Chris. I'm sure everything is fine. I don't have any pain at all anymore," I told him as I finished getting ready.

"I want to make sure you're okay," he insisted.

I sighed, not frustrated, but I didn't want to argue with him. "Fine," I chuckled and looked at the clock. It was after seven. "If you're going with me, we need to leave now."

Chris followed me to the hospital in his truck. We only had to wait a few minutes because of the early appointment.

"How are you, Sarah?" Doctor Morgan asked me as he examined my stitches.

"I'm great," I admitted. "No pain, no headaches, no memory loss."

"Everything looks good. No infections or swelling. Let's remove these stitches and you can be on your way," he told me.

"Great." I was happy to be "normal" again.

Chris piped up, "She's flying to Portland in the morning. Is she okay to fly?"

What was he doing?

"It's safe for her to fly," Doctor Morgan assured him.

"I wanted to make sure," Chris said, looking at me.

It only took about twenty minutes for the entire process to remove my stitches. We would be five or ten minutes late to work, but I had already told Valerie. I had planned on making up the time.

"What was that about?" I asked Chris as we took the elevator upstairs to the office.

"I wanted to make sure it was safe for you to fly. That cabin pressure can have a weird effect on your head."

"Hmm. Are you sure that's all it is?"

He laughed and held the office door open for me. "Yes, Sarah, that's all it is."

I walked in ahead of him. Kelly greeted us with a cheery smile, as usual. "How did it go? Are you free to go to Portland tomorrow?"

"Yes." I grinned at her. "I need to use your computer to clock in."

Chris excused himself and went down the hall to his office.

"Cool. How are you?" Kelly piped up after Chris disappeared.

"Great. No pain at all. The doctor gave me a clean bill of health."

"That's not what I meant, but I'm glad." Kelly smiled at me.

"I'm excited... and nervous. I'm going to be meeting Trevor and Karen this weekend."

"Andrew will be there. I'm sure it will be okay. From what I've seen on TV, they appear to be down-to-earth."

"That's what Andrew says. I hope they like me."

"How can they not?" She grinned at me.

"Thanks, Kelly." I looked at the clock. "I had better go to work. I have to be caught up before I leave tonight."

"Oh, that reminds me, Val wanted to talk to you."

"Is everything okay? Am I in trouble?"

"I don't think so. I think she wants to catch up." Kelly smiled again, and I walked to the back to Valerie's office.

"That didn't take long," she greeted me with a big smile.

I sat down across from her. "Nope. Everything's great." I smiled back at her.

"That's good to hear." She sat back and looked at me. "Are you getting excited? Tomorrow's the big day."

"Yeah. I'm nervous as hell. I'm meeting his co-stars this weekend."

"How are you doing with the media garbage?"

"They're actually behaving themselves." I chuckled. "I'm sure when I land in Portland, it will be a different story. They are aware I'm headed to Portland and Andrew will be at the airport waiting for me. I think I'm more worried about *him* being hassled."

"Well, have fun, and take a lot of pictures."

"I plan on it." I grinned big and stood up. "I need to go to work. I promised I'd get caught up before I left today."

"How close are you to that, by the way?"

"About half. I've been kicking butt this week. I'm going to stay an extra fifteen minutes today to make up the time I missed this morning.

"Don't worry about it. Tell me when you're all caught up. I might even let you leave early." Her smile was devious.

"No, that's fine, Val. You don't have to," I protested.

"I'm sure you have a lot of packing to do."

"Ugh." I groaned, frustrated. I hadn't even started packing. "Okay, we'll see where I am later, and I'll tell you."

The day was flying by. Before I realized it, it was noon. It was lunchtime, and I was a couple of hours away from being finished with my work.

I'd had a few pleasant interruptions during the morning, first from Anita wanting an update, and from Chris wanting me to go on break with him. He only wanted someone to walk with. We didn't even talk much. We walked, but I could tell he had something on his mind. I wouldn't push him. He would tell me when he was ready.

"What are you doing for lunch?" Marie asked, startling me as I clocked out. She was always doing that.

Once my heart stopped pounding, I told her, "I don't have anything planned. I thought I'd go for a walk or something. I'm too nervous to eat."

"You're going to lunch with me," she told me.

"I'm not hungry."

"Nobody said you had to eat. We need to catch up." She was ignoring my protests. "Let's go."

Marie dragged me to a small Italian restaurant around the corner from the office. The moment we walked inside, my stomach churned. What was wrong with me? I loved the smell of Italian food. It must have been nerves. Every moment meant I was that much closer to getting on a plane to meet Andrew's friends. It had to be nerves. The nausea subsided, and I never mentioned it to Marie, but ordered a ginger ale and bread sticks to be on the safe side.

"Tell me everything." She was leaning on her elbows on the table and grinning from ear to ear.

"There's nothing to tell. I haven't done anything."

"Chris, dummy." She slapped my hand. She was still grinning.

"Nothing to tell with him, either. We kind of do our own things."

"You're lying." She leaned back. Her expression was serious. "Come on, Sarah. He hasn't tried anything?"

"Nothing at all." I stared her down. "We're working on our friendship. He's being good. We eat dinner together and talk, but there isn't anything going on."

"Uh-huh. You said that about Andrew in the beginning, too."

"I did not." I frowned at her. "You dragged me to lunch that day, too, and I told you everything. This time there isn't anything to tell." I sipped my ginger ale. My stomach was returning to normal, so I ate some bread. "Why don't we have this conversation again on Tuesday, when I'm home?"

"Oh, I had already planned on that." She waved her hand and chuckled.

I smirked at her. "You're impossible."

"Whatever. Are you nervous?"

"Yes. I'm meeting Karen and Trevor."

"I want autographs and pictures."

"Of course, you do." I laughed at her. "You grew up in Southern California, too. Aren't you over the star-struck phase yet?"

"I didn't go to school with celebrities like you did. Besides, you're the one who flipped out when you saw Andrew that first day."

"Uh, yeah, but he's Andrew Collier, duh." I giggled.

"Point. And look at you now. You're engaged to him."

I sighed and grinned. "I am." I loved him so much, it hurt to be away from him.

***

On Thursday night, Chris asked me if I wanted to go out for dinner, sort of as a bon voyage dinner. I agreed. It couldn't hurt to have dinner with my friend. I was so wrong.

We went to Texas Roadhouse, one of my favorite restaurants. The paparazzi had followed us. Why was I not surprised? It was a little annoying. I didn't like the idea of being followed and photographed. My privacy was being invaded, and it bothered me. How did Andrew deal with it?

"Come on, guys. Give us some space. I'm not doing anything exciting," I told them as I passed by. I was holding Chris's hand.

"Sarah, who's your friend?" someone asked.

"Is this Chris?" someone else asked.

I stopped dead. How could they know that?

"Is it true he's living with you? Does Andrew know? Have you and Andrew split?"

The questions kept coming, but the only way I could stop them was by going inside, so I led Chris inside the restaurant, where it was safe.

"Sorry about that," I apologized to Chris.

"You didn't go off on them," he chuckled.

"I'm not in the mood." I eyed him, and said, "let's eat."

"How many?" the pretty blonde hostess asked before she looked up.

"Two, please," I told her with a weak smile. Dealing with photographers was draining.

The hostess looked up with a smile until she saw me. Her smile turned to awe. Great, I already have a fan, or an enemy, because of who I was dating. I wasn't sure yet. "You're Sarah Miller."

"Yeah." My face was expressionless.

"Wow. I've been following yours and Andrew's story for almost a month. I love you guys."

"Thanks." I smiled. "Um... can we please go to our table?"

"Oh, God, I'm sorry. Of course. Please, follow me." She led us to the back of the restaurant so we wouldn't no one would bother us. The hostess seated us and took our drink order. When she left, I nibbled on a roll and glanced at her out of the corner of my eye as she giggled with her co-workers.

"Do you think you'll ever be used to this?" Chris asked as he grabbed a roll and took a bite.

I shrugged. "It's annoying. I don't like being followed."

"And I'm kind of watching from the sidelines." He smiled at me.

"It's safer where you are. Trust me."

Our waiter brought our drinks and took our order. He seemed unaware of who I was or, if he was aware of my status, he didn't care.

"So, tomorrow's the big day, huh?"

"Yeah." I continued to nibble on the bread. "Listen, Chris. I want to tell you how much I appreciate everything you're doing." I touched his hand. Let the paparazzi outside think what they wanted if they were watching.

"I'm glad to help you, Sarah. You're my friend." He squeezed my hand and smiled. He took in a deep breath and sighed. He looked pained, as if he had something to say, but was afraid to. "Don't go." His voice was quiet.

"What?"

"Don't go to Portland this weekend?"

"Why not?" I pulled my hand away. I wasn't sure I liked where this was going.

"I sensed something bad. I can't explain it. Something isn't right." He shook his head and leaned back.

"What, exactly, isn't right?" I leaned back as well and crossed my arms over my chest. I was certain I didn't like where this was going.

"I can't explain it. It's like you're going to get hurt or something." I cocked my head and looked at him with a suspicious expression.

"It's not a jealousy thing. Don't worry."

"It isn't?"

"No. It's more in the pit of my stomach."

"I'll be fine. Andrew will be by my side to keep anything from happening." I grinned at him.

"Sure. I'm not worried about that. I'm sure he'll keep you safe, but it's something else. I can't put my finger on it."

"Please stop worrying, Chris. Everything will be fine."

We sat in silence for several minutes before the waiter brought our food. The silence between us was awkward, so I asked what his plans were for the weekend. He was planning to go to Windsor to see his kids.

"You'll have the house to yourself. You can bring them down here."

"I'm sure Haley won't let the boys out of her sight."

I nodded. "Well, the offer is open if she changes her mind."

ANDREW

On Thursday afternoon, I went to Avenue Five, an upscale jewelry store in Downtown Portland, to pick up Sarah's engagement ring. I had ordered it last week, making sure it would be ready before Sarah arrived. Per Sarah's request, not a single diamond graced the ring. The ring was beautiful. It had a solitary opal in the center, surrounded by twelve small emeralds. It wasn't gaudy. I felt anything bigger would look tacky on Sarah's small, delicate hand.

I had only been in Portland a few hours, preparing for Sarah's arrival. I had reserved a suite at The Benson Hotel, close to where we would film "Silence." Once Sarah left on Monday morning, I would go back to staying in my trailer on set.

I was so nervous and excited about her arrival. I wanted everything to be perfect for her; perfect for when I proposed to her for a second time. This time, however, I would do it the right way; on bended knee, with a ring in hand. We would spend the entire rest of the day in bed, making love. On Saturday, I would take her to lunch with Karen and Trevor.

I worried about that a little. They would love her, but I was afraid they would intimidate Sarah. Then I remembered Sarah was a strong woman. Karen and Trevor were good people, but Sarah was not used to meeting movie stars, although she grew up around aspiring actors. I hoped she would be alright with everything. She was a strong woman, but a little shy with new people.

As I was getting things ready in the suite late Thursday afternoon, after I had picked up Sarah's ring, someone knocked on the door. It was Karen.

"What are you doing here?" I asked. My tone was bitter.

"We need to talk. Can I come in?"

"Sure." I opened the door for her, and we went into the living room of the suite. "What's going on?"

"I have an issue with your girlfriend."

I looked at her, confusion washing over me. "I'm sorry?"

"Let me rephrase that. I have an issue with the two of you together." She sat down on the chair and looked up at me. "I didn't want to do this, Andrew. I wanted to let this pass and be over it, but it won't go away."

"What are you talking about, Karen?" I sat down on the love seat across from her. She stood and walked over and sat down next to me and took my hands in hers.

"I'm in love with you, Andrew. I always have been, and I don't want you with her."

"You're kidding, right? This is a joke?"

"Not even close. I love you and I want to be with you." She leaned in to kiss me, but I pushed her away.

"No." I stood and walked toward the door. "I'd like you to leave now."

"You're turning me down?" she asked.

"Cold. Please leave now."

"I don't think she's good for you. She's too old for you, and she knows nothing about the way we live. She doesn't fit in, but you and I are the same. We live in the same world. We should be together."

"How can you make assumptions about someone you've never met? I love her and nothing you do or say is going to change that. Nothing you do will break us apart. I would appreciate it if you left now."

Karen stood and walked toward me. "We could be so good together, Andrew. We would be. I can tell want me."

"Maybe at one time I did, but those feelings are gone. I'm with Sarah and I'm going to be with Sarah for the rest of my life. Now leave."

"We'll see about that." She ran her finger down my cheek and smiled. It was a devious grin. She walked out of the room, and I was left alone, confused, and frightened. What was going on in her head? What was she planning?

I needed a few hours to calm down before I called Sarah. I needed to talk to her, but I didn't want her to know I was afraid. Karen had me scared. I was afraid of what she might have up her sleeve. I went downstairs and out onto the busy downtown Portland street.

I found myself along SW Oak Street until I stood in front of The Willamette River. I stood and viewed the ferries cross the river. People were coming and going, enjoying the rare warm February afternoon.

I thought about the confrontation with Karen. It had me on edge, and I couldn't wait for Sarah's arrival. Tomorrow would take forever.

SARAH

"I missed you so much," I squealed as I ran up to Andrew and hugged him.

"I missed you, too, love." He held me tight, kissed every inch of my face until his lips landed on mine. We stood there for a long time, kissing. It felt so good to be back in his arms.

"These past two weeks took forever. I never thought this day would come," I whispered in his ear, and kissed him again.

"Let's go. I have a surprise for you." He smiled at me and picked up my bag and we walked together out of the airport.

Andrew didn't say a word most of the drive to the hotel. I thought it was because he wasn't familiar with the streets of Portland. He may have been concentrating on the route, but I noticed a pained expression. "Is everything okay?"

"Sure." He glanced at me and smiled.

"You're deep in thought. You haven't said a word the whole ride."

"I'm alright." His tone was a little stern. I stayed quiet for the rest of the ride.

***

In the hotel suite, he closed the door and set my bag down and grabbed me and pushed me against the wall and pressed up against me as he ravaged my neck. If anything had been wrong with Andrew, it had passed.

I grabbed his shirt and tried to pull it over his head. "Not yet," he groaned. He planted his lips on mine and kissed me with passion. "God, I missed you, Sarah," he breathed. He pulled away and took my hands. "Come sit down."

259

He sat me down on the love seat and sat next to me, staring into my eyes. The tears were forming in his eyes as he pulled something out of his pocket. I didn't look down; I kept looking into his eyes.

"Please say yes," he asked as he opened the box containing the most beautiful ring I had ever seen.

I cried and nodded. "Yes. Yes, of course." He slipped the ring on my finger and kissed me with passion.

Andrew lifted me off my feet and carried me to the bedroom, where he placed me on the bed. He undid the buttons on my blouse, kissing my breasts and stomach.

I removed his shirt, revealing his bare chest. He pressed his body onto mine, his lips tracing a path from my neck to my lips and then to my eyes. My hands roamed over his chest and back as I planted kisses on his neck. I tangled my fingers in his tousled hair.

"I love you, Sarah," he whispered as he looked at me. Tears were falling from his eyes.

"Don't cry. I love you."

"I'm so happy and I missed you so much."

"I missed you, too." I pulled his face toward mine and continued kissing him.

As he wrapped his arms around me, I felt my body being lifted off the bed. Without a word, he guided me towards the bathroom and turned on the shower. We stepped into the shower, the steam enveloping us as we explored each other's bodies with eager hands. The sensation of the hot water against our skin intensified the passion between us. With every kiss and caress, the desire between us grew more passionate.

Andrew's body pressed against mine, his movements strong and insistent. With each thrust, he drove himself deeper inside of me, eliciting a cry of pleasure from my lips. Our mouths collided in a passionate kiss, his lips hungry and demanding more of my mouth.

The room was filled with the sound of our ragged breaths and the scent of our desire.

We made love all afternoon and didn't stop until the sun was going down and our stomachs were growling.

"God," I panted as we lay on the bed, entangled in each other.

He looked over at me and smiled. "I love you so bloody much," he whispered again. "You don't know how long the past two weeks have dragged on."

"Yes, I do." I smiled back at him.

He looked over at the clock on the nightstand. "Are you hungry?"

"Starving."

"Would you like to go out, or do you want to order room service?"

"I want to stay in," I told him, and kissed him softly.

He pulled me closer to him and kissed my forehead. "I love you so much. No matter what, please remember I love you."

"And I love you." I held him tighter. "I knew something was wrong earlier. What is it?"

"Not now. I don't want to ruin this moment." He looked down at me and smiled again and kissed me with passion. We made love again before we got up and order room service.

ANDREW

"I need to tell you something," I told Sarah as we sat in the living room of our hotel suite. We had ordered room service and sat on the love seat together, eating dinner.

"What is it?" She looked at me with a curious expression.

"I didn't tell you last night because I feared you wouldn't come. And I didn't tell you before I proposed because I feared you would say no. And I didn't tell you before we made love because I feared you wouldn't want to." I paused and took a deep breath.

"Tell me, honey." She cocked her head and smiled at me. She looked so beautiful. I didn't want to lose her.

"Sarah, you know I'm irrevocably in love with you?"

"Yes, of course I do."

He let out a deep breath. "Karen was here yesterday. She came on to me."

"I see." Her smile faded.

"No, you don't. She told me she's in love with me and doesn't want you and me together. She thinks you won't fit in."

"And?"

"I turned her away. I told her I'm in love with you and I always would be."

The smile returned to her beautiful lips. "What made you think you couldn't tell me this?"

"I was afraid you'd be upset or afraid I might leave you."

"The news has me a little concerned, but I have no doubt you love me, Andrew. I'm not afraid you'll leave me, and I'm sure as hell not going anywhere. I'm addicted to you." She grinned at me, and I kissed her.

"I'm so glad I told you this."

"Don't be afraid to tell me anything. We have to be honest with each other and communicate."

"You're absolutely right, love."

We smiled at each other and kissed again.

***

It was overcast and threatening to rain on Saturday.

Andrew and Sarah decided that lunch with Karen and Trevor would be better than going out in the rain, and less intrusive in their hotel suite. Karen and Trevor agreed, since half of the teenage population of Portland was aware of their whereabouts every minute of the day.

"I'm glad to meet both of you," Sarah greeted Karen and Trevor when Andrew let them in.

"It's great to meet you, too, Sarah." Trevor greeted her with a big smile and a hug. "Andrew has been a train wreck for the past two weeks." He glanced at Andrew, who only smirked at his friend.

Trevor stood tall, his muscular frame towering over Sarah. His dark skin was a testament to his Native American heritage. As he ran his hand through his jet-black hair, Sarah noticed the muscles in his arms. His big brown eyes captivated her. She couldn't find the words to describe him, but one thing was certain: he was more than just handsome; he was irresistible.

Karen extended her hand. "Hi," she said, her smile on this side of cordial. Her chestnut eyes squinted with disdain, and they seemed almost vacant. Sarah was sure Karen didn't like her, and she knew Karen wanted to be with Andrew, but she trusted Andrew, even though her confidence had all but disappeared.

Karen stood at five feet-five inches. At twenty-three, she already exuded the air of someone more mature. Perhaps it was her life in the film industry.

"I've heard a lot of good things about you," Sarah told Karen, trying to stay cheerful and not allow her lack of self-confidence to show itself.

"Same here." Karen walked past her and toward Andrew and hugged him. Andrew pushed her away.

"Well, I'm starving," Trevor announced, trying to lighten the mood. "Where's the grub?" He grinned at Sarah. She smiled at him.

Andrew walked over to Sarah and put his arm around her. He could tell she was uncomfortable with Karen, knowing she had confessed her love for him. "It should be here soon, Trevor. Why don't we sit down so you three can talk?" Andrew suggested.

"Great idea," Trevor agreed. "I want to find out everything about this beautiful lady of yours." He put his arm around Sarah's shoulder and walked into the living room with her.

Andrew was glad Trevor had taken to Sarah. He only wished Karen would at least try to be friendly.

"So, Sarah," Karen spoke up, "how do you think you're going to handle all of this all the time?"

"Well, I..."

"What I mean is, having to hide out in hotel rooms and dodge the paparazzi, and let's not forget the screaming teenage girls grabbing at your boyfriend..."

"Karen, stop," Andrew interrupted.

She gave him daggers. "Are you kidding, Andrew? You're not even a little concerned about what you're doing to her?"

"I can take care of myself," Sarah said.

"I'm sure you can, but it's easier to have Andrew take care of you, isn't it? Nice ring, by the way." Karen smirked at her.

"Karen, knock it off," Trevor demanded.

"Why should I?"

Andrew glared at her. "Enough," he shouted.

She shot a nasty glance at Andrew and snapped back at Sarah. "I don't think you can cut it in this world, Sarah. You're too timid. You're after Andrew's money, aren't you?"

"How dare you," Sarah spat out, and stood and ran out to the hall. Trevor followed her. Sarah cried on his shoulder. "Why does she hate me?"

"She's jealous."

"So, she has to say hurtful things to me?" She dried her eyes. "Maybe she's right. Maybe I can't handle this kind of life. The past several weeks have been stressful for me. I'm not sure I can live my life like this forever."

"Don't talk like that. Do you love him?"

"Yes, of course I do, but..."

"But nothing. You'll be fine. He is so in love with you, it's sickening. Trust me. He won't let you get away that easy. I think he would shrivel up and die without you."

"I can't live without him, either."

"He won't let anything, or anyone, especially Karen, come between you."

"You're sure?"

"Positive." Trevor smiled and hugged his new friend.

They walked back into the suite, with Sarah leading the way.

Sarah stopped dead in her tracks when she rounded the corner to the living room. In front of her was Karen, with her mouth pressed hard against Andrew's. Her arms were around his neck, and it didn't look like he was pushing her away.

"I was wrong," Trevor said from behind her, his mouth agape.

Also by Shelly Meyer

The Letter Series
The Letter

Standalone
Deadly Healer

Watch for more at https://www.shellymeyerauthor.com.

About the Author

Shelly Meyer has loved writing since childhood. She has a collection of unfinished manuscripts she hopes to complete one day.

Her passion for romance novels began in high school and eventually led her to explore mysteries and thrillers.

Along with "Deadly Healer," she is also working on a thriller novel about the Illuminati.

Living in a suburb of Denver, Colorado, she continues to pursue her writing while working a full-time job during the day.

Read more at https://www.shellymeyerauthor.com.

Milton Keynes UK
Ingram Content Group UK Ltd.
UKHW021940281024
450365UK00018B/1194

9 798227 622440